LET SLEEPING DOGS LIE

Center Point
Large Print

Also by Rita Mae Brown and available from
Center Point Large Print:

Fox Tracks

**This Large Print Book carries the
Seal of Approval of N.A.V.H.**

LET SLEEPING DOGS LIE

Rita Mae Brown

illustrated by
LEE GILDEA, JR.

CENTER POINT LARGE PRINT
THORNDIKE, MAINE

This Center Point Large Print edition
is published in the year 2015 by arrangement with
Ballantine Books, an imprint of Random House, a division
of Random House LLC.

Let Sleeping Dogs Lie is a work of fiction.
Names, characters, places, and incidents are
the products of the author's imagination or are used
fictitiously. Any resemblance to actual events, locales,
or persons, living or dead, is entirely coincidental.
The text of this Large Print edition is unabridged.
In other aspects, this book may vary
from the original edition.

Printed in the United States of America
on permanent paper.
Set in 16-point Times New Roman type.

ISBN: 978-1-62899-403-2

Library of Congress Cataloging-in-Publication Data

Brown, Rita Mae.
  Let sleeping dogs lie / Rita Mae Brown. — Center Point Large Print
edition.
    pages ; cm
  Summary: "A century-old crime reawakens bad will—and stirs up a
scandal that chills Sister Jane to the bone"—Provided by publisher.
  ISBN 978-1-62899-403-2 (library binding : alk. paper)
  1. Arnold, Jane (Fictitious character)—Fiction.
    2. Murder—Investigation—Fiction. 3. Fox hunting—Fiction.
    4. Large type books. I. Title.
PS3552.R698L48 2015
813'.54—dc23
                                                       2014037667

Dedicated in Loving Memory
to
Idler, American Foxhound, Bywaters blood
Who patiently taught me to carry the horn

CAST OF CHARACTERS

THE HUMANS

Jane Arnold, "Sister" is Master of Foxhounds, MFH, of The Jefferson Hunt in central Virginia. In her early seventies, she's strong, bold, loves her life, the people and animals in it. Like many people who live a deep life, she endured a terrible loss, her son, which ultimately taught her to cherish life, especially the simple things.

Shaker Crown, the hunt's long-serving huntsman, is loyal, reliable, mostly quiet. He and Sister are two peas in a pod when it comes to hunting philosophy.

Gray Lorillard, retired from a powerful accounting firm in Washington, D.C. He grew up in central Virginia and even when working in D.C., would come to the old home place on weekends for hunting. He's smart, handsome, judicious. As an African American man in his late sixties he has a broad overview of how things really work. He's in love with Sister and she with him.

Sam Lorillard is Gray's younger brother. A wonderful horseman, a Harvard graduate who threw it all away thanks to a long tango with the bottle. Dried out, he works for Crawford Howard.

7

He and his brother share the old Lorillard house with its lovely graveyard embracing two hundred years of Lorillards and Laprades.

Mercer Laprade is the cousin of Gray and Sam. He's a successful bloodstock agent. His family has closely worked with an important family of Thoroughbred breeders, the Chetwynds. He, too, has hunted with The Jefferson Hunt since childhood. (Children and grooms ride in the rear, a hunting tradition that allowed latitude where social customs at the time did not.)

Daniella Laprade at 94 can run her son crazy. Proud, imperious, so proud that when she married in 1940 she kept her maiden name as her husband lacked social cachet. Her sister, Gray and Sam's mother, took her husband's name, Lorillard, being less enchanted with social standing. Graziella Lorillard has passed on. Daniella is triumphantly alive.

Walter Lungrun, M.D., Joint Master of fox-hounds, is a relatively new Master often amazed at what one must learn and do. His medical reputation is skyrocketing, his riding is much improved, and he loves Sister, has since a child. Walter is the outside son of Sister's late husband. Mr. Lungrun never knew or never let on if he did. Sister didn't know until shortly before tapping Walter to be her Joint Master. Made her love him more somehow.

Phil Chetwynd owns and runs Broad Creek

Stables, a Thoroughbred breeding operation that has ridden the ups and downs of that most daring of employments since the 1870s. He grew up with Mercer and his cousins. Loves Mercer, teases him incessantly, and vice versa. They've made good money together, too.

Betty Franklin, as Sister's best friend and a good twenty-five years younger, is also a whipper-in, honorary, which means she isn't paid. She is a kind woman and a good one.

Anne Harris, "Tootie" lives with Sister, taking night classes at UVA. She left Princeton to be with The Jefferson Hunt. Her dream is to become an equine vet and to be a whipper-in. She is sweet, determined, and shockingly beautiful. She is also African American, born to one of the richest men in Chicago who can't fathom why anyone would want to work outside or with animals.

Crawford Howard is probably as rich as Tootie's father and equally as stubborn and egotistical. When Sister did not choose him to be her Joint Master he flew off in a huff and started an outlaw pack that seems to be spectacularly unsuccessful. With all the faults of a self-made man and many of the virtues, he is a force to be reckoned with. He cares a great deal about young people and their education and gives generously.

Ben Sidell has been sheriff of the county for three years. Since he was hired from Ohio, he sometimes needs help in the labyrinthine ways of the South. He relies on Sister's knowledge and discretion.

Kasmir Barbhaiya, widowed and in his mid-forties, moved to central Virginia to be close to his college roommate after his wife died. He is impossibly rich, having made his fortune in pharmaceuticals in India. He is generous, loving, helpful, and finally able to think about truly living again. He's also a very good rider.

Ed and **Tedi Bancroft** are in their early eighties, ride to three hunts a week, and are dear friends of Sister's. The Bancrofts and Sister have seen one another through desperate sorrows as well as many joys.

Sybil Fawkes is the Bancrofts' daughter and the other Jefferson Hunt whipper-in. Always impeccably turned out and beautifully mounted, there's nothing she can't do on a horse. She's divorced and her two sons are close to grown.

Penny Hinson, DVM, takes Tootie with her on Mondays. She likes the young woman, loves her patients.

Alida Dalzell, from North Carolina, comes to central Virginia on a foxhunting vacation and to rethink her career. Perhaps tipping over into her forties, she is flat-out gorgeous, and better, she can ride and adores hounds.

Jane Winegardner, MFH of Woodford Hounds in Lexington, Kentucky, is a dear friend of Jane Arnold, so this Jane is known as O.J., the Other

Jane. An inspired Master, a natural leader, she gets things done and makes riding Thoroughbreds look easy.

Ginny Howard is O.J.'s hunting buddy; married to a man who knows horses as well as his wife, she hunts with his support. She has insight into people that she usually keeps to herself except for O.J.

Justin Sautter, new JT-MFH of Woodford, is young, good with people, and has the wonderful fortune of having a wife, Libby, who can ride right up there with him.

Meg Jewett is Justin's aunt. She loves all animals, being the proprietress of glorious Walnut Hall in Kentucky. She has an incredible eye for structure, beauty, harmony.

Alan Leavitt, married to Meg, presides over Walnut Hall and still breeds Standardbreds for which this lovely place is famous. It is in Lexington, Kentucky, and the Kentucky Horse Park is on former Walnut Hall land. Like his wife, Alan is public-spirited, farsighted, and generous.

THE AMERICAN FOXHOUNDS

Sister and Shaker have carefully bred a balanced pack. The American foxhound blends English, French, and Irish blood, the first identifiable pack being brought here in 1650 by Robert de la Brooke of Maryland. Individual hounds had been shipped over earlier, but Brooke brought an entire pack. In 1785, General Lafayette sent his mentor and hero, George Washington, a pack of French hounds whose voices were said to sound like the bells of Moscow.

Whatever the strain, the American foxhound is highly intelligent and beautifully built, with strong sloping shoulders, powerful hips and thighs, and a nice tight foot. The whole aspect of the hound in motion is one of grace and power in the effortless covering of ground. The American hound is racier than the English hound and stands perhaps two feet at the shoulder, although size is not nearly as important as nose, drive, cry, and biddability. It is sensitive and extremely loving and has eyes that range from softest brown to gold to sky-blue. While one doesn't often see the sky-blue eye, there is a line that contains it. The hound lives to please its master and to chase foxes.

Cora is the strike hound, which means she often finds the scent first. She's the dominant female in the pack and is in her sixth season.

Asa is in his seventh season and is invaluable in teaching the younger hounds.

Diana is the anchor hound, and she's in her fourth season. All the other hounds trust her, and if they need direction she'll give it.

Dragon is her littermate. He possesses tremendous drive and a fabulous nose, but he's arrogant. He wants to be the strike hound. Cora hates him.

Dasher is also Diana and Dragon's littermate.

He lacks his brother's brilliance, but he's steady and smart. A hound's name usually begins with the first letter of his mother's name, so the D hounds are out of **Delia.**

Giorgio is a young entry and just about the perfect example of what a male American foxhound should be.

Other hounds

Trinity, Tinsel, Trident, Thimble, Twist, Tootsie, Trooper, Taz, Tattoo, Pookah, Pansy, Dreamboat, Ardent, Parker, Pickens, Zane, Zorro, Zandy

THE HORSES

Sister's horses are **Keepsake,** a Thoroughbred/ Quarter Horse cross (written TB/QH by horsemen), an intelligent gelding of twelve years; **Lafayette,** a gray TB, fourteen now, fabulously athletic and talented, who wants to go; **Rickyroo,** an eleven-year-old TB gelding who shows great promise; **Aztec,** a ten-year-old gelding TB, also very athletic, with great stamina and a good mind; and **Matador,** a gray TB, also ten years old, sixteen hands, a former steeplechaser.

Shaker's horses come from the steeplechase circuit, so all are TBs. **Showboat, Hojo, Gunpowder,** and **Kilowatt** can all jump the moon, as you might expect. Betty's two horses are **Outlaw,** a tough QH who has seen it all and can do it all, and **Magellan,** a TB given to her by Sorrel Buruss, a bigger and rangier horse than Betty was accustomed to riding, but she's now used to him. Kilowatt is a superb jumper, bought for the huntsman by Kasmir Barbhaiya.

Nonni, tried and true, takes care of the sheriff.

Matchplay and **Midshipman** are TBs from Roughneck Farm.

THE FOXES

The reds can reach a height of sixteen inches and a length of forty-one inches, and they can weigh up to fifteen pounds. Obviously, since these are wild animals who do not willingly come forth to be measured and weighed, there's more variation than the standard just cited. **Target;** his spouse, **Charlene;** and his **Aunt Netty** and **Uncle Yancy,** and **Earl** at Old Paradise are the reds. They can be haughty. A red fox has a white tip on its luxurious brush, except for Aunt Netty, who has a wisp of a white tip, for her brush is tatty.

The grays may reach fifteen inches in height and forty-four inches in length and may weigh up to fourteen pounds. The common wisdom is that grays are smaller than reds, but there are some big ones out there. Sometimes people call them slab-sided grays, because they can be reddish. They do

14

not have a white tip on their tail but they may have a black one, as well as a black-tipped mane. Some grays are so dark as to be black.

The grays are **Comet, Inky, Georgia, Tollbooth,** and **Grenville.** Their dens are a bit more modest than those of the red foxes, who like to announce their abodes with a prominent pile of dirt and bones outside. Perhaps not all grays are modest nor all reds full of themselves, but as a rule of thumb it's so.

THE BIRDS

Athena is a great horned owl. This type of owl can stand two feet and a half in height with a wingspread of four feet and can weigh up to five pounds.

Bitsy is a screech owl. She is eight and a half inches high with a twenty-inch wingspread. She weighs a whopping six ounces and she's reddish brown. Her considerable lungs make up for her small stature.

St. Just, a crow, is a foot and a half in height, his wingspread is a surprising three feet, and he weighs one pound.

THE HOUSE PETS

Raleigh is a Doberman who likes to be with Sister.

Rooster is a harrier, willed to Sister by an old lover, Peter Wheeler.

Golliwog, or **Golly,** is a large calico cat and would hate being included with the dogs as a pet. She is the Queen of All She Surveys.

SOME USEFUL TERMS

Away. A fox has gone away when he has left the covert. Hounds are away when they have left the covert on the line of the fox.

Brush. The fox's tail.

Burning scent. Scent so strong or hot that hounds pursue the line without hesitation.

Bye day. A day not regularly on the fixture card.

Cap. The fee nonmembers pay to hunt for that day's sport.

Carry a good head. When hounds run well together to a good scent, a scent spread wide enough for the whole pack to feel it.

Carry a line. When hounds follow the scent. This is also called working a line.

Cast. Hounds spread out in search of scent. They may cast themselves or be cast by the huntsman.

Charlie. A term for a fox. A fox may also be called **Reynard.**

Check. When hounds lose the scent and stop. The field must wait quietly while the hounds search for the scent.

Colors. A distinguishing color, usually worn on the collar but sometimes on the facings of a coat, that identifies a hunt. Colors can be awarded only by the Master and can be worn only in the field.

Coop. A jump resembling a chicken coop.

Couple straps. Two-strap hound collars connected by a swivel link. Some members of staff will carry these on the right rear of the saddle. Since the days of the pharaohs in ancient Egypt, hounds have been brought to the meets coupled. Hounds are always spoken of and counted in couples. Today, hounds walk or are driven to the meets. Rarely, if ever, are they coupled, but a whipper-in still carries couple straps should a hound need assistance.

Covert. A patch of woods or bushes where a fox might hide. Pronounced "cover."

Cry. How one hound tells another what is happening. The sound will differ according to the various stages of the chase. It's also called giving tongue and should occur when a hound is working a line.

Cub hunting. The informal hunting of young foxes in the late summer and early fall, before formal hunting. The main purpose is to enter young hounds into the pack. Until recently only the most knowledgeable members were invited to cub hunt, since they would not interfere with young hounds.

Dog fox. The male fox.

Dog hound. The male hound.

Double. A series of short sharp notes blown on the horn to alert all that a fox is afoot. The gone away series of notes is a form of doubling the horn.

Draft. To acquire hounds from another hunt is to accept a draft.

Draw. The plan by which a fox is hunted or searched for in a certain area, such as a covert.

Draw over the fox. Hounds go through a covert where the fox is but cannot pick up his scent. The only creature who understands how this is possible is the fox.

Drive. The desire to push the fox, to get up with the line. It's a very desirable trait in hounds, so long as they remain obedient.

Dually. A one-ton pickup truck with double wheels in back.

Dwell. To hunt without getting forward. A hound who dwells is a bit of a putterer.

Enter. Hounds are entered into the pack when they first hunt, usually during cubbing season.

Field. The group of people riding to hounds, exclusive of the Master and hunt staff.

Field master. The person appointed by the Master to control the field. Often it is the Master him- or herself.

Fixture. A card sent to all dues-paying members, stating when and where the hounds will meet. A fixture card properly received is an invitation to hunt. This means the card would be mailed or handed to a member by the Master.

Flea-bitten. A gray horse with spots or ticking that can be black or chestnut.

Gone away. The call on the horn when the fox leaves the covert.

Gone to ground. A fox who has ducked into

his den or some other refuge has gone to ground.

Good night. The traditional farewell to the Master after the hunt, regardless of the time of day.

Gyp. The female hound.

Hilltopper. A rider who follows the hunt but does not jump. Hilltoppers are also called the Second Flight. The jumpers are called the First Flight.

Hoick. The huntsman's cheer to the hounds. It is derived from the Latin *hic haec hoc*, which means "here."

Hold hard. To stop immediately.

Huntsman. The person in charge of the hounds, in the field and in the kennel.

Kennelman. A hunt staff member who feeds the hounds and cleans the kennels. In wealthy hunts there may be a number of kennelmen. In hunts with a modest budget, the huntsman or even the Master cleans the kennels and feeds the hounds.

Lark. To jump fences unnecessarily when hounds aren't running. Masters frown on this, since it is often an invitation to an accident.

Lieu in. Norman term for go in.

Lift. To take the hounds from a lost scent in the hopes of finding a better scent farther on.

Line. The scent trail of the fox.

Livery. The uniform worn by the professional members of the hunt staff. Usually it is scarlet, but blue, yellow, brown, and gray are also used. The recent dominance of scarlet has to do with people buying coats off the rack as opposed to having tailors cut them. (When anything is mass-produced, the choices usually dwindle, and such is the case with livery.)

Mask. The fox's head.

Meet. The site where the day's hunting begins.

MFH. The Master of Foxhounds; the individual in charge of the hunt: hiring, firing, landowner relations, opening territory (in large hunts this is the job of the hunt secretary), developing the pack of hounds, and determining the first cast of each meet. As in any leadership position, the Master is also the lightning rod for criticism. The Master may hunt the hounds, although this is usually done by a professional huntsman, who is also responsible for the hounds in the field and at the kennels. A long relationship between a Master and a huntsman allows the hunt to develop and grow.

Nose. The scenting ability of a hound.

Override. To press hounds too closely.

Overrun. When hounds shoot past the line of a scent. Often the scent has been diverted or foiled by a clever fox.

Ratcatcher. Informal dress worn during cubbing season and bye days.

Stern. A hound's tail.

Stiff-necked fox. One who runs in a straight line.

Strike hounds. Those hounds who through

keenness, nose, and often higher intelligence find the scent first and press it.

Tail hounds. Those hounds running at the rear of the pack. This is not necessarily because they aren't keen; they may be older hounds.

Tallyho. The cheer when the fox is viewed. Derived from the Norman *ty a hillaut*, thus coming into the English language in 1066.

Tongue. To vocally pursue a fox.

View halloo (halloa). The cry given by a staff member who sees a fox. Staff may also say tallyho or, should the fox turn back, tally-back. One reason a different cry may be used by staff, especially in territory where the huntsman can't see the staff, is that the field in their enthusiasm may cheer something other than a fox.

Vixen. The female fox.

Walk. Puppies are walked out in the summer and fall of their first year. It's part of their education and a delight for both puppies and staff.

Whippers-in. Also called whips, these are the staff members who assist the huntsman, who make sure the hounds "do right."

THE JEFFERSON HUNT CLUB
EST. 1887

LATE WINTER 2014
FEBRUARY

Sat., Feb. 1	Jt. Meet Woodford Hounds in their Territory	10:00 A.M.
Tues., Feb. 4	Oakside	10:00 A.M.
Thurs., Feb. 6	Tattenhall Station	10:00 A.M.
Sat., Feb. 8	Mill Ruins	10:00 A.M.
Tues., Feb. 11	After All	10:00 A.M.
Thurs., Feb. 13	TBA	10:00 A.M.
Tues., Feb. 18	Prior's Woods	10:00 A.M.
Thurs., Feb. 20	Skidby	10:00 A.M.
Sat., Feb. 22	Orchard Hill	10:00 A.M.
Tues., Feb. 25	Close Share	10:00 A.M.
Thurs., Feb. 27	Punchbowl	10:00 A.M.

MARCH

Sat., Mar. 1	Foxglove	10:00 A.M.
Tues., Mar. 4	Litany Brook	10:00 A.M.

Thurs., Mar. 6	Oakside Jt. Meet	
	Woodford Hounds	10:00 A.M.
Sat., Mar. 8	After All	10:00 A.M.
Tues., Mar. 11	Beveridge Hundred	10:00 A.M.
Thurs., Mar. 13	Tattenhall Station	10:00 A.M.
Sat., Mar. 15	Roughneck Farm	
	Closing Meet	10:00 A.M.

Hounds Always Have Right of Way
Hunting 540-111-1111

Mrs. Raymond Arnold, MFH
Dr. Walter Lungrun, Jt-MFH
Mr. Shaker Crown, Huntsman

• • • • •

1. Hunting license and State Forest permit required by law.
2. Negative Coggins and signed liability waiver required.
3. Formal Dress, Saturdays and Holidays. Proper ratcatcher for Tuesdays, Thursdays.
4. Damage to fences, crops, lawns must be reported to the Field Master immediately.
5. No smoking in the hunt field.
6. Obey the Field Master and give staff precedence in the field.
7. Give every consideration to landowners, through whose kindness hunting is possible.

· · · · ·

CAP FEES

For adults on Saturdays and holidays	$100.00
For adults on Tuesdays and Thursdays	$75.00
Juniors (17 and under) & grooms	$15.00

· · · · ·

www.facebook.com/sisterjanearnold
Kennels: 540-111-1122

LET SLEEPING DOGS LIE

CHAPTER 1

Two women, both named Jane, heads down, horses' heads down, rode into driving sleet. Even their horses had sleety, icy bits stuck to their long eyelashes.

O.J., Jane Winegardner's nickname, standing for the Other Jane, shouted to the tall older woman riding next to her. "It's an ill wind that blows no good."

"So much for the weather report," said Jane Arnold, generally known as "Sister." Chin tucked into her white stock tie, collar of her heavy frock coat turned up, she blinked to keep the sleet out of her eyes.

A stone fence appeared up ahead, then disappeared. The two walked their mounts in that direction.

Sister turned toward O.J. "Can't hear a thing. You think we'd hear the horn."

"I hope Glen has the hounds up by now," said O.J., Master of Woodford Hounds, mentioning her huntsman.

When the joint meet started out on Saturday, February 1, low clouds blanketed the Kentucky sky, the temperature at ten in the morning hung at 34°F. The first cast started off hopefully: the Woodford Hounds, named for Woodford County,

29

found a coyote line right off. The Jefferson Hunt, central Virginia, rode right up with the Woodford people, a courtesy extended to them by their host. Eighty people charged up over a hill from the main barn at Shaker Village in Mercer County.

Upon well-groomed horses, the riders in their best hunt gear had little trouble negotiating the hill as the ground remained frozen. So far the two degrees above freezing had no effect. The slipping and sliding would start in perhaps an hour. The cold air felt invigorating, the cry of the hounds exciting.

Like The Jefferson Hunt, Woodford Hounds did not hunt to kill but rather to chase. The Virginia hunt chased more fox than the Kentucky group, who flew across fields on coyotes running straight and fast. Usually the quarry would speed out of the hunt's territory. Riders would pull up, waiting for huntsman and staff to bring hounds back, often grateful for a breather.

That's how both Janes thought the day would go: hard runs, retrieving hounds and then casting them again for another fast go. O.J., MFH, along with Robert Lyons and new Joint Master, Justin Sautter, asked Sister Jane to ride with O.J. The two ladies would whip in, which means riding at the edge of the hounds where the huntsman assigned them. This was a bit like playing first base or third. The Masters didn't expect Sister Jane to really whip in but all knew if she trotted out with O.J., she'd be rewarded with great views of the excellent hound work.

"The girls" were flying along when, within five minutes, a low howl came from the west: an unnerving noise. Neither woman paid much attention, the pace was too good. Sister Jane knew the sound of approaching wind well, as much as her huntable land nestled east, at the foot of the sensuous Blue Ridge Mountains. Sometimes the wind would howl overhead, not touching those below. Other times it cut you to the bone.

A few moments passed after the ominous sound, then trees bowed before the onslaught. The two Masters were hit full in the face. Clouds lowered, bringing an impenetrable freezing fog, what the tribes called a pogonip. The colonists kept the word. Sleet slammed the riders like the palm of a giant open hand. They could neither see nor hear.

O.J. knew this place intimately. She pulled up. She knew where she was when the sleet and fog hit but now had to feel her way, hoping a landmark would appear through the fog.

Turning her wonderful mare around, O.J. had the good sense to head back to the barn. The mare had a better sense of direction than she did.

The two women rode right up on the stone fence.

O.J. hollered, "Sister, if we back up to jump it, we won't see it until we're right on it. Let's walk around to the right. We should come up on a creek. There's a small hand gate there."

Slipping, sliding now as the ground sloped down, their horses carefully walked along, keeping their heads low. Finally, they reached the creek and O.J. saw the small gate nearby when a swirl cleared her vision for a moment.

Sister Jane dismounted before O.J. could protest. Once both horses passed through, the older woman closed the gate.

"I'll hold your horse," O.J. yelled.

Seeing that her saddle seat was already covered with sleet, Sister thought the better of plopping in the middle of it. Her hands throbbed. She couldn't feel her feet. "I'll be warmer walking." She ran up her stirrup irons, lifted Rickyroo's reins over his head to walk on his left between both horses. That would shield her a bit from the fierce winds.

She opened her mouth to add something, but in a second it was full of ice bits. Sister Jane loved foxhunting. She loved being a Master but at this exact moment she questioned her sanity. She questioned O.J.'s, too.

Shaker Village in Mercer County, Kentucky, flourished between 1806 and 1923 when Mary Settles, the last Shaker, passed away. Like all Shaker settlements, this one died out due to the fact that Shakers did not believe in sexual congress and therefore no children were born in the villages. People joined the sect with children in tow. Eventually those children became seventy, eighty, a few even ninety years old. Without new recruits, these visually beautiful communities died out. Time passed them by.

Americans lost interest in the spiritual, quiet development fostered by the Shakers. While the lack of sex surely deterred many, another cause for the demise of such an unusual sect was the Industrial Revolution. This force grew and grew, devouring much in its path, most especially the desire to live simply.

Sister patted Rickyroo on the neck. A ten-year-old Thoroughbred, nearing eleven, he'd learned his job, carrying it out with energy, but even this kind fellow had found the going difficult.

"Couldn't they smell it coming?" O.J.'s mare asked.

"No," Rickyroo replied. *"You have to think for them."*

Another seven miserable minutes and the two lone humans finally made it to the barn. They could just see the outline of the roof. Inside was a much-needed welcoming party, Betty Franklin, Anne "Tootie" Harris, and Ginny Howard.

Although one is not supposed to dismount inside a barn, O.J. couldn't stand one minute more of that lashing wind outside. Her friend Ginny Howard helped her down, putting O.J.'s hands between her own. Ginny took off her gloves, then rubbed the Master's hands. The mare stood by patiently, grateful to be inside.

Betty Franklin, Sister's best friend, quickly untacked Rickyroo, for Sister couldn't uncurl her fingers.

Tootie, a beautiful young woman, who had left Princeton in her freshman year to the horror of her socially conscious Chicago family to work with Sister, came up with a heavy blanket for Rickyroo.

"Honey, before you put that blanket on, rub some Absorbine on his back and down his legs," said Sister, teeth chattering. "Wet a chamois cloth, make it warm, good and warm. Put that on his back just for a couple of minutes. Then wipe him down and toss the blanket on."

Tootie spoke to both human and horse: "You must be frozen."

"Hateful," came the human's one-word reply.

"Hateful," Rickyroo echoed.

Betty took off Sister's gloves, blew on her hands to rub them as Ginny was doing. "Your hands are cherry red."

"They throb. The thought of taking my boots off fills me with dread."

"Gray went back to your room to get things ready for you," Tootie said.

"That's a happy thought." Sister loved her boyfriend for his thoughtfulness. That he was handsome didn't hurt. She called him her gentleman friend—ever proper Sister.

"Ginny, what happened?" O.J. asked. "It was like a curtain of fog, sleet, and wind dropped."

"That's what happened. There was no hope so we turned back, everyone turned back."

"Did Glen get the hounds up?"

"You bet he did." Ginny smiled. "They didn't want to be out either."

"Good." O.J. breathed relief.

Both Sister and O.J. loved their hounds. Being Masters, they were, in effect, the chief executive officers of their respective hunts. An overwhelming number of chores dropped into their lap but Sister sometimes thought her most important function was to patiently listen.

"Everybody ready?" O.J. asked.

"I haven't cleaned my tack yet." Sister wondered if her hands could do it.

Betty, saddle over her forearm, bridle over her shoulder, announced, "I'll do it in my room. You rest. Don't forget you need to be at your best at the dinner."

Sister smiled. "We all need to be at our best. Woodford never does things halfway."

Both Sister and Tootie, along with many other Jefferson Hunt members, stayed in the Long House at Shaker Village. Each of the original rooms remained as they had been built, though

35

were now guest rooms with a shower and sink. No TV. No radio. Scrubbed wooden floors, chairs hung up on pegs to create more space, a nice bed with blankets, all bore testimony to the pure design of Shakers.

Standing outside the door to their room, Sister knocked, wincing as she did so.

Gray opened the door. "Honey, I've been so worried about you."

Stepping inside, she allowed him to peel her out of her heavy frock soaked at the shoulders. She then wriggled her arms out of her vest. "The storms knocked out my cell phone, plus in that freezing torrent I couldn't use it anyway." She inhaled deeply.

"Here, sit in the chair." He pulled a second one down off the wall for her. "I'll undo your tie."

"You're an angel. There's no way I could unfasten the pin."

Gray expertly freed the long titanium pin, a gift from a friend, Garvey Stokes, owner of Aluminum Manufacturers, and also unfastened the two safety pins to hold down the ends of the tie.

She began to fill him in on the adventure. "A pogonip."

Gray, African American and well versed in the old stories, murmured. "A bad sign."

"Well, that's what the Virginia tribes always said."

"My grandmother, too." Their eyes met. "Okay,

beautiful. Be brave. You have got to get your boots off." He pulled the big bootjack over for her. They always took a big bootjack when they traveled, just as she always took a heavy down comforter, a real necessity in these rooms without insulation. A few of the Shaker lodgings had horse-hair in the walls but the wind rattled the hand-blown glass, finding every crack in the walls.

"Come on. I'll hold the handle along with you but you need to get your boots off before the warmth makes your legs swell."

"What warmth?" She felt a wedge of cold air from the window reach her as she stood with one foot on the bootjack the other in the slot where the heel would rest.

He laughed. "Come on. Better a short, sharp pain than a long, drawn-out one."

"Dear God." She gasped as she freed one foot.

"One more." He encouraged her and she did pull her foot out of the boot, pressing her lips together so she wouldn't scream.

"Will I ever walk again?"

He put his arms around her. "I don't know, but I know you'll ride again. You get the rest of those cold, wet things off. I'll start the shower. All you have to do is step inside. I'll have your Constant Comment ready when you step out."

"Weren't we smart to bring the electric teapot?" She gingerly stepped to the bathroom as he preceded her.

Feeling had returned to her frozen feet and they hurt like hell.

Once cleaned up, wrapped in her heavy robe, she sat on a ladderback chair across from him.

Gray scanned the room. "I admire Shaker design, don't you?"

"I do. It reminds me that I have too much stuff. Whenever we come here, I feel cleansed."

Holding the heavy mug in her hands felt restorative as did a sip. Tea always lifted Sister's spirits as did the sight of a horse, hound, or Gray.

"Funny, how we remember the old tales, isn't it? I mean the stories about freezing fogs."

"I wouldn't disbelieve them and you were lucky to get through that pogonip, those damn winds. What in the hell were you doing out there?"

"I told you. We whipped in on the left side and within five minutes, *whammo*."

"Actually, it was pretty much that way in the field, too. I don't remember anything quite like it." He took a sip of his own tea. "I'm looking forward to the dinner at Walnut Hall. I've never been inside."

"It's fabulous. But then everything that Meg and Alan Leavitt do is pretty fabulous," she said, referring to the owners of Walnut Hall.

Meg Jewitt was the aunt of the new, young Joint Master, Justin Sautter, about whom O.J. was thrilled. Well, she should be. Young people bring with them energy, new ideas, and physical strength.

"I remember a pogonip when I was in grade school," said Gray. "The teacher wouldn't let us walk home. Took forever for our parents to fetch us and, of course, my mother had to go on about unhappy spirits being released during a pogonip." He paused. "And you know, it was February first like today."

Sister sipped again. "Do you believe that stuff about unhappy spirits?"

He shrugged. "I don't know."

In a sense, they were about to encounter one.

CHAPTER 2

Nestled in Gray's big-ass Land Cruiser, Sister felt warm at last. The SUV's heater was a godsend. He exited the drive from Shaker Village, turning right.

"It's more scenic if you turn left," Sister offered.

"Takes longer, too." His iron-gray military mustache curved up at one end as he teased her, "You know, I could install a steering wheel on your side."

She turned to face him, as always admiring his handsome profile. "You say."

He laughed. "So, I do. The sun won't set until five-thirty. I love the light. I mean, winter has its beauty but sometimes the darkness gets me. We now have an hour's more light than on December twenty-first. Never seems to bother you."

"Doesn't. How do people live without the seasons? That would get me. I'd go stark raving mad. I measure time, even emotion, by those shifts."

"Mmm." He paused for a moment, then turned another right onto one of Kentucky's highways. "Boy, this state has done a lot of work on the roads."

"Yes, it has. They have a good governor in

Beshears and they have had some good ones before. Some real stinkers, too."

"It's the legislature that's the problem." Gray, a retired accountant from a high-powered firm in D.C., kept up with financial incentives and disincentives in government. Although he'd made a career as a tax lawyer of impeccable repute, he knew only too well how the system could be gamed from either end.

"Right now we Virginians can't really hold our heads up either. Hopefully, McAuliffe will prove more rigorously honest than the governor before him, who I thought was pretty good until the stories came out about accepting money, a watch, etc., for favors. So very foolish." She noticed a huge sycamore in the middle of a field that meant water was nearby. "What is it about old trees that call to one?"

"Old spirits."

"That's one of the things I liked about the Harry Potter movies; the trees talked and moved. Well, all that started long before that, remember the story about Apollo chasing Daphne? Just as Apollo grabbed her, Daphne called to her Mother Earth, who snatched her out of Apollo's arms, putting a laurel tree in Daphne's place. Apollo created a laurel wreath to console himself. Somehow the laurel wreath was used ever after to crown victors in the real Olympics. It was used for artistic contests, too. I'd love to see that now.

You know, current Olympians crowned with laurel leaves, the Wimbledon winner, the winner of the golf U.S. Open, that sort of thing. There's some-thing beautiful about it."

"You think about things that would never occur to me." He loved that about Sister most times.

On a few occasions, it became tedious.

"I'll take that as a compliment. Gray, we've got the Chetwynds and the Bancrofts coming to this. Those families once raced against Meg's grand-father, when everyone raced harness horses. There were a few Thoroughbreds at the farm, too."

"I thought L.V. Harkness was a Standardbred man through and through," Gray remarked.

"He was, and Meg and Alan still are. Every now and then I think Mr. Harkness slipped in a Thoroughbred but in those days, the turn of the last century and before, sulky racing was the thing. Think of Dan Patch," she continued. "As big a star as later Secretariat was." She wrapped her arms around herself, beaming. "How it pleases me to be driving through Kentucky knowing the last winner of the Triple Crown, one of the greatest Thoroughbreds ever, was bred in Virginia."

"I'd keep that to myself tonight."

"I will." She frowned for a moment. "Harness racing ought to prove to all of us not to take anything for granted. You and I could live to see the fraying of flat racing."

"Don't you think it already is?"

42

"Yes, but there's hope for it being reversed. It comes down to three things, honey: visionary leadership, unimpeachable training practices, and slots."

"Well, that's another subject we'd best not get on tonight. Too close to home. Don't get Mercer on it." He mentioned his cousin, who did business in Kentucky and elsewhere as a bloodline/ breeding consultant. Gray's mother and Mercer's mother were sisters.

It was a sore subject since the Kentucky legislature repeatedly voted down, always with a terrific fight, not to allow other forms of gambling at the racetracks. As to good treatment of horses by trainers, the issue was made more difficult as each state had different drug rules. Barn practices, cleanliness, proper food, and so forth proved far less difficult to monitor than drugs.

Many members of Woodford Hounds made their living through breeding, selling, and racing Thoroughbreds. Phil Chetwynd, one of The Jefferson Hunt's members, had kept up his family tradition and stayed in the Thoroughbred business, which was small in Virginia compared to Kentucky. The Chetwynds, four generations' worth, were kept afloat financially through their stallions. People still vanned mares from New York, Pennsylvania, Maryland, West Virginia, and even Kentucky to breed to Broad Creek Stables stallions, each of whom carried impeccable blood.

"For Kentuckians, the frustration has to be wild. All anyone needs to do is cross the Ohio River into Indiana and walk onto a riverboat." Sister shook her head.

"As an accountant, I have mixed feelings about gambling."

"Gray, I don't. No one puts a gun to someone's head and says you will wager away your salaries. And face it, there is a thrill."

"There is no thrill to bankruptcy."

"You've got me there, but really, do you think we can protect people from themselves?"

"No. On the other hand, we don't have to enshrine foolishness."

"You are so right. That's why we elect it."

He laughed. "Now I know you're warmed up."

"Slow down. No, I'm not backseat driving but we're only twenty minutes from Walnut Hall and we don't want to be the first ones at the do." She thought for a moment and reconsidered. "Oh, don't slow down. Having a few moments with Meg and Alan, Justin and Libby, too, surely they'll be there early, that's a treat. They are so literate. I love being around people who read."

"It's always an elite, you know. Throughout history. One can know how to read but not exercise the ability. Now people look at their phones, their iPads, their computers."

"Useful stuff but makes you passive." She announced this with conviction, absentmindedly fingering the pearls at her throat. God forbid a Southern lady be without her pearls.

"I understand how film and TV makes one passive but I'm not so sure about the other stuff."

"Okay. When you read a book, it's just you, a white piece of paper with black marks on it. You know what the black marks mean but they explode in images in your head. So you and I can read the same passage from *Moby-Dick* but your whale looks different from mine. We use our imaginations. When the image is preselected as it is in electronic media, you are looking at someone else's whale. I mean, some of the electronic books even have moving images."

"Ah." A few moments passed. "You're certainly philosophical."

"The near-death experience in the pogonip. Crystallized my mind."

He burst out laughing as he turned down Newtown Pike. Kentucky Horse Park was at one time part of Walnut Hall. Now Walnut Hall as well as the Sautter house were behind it. Originally the giant property was granted to William Christian in 1777. Christian moved his family near Louisville in 1785 but was soon killed by Indians that same year. The western territories seethed with danger. Over time, as those dangers abated and Christian's daughter Elizabeth Dickerson persevered, more settlers moved to the lands.

Dickerson sold a section of her land. Down through the nineteenth century it was passed along, being subdivided over time. L.V. Harkness bought the land in 1895 from the estate of Captain Sam Brown who had won the Kentucky Derby in 1884 with his horse, Buchanan. Harkness renamed the place Walnut Hall, owning 2,000 acres.

A late sun drenched the large still-bare trees in pale light, for the skies had cleared and the winds stood still. Just another demonstration of the variability of Kentucky weather.

The manicured grounds exuded a subdued grace.

"What's going on over there? No one dead, I hope." Gray knew no person was, for they slowly drove by the oldest horse cemetery in America, where rested fifty-eight of the greatest of the early Standardbreds. A statue of the horse Gus Axworthy, 1902–1933, announced the lovely final finish line of their lives.

At the edge of this hallowed ground, Sister observed two men working to dislodge a huge shard of engraved slate. The slab had broken over the only Thoroughbred there, Benny Glitters, 1892–1921. A large tree limb could be seen upturned at the side of the large flat tomb marker that covered the entire equine grave. So great was the force of the earlier wind that the branch must have fallen onto the slate with such ferociousness that it drove the broken sharp edge into the grave itself. The odd rise of the temperature after the storm was turning the hard frozen ground into mud.

Arriving at the door to Walnut Hall, Gray handed the keys to the gentleman there to park the cars.

"We aren't the first." He took Sister's arm as he escorted her to the door.

"And it's six o'clock. If people are that eager to get here you know it will be some party."

Standing by the door to greet his guests, Alan Leavitt kissed Sister on the cheek, shook hands with Gray. "How good to see you. Sister, you light up every room you enter." Alan meant that, but as he was a gentleman he wisely knew to flatter the ladies.

People were pushing in behind them. Alan continued greeting guests. Meg was easy to find, you followed the laughter.

The party, in full swing at 6:30 P.M., was the typical foxhunters' gathering. There were people there of great wealth like Kasmir Barbhaiya, a portly Indian gentleman who had moved to Virginia to be part of The Jefferson Hunt. He'd made a billion dollars plus in pharmaceuticals in his native India. A widower, he was beset by many women who liked his money and therefore liked him. No fool, he trusted that when he did find a person to whom he could give his heart, his late wife would tell him. This he firmly believed and, having told Sister, she believed it, too.

The deepest things in life are not logical.

The elegant rooms filled with Woodford people and Jefferson people. Old silver trophies, continually polished over generations, reflected light, adding their own silver glow. Old and new gossip was rapidly dispensed with so folks could get to the real conversation: horses and hounds.

Walnut Hall represented both accumulated wealth and excellent taste. In a sense, it was like an old European home where generations refined the art of living and in the case of Meg, of giving. Kasmir was another giver.

Mingling among those who had financial great fortune in their lives were those who barely had two nickels to rub together. Apart from those two poles, the bulk of the group watched their pennies, got along, and enjoyed life with what they were able to earn.

Exuberance, love of nature, physical energy counted for more than money. And of course, character counted most of all. Foxhunters, like any group of humans anywhere in the world, provided a rich assortment of the good, the bad, and the plain old rotten to choose from.

O.J. found Sister in the scrum. "Took me two hours to thaw out."

"I'd still be blue if it weren't for Gray," said Sister. "He helped me take my boots off, got me in the shower, then handed me a cup of tea. I think that's the coldest I have ever been. Then he picked out tonight's clothing, insisting I wear this cashmere sweater with a wraparound skirt. He said I needed to stay warm."

Eyes twinkling, O.J. laughed, then said low into Sister's car, "Remind me of the connection between the Chetwynds and the Laprades? Didn't the Laprades work for them since World War One?"

"Before and after. The Laprades had and still have a great eye for a horse. The Chetwynds were smart enough to use it."

"As long as they stand Guns and Roses and Loopy Lou, people will haul mares to Virginia. They've also got St. Boniface, young, his first year crop looks good."

"O.J., you remember your horses."

"So do you. So much of what's good in Virginia goes back to Mr. Mellon's stud, the Chenerys, of course. But tell me about the Laprades." O.J. leaned in closer.

"Related to Gray. Gray's mother, Graziella Lorillard, and Daniella Laprade were sisters. I add, they weren't close but they more or less got along. The Laprades made a lot of money with the Chetwynds. Not so much in salary but in betting at the track, or so I'm told. Mercer"—she indicated a well-dressed man in his fifties—"still advises Phil Chetwynd as well as others. Gray says he makes money at the track as well."

49

"Well, he doesn't look poor," said O.J. "Anyone riding in a Hermès saddle isn't poor."

"Drives Gray nuts." Sister shook her head. "Gray does not believe in flash."

"You might remind Gray that a Hermès saddle will last at least three generations and if it fits you and your horse, it's worth the price." O.J. grinned. "The Chetwynd money isn't all from horses, right? I thought their fortune started with coal in West Virginia."

"Did. They still own the mines. Phil"—she nodded at the Chetwynd standing nearby next to Gray, towering over him actually—"doesn't run the mines. His brother does. Phil is in charge of the breeding and racing operation, Broad Creek Stables. Phil works closely with Mercer. There's always been the thought that they are related back through Phil's grandfather and Mercer's grandmother. No one says this outright but Gray told me and he wondered if it ended there. He's good about so-called sexual sins but prior generations lied through their teeth. Phil comes to Kentucky regularly for the big races but he does most of his business in the mid-Atlantic."

"Dear Lord, Sister, the way things are going, racing might shift to the mid-Atlantic."

"Kentucky will always be first in Thoroughbreds," Sister predicted.

"Sister, each year over five hundred million dollars shoots out of this state into Indiana casinos. And we can't get slots in the racetracks. It's crazy."

"It's kind of like killing the goose that laid the golden egg." Sister had no idea how immense was the financial drain Kentucky was experiencing.

Both their heads turned when they noticed their host Alan Leavitt opening the front door to the two men, Fred and Arnie, who had been at the graveyard. After a quick conversation, Alan hastily threw on his overcoat and left with them, shutting the door behind him.

He returned within fifteen minutes, said something to Meg.

Meg's expression changed from calm to disbelief. "Alan, that can't be," Sister heard her say.

"Well, come see."

As others overheard this exchange, curiosity rose.

Alan looked over his shoulder as he stepped outside the door. "Come on. Might as well see this, but put on a coat. Sun has set and it's getting cold again."

Sister, Gray, O.J., Betty, Phil Chetwynd, Mercer Laprade, who was in the front hall, Tootie, Kasmir, and a group of the Woodford members dutifully put on their overcoats and went outside to trod upon the sodden ground squishing beneath their feet.

For the ladies in heels, this was not a good idea.

At the Walnut Farms burial grave site, Fred and Arnie pointed down. Fred held a strong flashlight while Arnie knelt down, slinging away mud.

"Who was Benny Glitters?" Tootie asked, then quickly shut up.

"What's that?" Meg exclaimed, for a smashed gold pocket watch and chain caught the gleam from Fred's flashlight.

Arnie scraped around a bit more and a dog skull appeared, possibly that of a small terrier, then a thumb and human forefinger also appeared not far from the watch. The forefinger was bent toward the unseen palm.

Sister inhaled sharply, then whispered. "Death beckons."

CHAPTER 3

Tuesday, February 4, some clouds and some sun hinted that the weather might turn in the foxhunter's favor. Sister Jane knew better than to be too hopeful. She'd lived through whopping snowstorms as late as mid-April in central Virginia. As a rule of thumb, though, the last frost was around April 15 and she fervently hoped this year would run true to form. However, it was now February, a notoriously difficult month.

Tuesdays, Thursdays, and Saturdays were The Jefferson Hunt days. Back from Kentucky, Sister, her hounds, her huntsmen, and two whippers-in prepared for what they hoped would be a good day. As so many people worked, Tuesdays and Thursdays drew smaller numbers. When the season passed New Year's Day, the diehards slipped away from work as they knew the last half of hunt season always flew by faster than the first half.

As Field Master, the seventy-three-year-old Sister led the riders in First Flight, those who took the jumps. Bobby Franklin, Betty's husband, a man of prudent judgment, led Second Flight. Mostly they didn't jump, although they might pop over a log.

The pasture—dull brown, patches of old snow here and there—lay below them. Within two months it would shine bright green.

Another reason people came out on this particular Tuesday was that they were hunting a new fixture, Oakside. It takes a season to learn a fixture, sometimes more, both for hounds and staff.

Led by Cora, an older, wiser hound, the pack fanned out over the lower pasture. They'd lost the line, easy to do in even the best of conditions, for the fox is every bit as smart as the old myths and stories tell us.

Noses down, concentration intense, the Jefferson pack made Sister proud. Shaker Crown, her huntsman of many years, knew when to urge them on and when to sit tight and shut up. This was a sit-tight-and-shut-up situation.

Pookah, young, a trifle silly, was momentarily distracted by the pungent odor of a bobcat. *"Hey, this smells kind of interesting."*

Diana, an outstanding hound in her prime, walked over, checked it out. *"Pook, that's a bobcat. You know that's a bobcat. Why waste your time?"*

"Well, if we can't pick up the fox again this could be fun. I want to have fun."

"Shut up. Forget it and go to work." Cora growled convincingly.

Pookah immediately did as she was told. You didn't cross Cora.

Most members of the field want to gallop along.

The more they gallop, the better they think the hunting. Granted, moving along at pace is always a thrill, but for Sister, staff, and those foxhunters who loved hounds, they marveled at the work below. This pack performed beautifully.

Dreamboat was one of the D line, for foxhounds take the first initial of their name from their mother's name. He stopped, sniffed, sniffed more, his tail started to flip like a windshield wiper. Now Dreamboat was not a particularly brilliant hound. He was the good foot-soldier type. He had always been overshadowed by his littermates, Diana, Dragon, and Dasher. He did his job, was always in the middle of the pack but today was his day.

"Here he is!" he sang out in his resonant voice.

As Dreamboat was a reliable fellow none of the lead hounds bothered to check the line. Within seconds, Dreamboat up front, the pack spoke in unison.

Shaker, on Hojo, the perfect huntsman's horse, bold, fast, and handy, fell in behind the pack. Way out on the right of the pack rode Betty Franklin, whipping in. On the left, just now dipping down into a swale, rode Sybil Fawkes, also whipping in.

Sister waited for a moment before trotting down the hill, riding behind Shaker by about thirty yards. Just behind her rode Maria and Nate Johnson, owners of Oakside. Out of the corners of their eyes they caught sight of their daughter, Sonia, behind Sybil by about a football field in length, riding tail. Sister wanted to train young people for staff positions and as Sonia was in her early twenties and could ride, this was working out.

The Johnsons rode up to direct Sister, who did not yet know the territory that well. Good thing, too, because the fox crossed a shallow creek, headed into a woods, and burst out again. Of course he didn't run in a straight line, so everyone looped in the woods a bit. When they emerged, an old fence line dividing the Johnsons' property from their neighbors' appeared and so did the fox. The crafty fellow paused for one moment, looked back at the approaching hounds, then scooted under the fence and put on the after-burners to create havoc.

Knowing that the neighboring farm wasn't available for hunting, Shaker had to halt his pack. Taking hounds off a hotline is miserable work because, in a sense, you are punishing them for doing their job. Hounds have little sense of human boundaries and if they did, they wouldn't care.

To make matters worse, the entire field could view this beautiful red while watching the whippers-in jump the three-board fence to bring back the hounds.

Shaker pulled up to blow them in. Had he gone on, the hounds would have taken that as a signal they could continue. If the huntsman was right behind them, they were right. Like any huntsman, Shaker, frustrated, blew his horn three long notes in succession, and prayed his whippers-in could do their job. Not an easy one.

Betty rode right up on the pack's shoulder, looking down at Thimble and Twist. "Leave it."

"It's red-hot!" Thimble protested.

On a blindingly fast Thoroughbred, Sybil called out the same order on the left side where Giorgio, a hound of stunning beauty, obeyed.

Sonia, without being told, rode past Sybil, got in front of the pack, slightly turned toward them and cracked her whip. That sounded like rifle fire and scared the hounds. They slowed down.

Then Betty and Sybil, who had worked with the pack for decades, knew everyone and vice versa, called again. "Leave it!"

Diana stopped so the others did, too, as Diana and Cora had the respect of all the hounds. Hounds, like humans, are pack animals. Some have natural authority and often they build on this, earning trust by their work.

"Not fair! Not fair!" Trident howled.

"How could they do this to us?" Dasher cried.

"Good hounds. Good hounds." Betty praised them, which offered some salve.

"Come on. Come along," Sybil pleasantly ordered, turning her horse back toward the fence.

"Why do they do this? Why?" Trident, who had been right behind Dreamboat, spoke in misery.

"Humans are perverse," Trooper replied.

"True, but you have to admit, they rarely break us off a line," Cora counseled.

Back at the fence, the hounds wiggled back under it while Betty, not under pressure, looked for a place with a top board off to jump. Yes, she could and just did jump a three-board fence, but it wasn't her preference. She rode Outlaw, her tough Quarter Horse, who had that odd little engine push when he jumped.

Thoroughbreds' jumps were usually smooth, often seemingly effortless; they spoiled their riders. Quarter Horses could jump without a doubt, but they always felt—to Betty, at least—as if there was a little extra wiggle there in the rear.

Sybil didn't think anything about the fence being three boards. She leapt back over, as did Sonia.

The hounds gathered around Shaker, who lavishly praised them.

The medium-built, muscular huntsman leaned over, citing Dreamboat directly for all to hear; hounds, horses, and humans.

"Dreamboat, you were a star."

"Me?" The good fellow gazed up, then realized *"Me!"*

Dreamboat stood on his hind legs as Shaker leaned over, reaching down, and took the offered paw.

The happy hound rejoined the pack. Shaker paused for a moment, looking to his master.

Sister asked Maria, "If we follow the creek south then turn back toward your farm, think we'll be okay?"

"Sure."

"If we find another fox that runs out of the fixture, we'll just deal with it," the elegant Master said.

A narrow path followed the creek. Resuming the search, hounds headed south, a few floated into the woods.

As Sister rode along, she memorized suitable crossings on the new fixture's creek. As the waters were clear she could see the bottom, a big help. Nothing like getting into water only to sink in nasty silt.

Fifteen minutes passed, then twenty. Betty, on the other side of the water, picked her way through, as there wasn't a path on that side. The problem was always those tendrils hanging from trees, Virginia creepers, and little bushes with loathsome thorns. It was a good horse that willingly plunged into the stuff, which Outlaw did. Not that he didn't complain about it.

Twenty minutes. Twenty-five. The temperature, midforties, felt warm, especially if one had put on extra layers, since it was below freezing at ten o'clock when hounds were first cast.

Thirty minutes.

"Hey, gray," Dreamboat called out, having picked up a scent. *"Fading,"* he cautioned.

He moved along a bit faster, hooked into the

woods on the path side, then opened in earnest, his resonant hound baritone sounding beautiful.

Another run, maybe ten minutes followed, but it seemed longer as there were many obstacles to dodge. Finally the scent pooped out.

By now it was twelve-thirty. Two and a half hours seemed sufficient, given conditions and the newness of the fixture. Sister didn't want to risk heading into forbidden territory should they get another line.

So many times a decision a Master must make isn't good for hunting but necessary for land-owner relations. She hoped, in time, the neighbor would learn that the club did no harm and was happy to do some good if you needed a gate fixed or perhaps useful information. She would call upon the neighboring farm after this first season down here and hope for the best.

Oakside's neighbors, new people, were not country people. Like most new people, especially those moving from cities or suburbs, their property lines seemed inviolate to them. This is deeply unrealistic but it was best folks learn this lesson in a gentle manner. That didn't necessarily mean Sister would someday be able to hunt that land but it did mean that hounds can't read. You can post all the NO TRESPASSING signs you want, won't do a bit of good to four-legged hounds with a snoutful of scent.

Walking back, the group came up to the old,

now unused Saddlebred barn. The Johnsons had their hunting barn up by the house. The five-stall Saddlebred barn, built decades ago by an owner of these lovely horses, rested farther away and had been let go by an interim owner. The abandonment gave it a sorrowful air.

As she rode by, Sister noticed glowing skulls with red eyes pushing up from the ground, red paint on the sides of the barn reading, Murder, Help, I'm Being Held a Prisoner, plus a mannequin hanging from the rafters.

Maria and Sonia, with Nate's help, had created a haunted barn as a fund-raiser for the pony club last year. A haunted barn it remained.

"Those darn skulls get me. It's the damned red eyes," Sister remarked to Maria.

"Scared the devil out of the kids." Maria laughed.

Walking behind Sister, Phil Chetwynd teased Maria, "If you ever have a big fight with Nate, we'll know where to look."

Mercer, next to Phil, chirped, "I don't know, Phil, I'd worry *more* about you. Taking all those road trips."

Phil grinned. "Truthfully, I think sometimes my wife is glad to get rid of me."

"Hear! Hear!" Sister called out and people laughed, most especially Phil.

Once back at Roughneck Farm, a forty-five-minute drive from Oakside, hounds were carefully checked for barbed-wire cuts, sore pads, anything unusual.

Betty and Tootie untacked horses to clean them as Sister and Shaker checked, then fed hounds.

The Master and huntsman watched the boys eat. The boys ate first, then the girls. Shaker figured if any of the girls were going into heat early the scent would linger and might cause a ruckus among the boys. And the boys always knew before humans had a sign. Of course, given that all had just hunted together without a hint of someone coming into season early, hounds were safe but Shaker stuck to his program. Sister rarely interfered. Her philosophy was if you have a good huntsman who doesn't drink, run women, or is cruel to horses, leave him or her alone.

Shaker hadn't gone to Kentucky. Sometimes he'd go along to away meets but mostly he didn't want to be far from his hounds. He did enjoy riding with other huntsmen and had struck up a friendship with Glen Westmoreland at Woodford as well as Danny Kerr, huntsman at Camargo Hunt, another rousing Kentucky hunt. Shaker enjoyed talking shop. Most huntsmen did, especially as they were few in number, 162 in North America, give or take one or two depending on circumstances.

"Dreamboat, this was your day. It was the best day you ever had," Sister called to the racy-looking hound as he enjoyed his food, drizzled with corn oil for the taste and also the shine it put on the coats.

"Funny, isn't it?" Shaker smiled, for he liked the hound so much. "He really did me proud."

"I love this pack. It's taken a lifetime of breeding and work and I've always loved my hounds, but Shaker, I think this is the steadiest, hardest-working pack I've ever had and of course, much of the credit belongs to you and our whippers-in."

"No shortcuts." Shaker appreciated the compliment and she knew it.

The two of them had spent many an hour poring over bloodlines and performance. They also attended other hunts, singling out the special hounds there. The research never ended, the study, the planning, and they never wanted it to.

Sister's cell phone beeped. She fished it out of her barn jacket, as she'd already taken off her good hunt coat. Peering down, she read a text:

"Call me. O.J."

"Excuse me a minute." She walked back into the tidy office and called Kentucky.

"Hey."

"Sister, Alan and Meg notified the authorities as you would think they would. So Benny Glitters's tomb has been opened with, oh, I don't know what you call them, forensic people, I guess were there. Anyway, they found an entire human skeleton. Found the watch chain, no other jewelry. Bones and a watch."

"What about the dog?"

"Buried with the human skeleton. No one can say for sure but it looks like the skeleton of a little terrier, you know, like a Norwich. The snout wasn't long enough to be a Jack Russell. Oh, the human skeleton is male."

"I'll be damned. Did they find anything else?"

"Well, Benny Glitters."

"Yes. Remind me again about Benny Glitters."

"The owner, Captain Brown, of Walnut Hall before L.V." Like most people, O.J. called Mr. Harkness by his first initials, as though he were still alive. "Brown was a very successful Thoroughbred horseman."

"Right."

"Before he died, he'd bred Benny Glitters. Everyone thought this would be the next great one. It surely looked like it. Well, Captain Brown died in 1894. The year Benny was eligible to race, he was sold along with the farm to L.V. L.V. was a harness-racing man but he wouldn't have minded winning the Derby. Anyway, Benny started out brilliantly, winning everything and then just fizzled. No one knows why. He was sound. L.V. retired him, hoping he might prove useful as a stud. But then Lela, L.V.'s one daughter, he had two, fell in love with Benny, who was sweet. He became her favorite horse. She foxhunted him and when he died in 1921, she created a memorial. Benny is the only Thoroughbred buried in that graveyard, placed a little off to the side, under the trees."

"She must have loved him very much."

"It's a wonderful story. The Chetwynds, your Chetwynds, did a lot of business in Kentucky, as you said. Old Thomas Chetwynd and L.V. were pals, according to Meg. Kindred spirits perhaps. Thomas had the big slate covering the tomb made, cut, engraved, and brought it out from Virginia to here. I guess there are a lot of slate quarries in central Virginia."

"Yes. We hunt a fixture with an abandoned quarry on it. A seam of land running under a few counties, kind of like your limestone, I guess."

"Anyway, that's how Benny came to rest. The first Standardbred buried in what we all now know as the cemetery was Notelet, who died in 1917, and of course by then L.V. was gone. He died in 1915."

"I don't suppose anyone has an idea who it was down there with Benny," said Sister, her interest piqued, inflamed really.

"No. It surely seems to be murder. You don't just reopen a grave and stick someone and their dog in it."

"True enough and it couldn't have been a robbery. No one would leave a gold watch."

"Meg said police took the watch with them after looking it over carefully at the site. No initials on it but a horsehead is engraved on the back. So I suspect whoever was down there was in the business."

"Or an inveterate gambler," speculated Sister.

"Didn't think of that."

"No good will come of this. I don't care how long someone has been entombed, when you disturb them, troubles follow." Sister shivered for a second as she felt the old evil of the deed.

"I wonder if troubles will follow finding and moving Richard the Third." O.J., an avid reader and history buff, had followed that recent news story with great interest. The bones of the former English king—killed in 1485 in the Battle of Bosworth Field—were found under a parking lot.

"In one way or another it will, but I'm sure the British are equal to it. My worry is this is our problem. Well, I certainly hope it doesn't bring trouble to Meg and Alan, or others that we know."

"Sister, isn't it creepy to think someone has been down there for one hundred and thirteen years and no one knew?"

"That's just it. Someone did know."

CHAPTER 4

Clutching a bottle of hyaluronic acid, Crawford Howard leaned over the counter of the Westlake Equine Clinic. Barbara Engles, the receptionist, printed out the receipt just as one of the partners in the clinic emerged from the rear of the facility.

"Crawford, how are you and how is Czpaka?" asked the veterinarian, Penny Hinson.

"Good. This stuff works. I take it myself. Physicians warn us not to use vet products but hyaluronic acid is hyaluronic acid and it's a lot cheaper here."

Wise in the ways of bumping up any human pharmaceutical cost, Penny nonetheless didn't want to counter a human doctor's caution. She smiled. "So both you and your horse have good working joints."

"Marty's horse, too," he said, mentioning his wife and her horse.

Kasmir Barbhaiya came through the door. "A convocation!" he exclaimed.

Crawford Howard, a self-made man originating along with his fortune from Indiana, respected Kasmir. Crawford felt that anyone who made wagonfuls of money was smarter than someone who didn't. "How's Nighthawk?"

A large smile wreathed the kind fellow's face, for Kasmir, like most foxhunters, dearly loved his equine partner. "A bad boy. Oh my, yes, a very bad boy."

Penny unzipped her coveralls, smears of mud and some blood on them. "What did he do now?"

"Stole my Borsalino. Oh, a lovely navy hat it was, and he snatched it right off my head."

"Did he put it on his?" Penny smiled at Kasmir.

"No, he ran all the way to the end of his paddock, all the way back, then dropped it in his water trough."

Crawford chuckled. "Give him credit for good taste. You never wear anything shabby."

"You are too kind," Kasmir demurred. "I wish you would rejoin the hunt club, Crawford. Yes, I do." Kasmir held up both hands palm outward as this was a vexing subject. "You must hear what happened in Lexington, Kentucky. A most remarkable thing."

He told the three about the sudden pogonip, the sleet, the long ride back to the barns and then the discovery at the Walnut Hall dinner.

"A gold watch?" Crawford stroked his chin.

"Oh, that poor little dog." Barbara couldn't care less about the watch.

"Did they find a body?" Penny got down to business.

"I read *The Lexington Herald* online," Kasmir informed them. "They did, but whose body they don't know. A stray skeleton, ah, too many deaths, I think."

"How do they go about notifying the next of kin if they can't identify the remains?" Crawford remarked.

"Who would know?" Kasmir replied.

"Exactly," Penny sensibly said as Mercer Laprade came through the door.

"Ah, Mercer," said Kasmir. "I was just telling the ladies and Crawford about the branch cracking the slate covering the horse's tomb."

Mercer was careful around Crawford, as he hoped one day the rich man would breed Thoroughbreds to Mercer's profit. "It was a joint meet with one excitement after another."

"You two should come hunt with me." Crawford then added with vigor, "The hell with the MFHA and who would know? My Dumfriesshires are good hounds."

He mentioned the Master of Foxhounds Association of America and a type of hound that originated in Scotland, hence the name. As Crawford ran or tried to run an outlaw pack, members of recognized hunts could not hunt with him without jeopardizing their status with other recognized hunts. The rub was how does one enforce this and Crawford well knew it. He had no intention of submitting to MFHA rules, hence the term outlaw pack.

Kasmir inclined his head in a small bow. "You are most hospitable." Then he quickly changed the subject, turning to Mercer. "You would remember, what was the name of the horse whose memorial covering was smashed?"

"Benny Glitters," Mercer quickly answered as he, too, wanted to slide away from the outlaw pack discussion.

"Yes, yes, that's it."

Mercer was eager to share his knowledge, hoping Crawford would be a bit impressed. "Benny Glitters was a son of the great Domino. Captain Brown, who owned him and the farm then called Senorita, thought he would equal his sire on the track. A beautiful fellow, Benny. Alas, he went up like a rocket and came down like a stick, which was unusual since Domino usually passed on talent. His son, Commando, for example, another great horse."

Crawford placed the bottle back on the counter. "Benny washed out?"

"The farm was bought by L.V. Harkness, who changed the name to Walnut Hall," said Mercer. "One of his daughters fell in love with Benny, who more or less went with the farm. He lived to a ripe old age, twenty-nine. He was so loved he was buried at the farm, the only Thoroughbred in the graveyard. So that's how Benny wound up where he did. His father, by the way, is buried at Hira-Villa, Kentucky. Domino died in 1897. A great, great horse. You can never trace pedigree back far enough."

"It's worked for you." Crawford nodded, acknowledging Mercer's success. For Crawford, success meant money, which led to prestige.

"A bit of care and most people can see some profit in Thoroughbreds." Mercer was shrewd and knew not to push it. He also did not expand on his views concerning the upsetting graveyard incident.

"Um." Crawford picked up the bottle again. "Well, I'm on my way to Old Paradise."

Both Kasmir and Mercer held their breath for an instant, and Penny's eyebrows rose.

"A place steeped in history." Kasmir always felt the romance of Old Paradise. His holding, Tattenhall Station, lay across the road from Old Paradise. Both places encompassed thousands of acres.

"Steeped in history and stupidity," said Crawford. "The DuCharme brothers, thanks to their ridiculous feud, never realized the profits the place could bring. The last smart DuCharme was the one who created the place and that was after the War of 1812. The rest drifted along." Obviously, he disdained the distinguished old family.

"Perhaps," Kasmir said noncommittally. Although a recent resident of this beautiful area, he took pains to learn the history of the farms as well as the people.

"Perhaps? The brothers are idiots and all over a

woman. This was back in the 1960s." He laughed. "And it's not like Binky's wife is Helen of Troy."

No one said a word.

Then Penny remarked diplomatically, "Your efforts are bringing the place back. The sad Corinthian columns, all that's left from the great fire—the sight of them always gives me chills."

"Marty says that, too." Crawford had often heard this from his wife.

"Crawford, you like history." Mercer fed him a compliment. "The boars on top of the pillars to your entrance were the symbol of Warwick the Kingmaker, the man who put Edward the Fourth on the throne."

Crawford lapped it up. "A man who knew how the world truly works. I have always admired him and when I first went to England I visited where he is buried."

"Back to dead bodies again." Penny giggled.

"The truth will all come out sooner or later," Mercer replied.

"Did the dog carry the gold pocket watch?" Barbara couldn't resist.

They all smiled.

"Well, I'd better get over there to see Arthur and Margaret." Crawford named Arthur DuCharme's daughter, a sports physician. Arthur was Binky's brother.

"I do hope you will allow us to continue on to

Old Paradise if the hunted fox leaves Tattenhall and crosses the road." Kasmir smiled.

As Kasmir had more money than Crawford, the late-middle-aged man softened his words. "Of course. I respect the traditions, but it goes in reverse, Kasmir. You won't throw me off of Tattenhall if my hunted fox heads east."

"Never." Kasmir smiled broadly.

"Good to see you all." Crawford left.

Mercer breathed out through his nose, then said, "He lives to make us miserable."

"Not us," Kasmir corrected him. "Sister Jane."

Penny knew the story. "And all because she didn't choose him to become Joint Master."

"How could she?" said Mercer. "He's like a bull in a china shop. Every week she'd have to put out brush fires started by his ego. She's a good Master and yes, his money would have been terrific and he would have spent freely but my God, we would have paid for it."

Penny nodded. "Subtlety isn't his strong suit."

"The first time he met me, he looked into my eyes and said, 'You must have a lot of white in you.'" Mercer's light hazel eyes flashed.

"I hope you said, 'Sure, my bad half.'" Penny looked at the wall clock.

"You know, I didn't say anything. I figured why bother on someone that dense? You know, it is possible to be rich and stupid."

Kasmir burst out laughing. "I know."

"Kasmir, I never meant you," Mercer quickly apologized.

"A man can be smart about one thing and dumb about another, or as my late wife used to say, 'A man can be smart during the day but dumb at night.'"

CHAPTER 5

Wednesday, February 5 was fair, in the midthirties, and began with a glorious welcome sunrise. Sister, Shaker, Betty, and Tootie walked the hounds from the kennels along the farm road. On their right was a large pasture with stone ruins in the middle of it, a huge tree beside the ruins. The old fence line had three stout logs as a jump not too far from the ruins, all that was left of the first tiny dwelling from the mid 1780s. Horses took this log jump seriously, whereas an airy jump, some spindly sticks, often set them off.

The group walked on foot. To their left reposed a lovely apple orchard, its trees gnarled. Inky, a black fox, kept a cozy clean den here, from which she would sally forth at night for hunting as well as to visit the kennels. She enjoyed chatting with hounds as long as they were on the other side of their heavy chain-link fencing.

A huge old walnut growing at the edge of the ruins provided a spacious accommodation for Comet, a gray fox. While not as good a house-keeper as Inky, he wasn't a total slob like Uncle Yancy, a red fox who threw everything out of his den. Even a human not well acquainted with wildlife would know whoever lived in Uncle Yancy's den was messy.

Foxes, like people, evidenced distinct personalities and habits.

Asa, an old hound beloved by all, walked up front. He could only hunt one day a week now but he still hunted well. Then, like many an old gentleman, he needed some extra rest, the canine version of Motrin, and a bit of extra love.

"Inky, I know you're in there," Asa good-naturedly called as the pack walked by.

A voice from within the den hollered, *"And I'm staying in."*

"Saucy devil." Sister laughed as she heard the little yip.

On the right side of the pack, Shaker grinned. "The only thing better than being a fox on this farm would be being a hound or a horse. Then again, being a human isn't so bad." He looked over toward the ruins, where Comet did not stick his head aboveground. "Give any thought to breeding Giorgio?" The huntsman greatly admired this hound.

"I have. I'm not sure yet to whom or if we should take him to another club. You know, Princess Anne has some wonderful girls, old Bywaters blood." She mentioned an exciting hunt located on the mighty Lower James River.

Sister, like any Master who breeds, studied bloodlines. Since childhood, she had favored Bywaters blood, a hound bred for Virginia's demanding conditions. She also strongly liked

Orange County blood, another Virginia hound bought from William Skinker, the Virginian who bred them, by a rich northerner, Harriman, over one hundred years ago. That old, fine blood coursed through Orange County's kennels.

They walked on, the dirt road firm.

Tootie glanced up toward the top of Hangman's Ridge. "Looks like it's blowing up there."

Betty also looked up. "Hard."

"That's what's so odd," said Sister. "Sometimes the wind will barrel right down the edge to us and other times it literally skims over our heads. You'd think after living here all these decades I'd have figured it out."

Walking out hounds, always a high spot in the day for the staff of The Jefferson Hunt, seemed to put things in perspective. Each time Sister would walk along with her friends and hounds, she knew how lucky she was to be strong and healthy and, best of all, to live out in the country where she could open her door to a beautiful world unfolding before her. She often thought of the millions of people all over the world whose primary view was a set of red taillights in front of them only to be followed by a computer screen. And then there were how many millions of women in Africa who walked miles to a well for a bucket of water? Were taillights an improvement over such hardship? Sister feared urbanization and had no answers to counter the destruction of so many unique environments. But she did know she'd fight like the devil to protect Virginia.

"Did you read in the paper about the next bypass meeting?" Betty inquired. "This western bypass has been in contention for, what, forty years?"

"Actually, I didn't read it," said Sister. "I did find out from O.J. that there was an entire man's body in the horse's grave. I told you that, though, didn't I?"

"You left a brief message. Well, whoever he was, God rest his soul," Betty intoned. "Seems to me all they have to do is go through the papers from 1921 to see who went missing."

"I don't know but I do know we'll be hunting from Tattenhall Station tomorrow and I will bet any of you one hundred dollars that Crawford will hunt from Old Paradise."

"He did that last season and at the beginning of this one, and made a fool out of himself both times," said Shaker. "He can't be that stupid." He laughed because Crawford would lose his pack or more accurately, whoever was hunting his hounds would lose the pack. Now on his fourth huntsman in three years, Crawford couldn't stop from meddling, from thinking he knew more than the person he hired to hunt his hounds.

"No one's going to bet me one hundred dollars?" Sister wheedled.

"I will." Tootie took her up on it.

"And if you lose the bet, where are you going to find the money?" Sister smiled at her.

"Betty will lend it to me," the beautiful young woman teased.

"Ha." Betty loved Tootie, as did they all.

"I'll bet one hundred dollars," Trident offered, the young hound listening in.

"You don't have anything worth that much," Dragon, a few years older, taunted him. *"You aren't even worth a hundred dollars."*

At that, the pack laughed that funny dog laugh where they puff out a little air, their eyes brighten.

"Just wait," said Trident. *"I'll show you all tomorrow that I'm worth more than one hundred dollars."*

And so he would.

Tattenhall Station, a clapboard train station with lovely Victorian flourishes, rested on the west side of the Norfolk and Southern rail line. The Western County Volunteer Fire Department sat across from this on the eastern side of the tracks. It was the westernmost fire station in the county.

Tattenhall, once busy thanks to passenger trains, had fallen into disuse, and was finally abandoned by the railway in the early 1960s. Kasmir Barbhaiya bought the station, all the land abutting it on the south side, and had added bits and pieces of more property over the last two years. His holdings, now two thousand acres, give or take, bordered such historic properties as Old Paradise to the west, Little Dalby and Beveridge Hundred to the south.

Across from this charming station, restored by Kasmir, sat the picturesque Chapel Cross on the northeast quadrant of the crossroads that bore its name. Apple orchards abounded along with pastures. Across from the church, shielded by pines, Binky and Milly DuCharme's Gulf Station still sported the old blue and orange Gulf sign. His son, Art—in his midthirties, often called Doofus behind his back—sometimes acted as a go-between for the brothers, as did Margaret, Arthur's daughter. The two cousins got along just fine, despite feuding fathers.

Horse trailers parked in the paved lot at the station. Sister knew the fixtures around here as well as her own farm. She'd hunted them for over forty years, thinking of her landowners as a large family, filled with old stories, resentments, loves, dreams.

Across from the fire station, Mud Fence was yet another fixture, so Sister had thousands of acres at her disposal, barring Old Paradise now controlled by Crawford. Recently, she'd also picked up some new fixtures.

The DuCharmes were desperate for money; what choice did they have but to turn out their old friend Sister when Crawford offered to pay big bucks to hunt there? This was also a violation of

MFHA strictures. Land had to be offered, not paid for. Knowing this, Sister bore no grudge but she sorely missed Old Paradise. Crawford rented it, improved it, but did not own it . . . yet.

Phil Chetwynd, Mercer Laprade, Ronnie Haslip, Gray, the Bancrofts, were a few of the people whose trailers Sister had noticed as she drove in earlier. People were out in full force, for the day looked promising and February could wind up with snowstorms canceling hunt days. Why miss a good day?

Once everyone was mounted, Sister quietly said to Shaker, "Hounds, please," the traditional request from Master to huntsman meaning, "Let's go."

Looking down at all those upturned faces, Shaker smiled, and replied, "Hup-hup."

He trotted up the slight hill behind the station, calling out, "Lieu in," then blew the note followed by four short ones. Hounds moved out in a semi-circle going forward, noses down.

Trident spoke loudly. Never one to be outshone by any other hound, Dragon checked the line. Trident was right. Dragon, fussy because he didn't go out Tuesday, tried to push ahead of the well-built tricolor but Trident was a touch younger and fast. All of Sister's younger hounds had speed. She had deliberately picked up the pace in these last three hound litters.

The pack ran so close together one could have

thrown a blanket over them, as the old foxhunting saying goes. The horses followed. Shaker rode Kilowatt, purchased for him by Kasmir, and felt as though he'd gone from 0 to 60 in three seconds. A few in the field parted company from their mounts, as the acceleration caught them off guard.

Bobby Franklin always assigned someone to ride tail to pick up the pieces. Fortunately, no one was hurt, but there's always that delay for a person on the ground to mount, which is why someone stays back. The field must move on, and move on they did.

Happy for a fast start, Sister felt Aztec stretch out underneath her. Like so many Thoroughbreds, Aztec had a long stride, so compared to other horses in the field it looked as though he wasn't laboring or trying very hard. And like all Thoroughbreds, he was born to run. The hounds charged into the thick woods a half mile from where they picked up the fox. Narrow trails necessitated slowing and taking some care, lest you leave your kneecap on a tree trunk.

Even with leaves off the deciduous trees, Sister couldn't see well. Behind her, Bobby's voice, loud and clear, stopped her short.

"Tallyho," came his booming, deep voice.

This was followed by a chorus of the same.

Sister couldn't easily turn around. She heard hoofbeats coming toward her. Aztec didn't want to back into the woods with its low bushes, but a hard squeeze did the trick.

"Huntsman!" Sister shouted.

With difficulty, people got their horses into the woods, heads pointing outward. In this way, the huntsman and Kilowatt didn't risk a kick. A hard kick could break a leg.

Flying as fast as he could given conditions, Shaker, mindful of the members, touched his crop to his cap. As he burst out into the open he saw Bobby, horse turned toward the north, cap off in his right hand, arm extended fully. This told the huntsman the line of the fox.

Sister was still in the woods and not liking it. She shot out of the underbrush to Aztec's delight, then thundered past the people in the woods. Following by placement, one by one, they emerged. Phil Chetwynd, who had ridden right behind Sister, was the next out. Ronnie Haslip, the club's treasurer, was next, and so they went. This is a sensible arrangement because usually horses in the rear are slower than horses in front, so if the people in the back came out first they would slow everyone down.

As she reached the pasture, Sister saw nothing. Bobby, as he should, followed the huntsman. She hit the rise, looked down and saw hounds, huntsman, Betty on the right, Sybil on the left, and Bobby leading Second Flight behind. As Sister rode down, hard, Bobby veered off to the side so she could slip behind Shaker, leaving a good forty yards between huntsman and herself. The faster you rode, the more space you left, just in case.

Once the entire First Flight emerged, Bobby fell in behind them. The fox, which no one saw, crossed the railroad tracks and cut north into Mud Fence farm.

The riders had to cross above the railroad tracks, then carefully cross the tertiary road, climb a small bank, take three steps, and pop over a coop that, having sunk with age, couldn't have been more than two and a half feet high. Sister was over in a flash, as were those close behind her, including the Bancrofts who, nearing eighty, were always perfectly mounted for their abilities, high, and their ages, also high.

Bobby knew where a hand gate was. This cost him a good ten minutes even though the last person with a companion closed it so he could get forward. You never leave anyone alone at a gate when horses are moving off. So it's always two people.

Bobby heard the horn blowing "Gone Away" again. Standing in his stirrups to see over the rise, he beheld all in front of him and pushed on.

Sister, flying, just flying, reveled, in her element. The fact that this was a fox they didn't know also excited her. Given the hard winter, breeding season had been interrupted by heavy snows, so she was sure this was a visiting dog fox.

She passed a collapsed shed, then the entire pack, Trident still in front, turned west, headed for Chapel Cross. A narrow ditch divided the church land from Mud Fence and it was full of running water from melting snows higher up. Aztec leapt it. Sister didn't look down. Never a good idea to look down.

They clattered by the graveyard, right past the small lovely church and had to cross the north/south road, which meant Sister was right at the Gulf station. Apron on, Milly stood in the picture window with DuCharme Garage written in the top. She waved to the people, which made a few horses shy.

Sister waved back but kept moving. The fox crossed the east/west road almost at the crossroads, shot into the edge of Old Paradise, and ran along the snake fencing. A roar above them announced Crawford Howard's Dumfriesshire hounds, who joined them.

To Sister's relief, the two packs ran together. The music was incredible. The cry of these hounds must have reverberated over the mountain all the way to Stuarts Draft.

The new, larger pack soared over the snake fencing, crossed the road again, this time a good mile from the crossroads. Trident was still in the lead and to Sister's surprise, Dreamboat was pushing his way forward.

Sister was so proud of him. His great day at

Oakside had emboldened him. He now believed he could lead and he was right up there.

She easily jumped over the snake fence, hit the road, slowed for a moment, then rode along the three-board fence marking Kasmir's land. A new coop beckoned; it was stout. Again, as it was close to the road, she had only a few strides to hit it right and sail over, which she did; but like any rider, a little wiggle room was always desirable.

Within seconds she was right back in the woods and hounds just tore through those woods, finally losing their fox at a small meadow with large fallen trees on it bordered by a tributary feeding into a larger creek.

How did the fox lose them? Scent vanished.

Hounds cast about, Shaker patiently waited, moving a bit here, a bit there, but that boy was gone.

Everyone pulled up. Some slumped over, trying to catch a deep breath.

The two packs kept trying to pick up a lead. Shaker called them over and Crawford's hounds followed, as though part of the Jefferson pack. He headed the group south, and try as he might for the next hour, their efforts were fruitless.

They'd been out for three hours, so Shaker turned back toward Tattenhall Station. Once again, hounds opened.

This brief run took them down to the larger creek. After fifteen blazing minutes, that was over.

Although she had hunted since childhood, Sister never deluded herself into thinking she understood scent. Only the fox understood scent. Hounds could smell it but they didn't understand it either.

Oh, she knew the basics. She knew a fox could jump into the creek and run in the water to destroy scent, which this fox may well have done. A clever fox with some den openings into a creek bed could get in and out without leaving much of a trace, or so Sister thought. He could roll in running cedar or cow dung, which threw hounds off for a time. He could also, if he knew where one was, go straight to a carcass. That never failed to confuse hounds.

But those thoughts were the thoughts of reason. The fox didn't care what she thought.

The group of humans chatted excitedly on the way back to Tattenhall Station. If hounds had spoken, the people would have quieted. Sister had them well trained. Crawford's hounds merrily tagged along. A gabby field drove her bats. Her people respected tradition. The human voice can bring a hound's head up, the last thing you want to do. They need their full powers of concentration. The only thing worse than bringing a hound's head up was kicking one. Turning a fox back into the hound pack ranked right up there with these cardinal sins as it meant certain death for the fox. Sister didn't want to kill foxes nor did most other Masters.

Fortunately The Jefferson Hunt people, most all of them, rode to hunt as opposed to hunting to ride. Observing hounds when they could was a goal for many of them.

Sister motioned for Tootie to catch up to her.

"See anything?" she asked.

The younger woman shook her head, then added, "Well, I did see Lila Repton take that coop on the road. Her horse didn't."

"She all right?"

"Yes. I stayed back to get her up."

"Could she make the jump then?"

"She was a little put off so I jumped her horse over. She climbed on the coop and mounted up while I untied Lafayette from the fence line. He's so good, that horse."

"Well, that was good of you."

"Lila is desperate to ride First Flight. I figured maybe this would help."

"Mmm. Good run." Sister beheld both packs walking quietly up ahead. "How long before he tears down here with his hound trailer and raises holy hell?"

Turns out, Crawford didn't show up.

Sister, Shaker, and the whippers-in put up the Jefferson Hounds and Phil Chetwynd kindly allowed Crawford's hounds to rest in his horse trailer. His horse and Mercer's horse, Dixie Do— tied outside, happily munching away at feed bags—didn't mind.

The station had a long kitchen at one side. Kasmir had outfitted the place so the club could enjoy hot breakfasts. Old railway benches pushed up to long tables provided seating. Once people selected what they wanted from the food tables outside the kitchen, they were glad to sit and not stand holding plates. There was also a cook in the old kitchen to scramble eggs, flip pancakes, fry bacon. This was pure luxury.

The old station exuded an ambience of time gone by. To Kasmir's credit, he did not dispense with the sign over a door that said Ladies Waiting Room nor the old one that spelled out Colored. He talked to many hunt club people about it but Gray settled the issue for him. Gray simply said, "It's our history. Let's not hide it."

History infused the place. As people excitedly replayed the hunt, some could imagine ladies in long dresses, bonnets, repairing to their waiting room where their delicate sensibilities would not be offended by the unwanted attentions of men.

The Southern concept is that every man surely wants to be in the company of a lady.

Sister figured there was some truth to that and she swept her eyes down the long tables to see the women, flushed from the exercise, exuberant. Even those not especially favored by nature became attractive. And then there were the ones like Tootie, so beautiful, so young and sweet, that she took a man's breath away. Tootie had no idea of this. That made her even more beautiful.

Unfortunately, not enough young men hunted but when one did show up in the hunt field he gravitated toward her.

Tootie's dream was to hunt hounds one day after becoming an equine vet, a dream that infuriated her ever-so-rich Chicago father and didn't much please her socially-conscious mother either. Why would their beautiful, brilliant daughter want to operate on horses as well as be an unpaid amateur huntsman?

On and on the assemblage chattered. Sister, coat hanging on the rack at the door along with everyone else's, pulled her grandfather's gold pocket watch from her vest. Snapping it shut with a click, she laughed, for Phil, Mercer, Gray, and Betty had imitated her with their pocket watches.

"Grandfather's." Phil smiled. "I know that's our grandfather's."

Betty chimed in. "Dad's."

"What about you, Mercer?" Sister asked.

"Bought it at Horse Country. You know the case of antique jewelry? Couldn't resist." Mercer smiled.

"The workmanship on those old pieces is, well, I don't know if people can make jewelry like that anymore." Sister again pulled out her grandfather's pocket watch, admiring the filigree and his initials in script, JOF for Jack Orion Fitzrobin.

Sister was a Fitzrobin on her mother's side and an Overton on her father's. She'd had a wonderful childhood of hunting with both grandfathers and grandmothers.

Betty, Phil, and Mercer again pulled out their pocket watches, opened them, and then all four clicked watches together, which gave them a good laugh.

After the breakfast, Sister kissed her Thorough-bred Aztec, then along with Betty and Sybil, rendezvoused at the hound trailer, also known as the party wagon.

Betty asked the obvious, "What do we do about Crawford's hounds?"

"Take them to him. I think they'll load into our trailer." Sister put her hands on her hips. She had no desire to see Crawford. However, she would always help hounds.

As his trailer was near the hound trailer, Phil overheard. He and Mercer usually hauled their horses together using a top-of-the-line four-horse conveyance.

"Sister, I'll take them to Crawford. I pass his farm on the way to mine and our guys will be fine with hounds all around them, plus we have the dividers. As long as they have their hay bags they don't care."

Dividers, a padded type of guard hung on a hinge, could be used to separate horses.

"That's kind of you."

"I don't mind a bit." Phil smiled broadly.

When Phil rumbled down Crawford's long drive, at the turnoff, Sam Lorillard met him with a truck and led him back to the kennels, on which—like everything else—Crawford Howard had spared no expense.

Phil had called ahead to Sam, Gray's brother, who worked for Crawford. No one else would give the former alcoholic a job, including his brother. Crawford took a chance on him, paid him handsomely, and was well rewarded by Sam's loyalty and labor.

Sam unloaded the hounds. "How was the hunt?" he asked.

"Good," Phil replied. "Where's Crawford?"

"Up at the house. He drove in about an hour ago."

"Well, his hounds hunted nicely under Shaker, if that matters to him," Mercer piped up.

Sam nodded. "He fired the huntsman in the middle of today's hunt. We will now be looking for number five."

"Man would have to be a fool to take that job." Mercer didn't monitor his opinion.

Grateful as Sam was to Crawford, he knew Mercer was right.

"He'd do better with a woman," Phil declared.

"Why's that?" Sam watched the last hound walk into the well-lit kennel.

Phil folded his long arms over his chest. "I think women are better at dealing with difficult people."

Mercer pulled out his pocket watch and as he did so he told Sam about the four people closing their watches at the same moment. "You know we'd better shoot out of here before he sees us and we hear the lamentations of Crawford Howard," Mercer advised.

"Something elegant about a pocket watch," said Sam.

Mercer said, "One of our relations had a gold pocket watch and he walked into a whorehouse and never walked out—remember that old story?"

Phil tilted his head. "Must have been a hell of a transaction."

Eye on the big house, Mercer recalled, "Great-Aunt Jessamy would shake her head and say they never found anything of Grandpa Harlan's. They found an empty wallet and his clothes were neatly folded in the laundry room of the establishment. Of course, the authorities couldn't tell Jessamy that, but they told enough others. Word got around." He looked at his cousin. "Funny what one remembers."

Moving toward the driver's door, Phil said, "Maybe some things are better forgotten."

CHAPTER 6

The long polished table gleamed under the soft lights which, though subdued, were bright enough to take notes by. The board of trustees for Custis Hall met regularly once a month, more if the occasion demanded. The paneled room was in the original building.

Founded in 1812 as a school for young women, it remained true to its originating principles, now being one of the best prep schools in Virginia. The original funding came from the owner of Old Paradise, a grand lady who had made a great fortune running supplies through the British lines during the War of 1812. Had this indomitable woman been able to return she would have been satisfied, thrilled even, at how the school had flourished over the years. She would have been much less impressed had she visited Old Paradise.

These days, Crawford Howard, a board member, was slowly putting the holding's owners, the DuCharmes, in his back pocket with money and improvements calculated to help Arthur again keep cattle. Crawford's long-term goal was to buy Old Paradise. The DuCharmes would first fight among themselves but he could play a waiting game.

On moving to central Virginia, Crawford

committed the mistake of building a garish new home designed to look old. He garnered attention. Not a penny was spared. Over time he learned that showing off his riches like this put a mark by his name as a vulgarian, even though he tried to make the place look historic. Far better to buy an historic estate. Even if one lived in one that was falling down, that still trumped the look of new money. Every place has its ways and Virginia remained steadfast in her habits, for both good and ill.

To Crawford's credit, he cared about young people. One of his passions was education and he gave generously—as in six figures per annum—to Custis Hall. Young and attractive, Headmistress Charlotte Norton proved adept at managing him, a quality Sister Jane admired since she had failed to pacify Crawford when he was a hunt club member. Crawford's business acumen also proved vital to Custis Hall.

Sister was now in her fortieth year on the board of trustees, for she kept getting re-elected. She valued Crawford's contribution even as she disdained him personally. While lacking his degree of business sense, she had a bit. Moreover, she was one hundred percent committed to a strong humanities curriculum, which meant foreign languages, structured classes, knowing your country's history along with world history. As a former professor of geology at Mary

Baldwin College, the huntmaster was passionate about the natural sciences.

The board had wisely corralled a bank president, head of one of the best local law firms, and one music star—who worked very hard, to everyone's surprise, as they thought she'd more or less show up for one meeting a year. Turned out that Mary Sewell Wainwright was as enthusiastic about all the arts as Sister was about the natural sciences.

The two women clicked, despite a thirty-year age gap.

Elected just last year and still finding their way were Phil Chetwynd and Mercer Laprade. The Chetwynds served on many boards but this was Phil's first turn at Custis Hall, where his oldest daughter was a sophomore. Mercer was determined to create scholarships for young women of color, a much cherished goal.

Nancy Hightower, also African American, addressed the gathering. "My fear is that this interference will create a backlash."

She referred to the S.O.L.'s, the Standard of Learning rules laid down by the federal government and then enforced by the state government.

"Not for us." Phil put his pencil down. "Custis Hall exceeds all the criteria."

"Let me be more clear, the backlash I fear is accusations about elitism. We outperform most every state school and we are right up there against St. Catherine's and St. Christopher's, Collegiate, St. Gertrude's, Foxcroft, Madeira. We hold our own and better."

"Private schools can't be compared to state schools," said Phil. "We can be far more demanding than the state."

"Yes, we can and we should be," Mercer agreed, his light voice clear, pleasant. "But the bulk of our students come from homes that are stable, value education, and strongly support same. We need more scholarship students."

"Mercer, forty percent of our students receive some form of student aid," said Isadore Rosen, head of personnel.

Now in his midfifties, Isadore had taken his job decades ago, thinking it would be temporary. But he had found his calling and stayed, to the benefit of all.

The six o'clock news anchor at a network station in Richmond and a Custis Hall alumna, Frances Newcombe agreed. "Mercer has a point. Private schools are seen as elitist and there is resentment about children not getting in because they can't afford it. We all at this table know it takes more than money, what it really takes is aptitude, a willingness to work hard and frankly, there's not enough of that as I would wish. This is a generation that expects to have everything given to them."

Sister weighed in. "With all due respect,

Frances, there are plenty of young people out there who would make good use of an education here if they could swing it. Custis Hall is expensive as are all the prep schools. It's not just the expansion of scholarship funding, it's also the housing, the food. You all see our budget statements. Lord, just keeping the physical plant and the grounds up to form costs us thousands upon thousands. And then if we could increase enrollment of scholarship students, could we raise the money to pay for it? Where would we build a new dorm without risking the historical character of this place? Custis Hall is one of the most beautiful secondary schools in the United States."

In his commanding voice, Crawford said, "There is another way."

The eleven other trustees stared at him as did the headmistress, Isadore, and the two other school administrators present.

"How?" Charlotte asked.

Never averse to being the center of attention, Crawford paused for a moment, then launched in. "We can't create scholarships without creating more infrastructures as has been noted." He couldn't bring himself to credit Sister but she enjoyed that he had to acknowledge her concerns. "Custis Hall can create outreach programs. There's no reason why we can't rent space for early evening classes, weekend classes in Charlottesville, Waynesboro. Bringing in students who don't live on campus is cheaper than construction. Yes, it takes planning and we would need to augment salaries for those on the faculty willing to do this. But even if we had to hire some new people, it's more cost-effective than housing twenty or thirty new students on campus."

A long silence followed this, then everyone talked at once, sparked by Crawford's vision.

Sister, who always made a point of sitting next to him on the principle that you keep your enemies close, touched his forearm. "Brilliant, Crawford. Thank you."

He nodded, then looked up as Phil called over the chatter, "Crawford, the old Chetwynd offices are serviceable in downtown Charlottesville. They need a bit of rehab but I could do that as a gift to Custis Hall if the board pursues this."

Charlotte pounced but softly. "Phil, that is extraordinarily generous. Well, Crawford, you've given us all something exciting to consider. I don't want this to slip away, frittered away in committees, so may I ask the following to be done for our next meeting? Crawford, would you examine our curriculum and determine what you think would be suitable for satellite locations or even e-courses? Most all students have access to a computer now."

Apart from the reception to his idea this flattered Crawford, who assumed she'd always limit his input to financial matters. "Of course."

"Phil, given your family's long association with the area, might you explore other potential locations?"

"Are you willing to decentralize enough so that we could offer classes in Waynesboro and over by Zion Crossroads?" Phil inquired. "In that way, we could bring in students from western and eastern counties. Zion Crossroads could serve Louisa, Fluvanna, possibly even Orange. There are a lot of bright kids out there."

"Hear. Hear," Mercer said.

"Mercer, are you willing to secure, or even procure, the numbers of students in area schools who score in the top ten percent at their school, the ones with good grades?"

"Of course, but Charlotte, there are kids who aren't doing well scholastically who would if we could just reach them." Mercer truly cared.

The headmistress smiled for she, too, wanted to find those diamonds in the rough. "You're right, but we may have to work up to that or find an efficient way to identify them. I know test scores aren't always the answer; the answer is and always will be educators who take an interest in their students, which brings me to you, Lucas." She addressed Lucas Diamond, who had worked in the State Education Department. "Find those teachers."

He looked up at the ceiling, then around the table. "Well, if you all can do what you're going to do, I will do my part." Then he laughed.

"What about me?" Mary Wainwright asked plaintively.

"Mary, this board and me in particular are going to shamelessly abuse you." That got everyone's attention. "Once we have a plan, you are going to give a concert to raise money."

All eyes were on Mary as she dramatically breathed in, then said saucily, "I will raise so much money you'll be able to build a satellite campus."

The room cheered. Sister thought it was the best board meeting she'd ever attended.

As it broke up, knots of people conferred and she found herself with Phil and Mercer by the long polished sideboard against the wall.

"Hey, to switch the subject, Sister, I know Lafayette is getting on. That fellow has to be fourteen or so, right?" asked Phil.

"We're both getting up there." She smiled at the thought of her aging horse.

"Keepsake and Rickyroo must be close to their early teens, too, if I recall," Phil continued.

Mercer teased, "I feel a horse deal coming on."

"I have a two-year-old and a three-year-old. One is by Guns and Roses and the other by St. Boniface, out of solid mares but they don't have the speed for the track. They have good minds. Why don't you come have a look?"

Crawford joined the group. "Phil, thank you for bringing my hounds back the other day."

Knowing the history between Crawford and The Jefferson Hunt, Phil said, "It was Sister's idea."

As this transpired, Mercer glanced at his iPad, which showed he had a new e-mail. He checked on the message. "Sister, thank you," Crawford said, doing the right thing.

"Crawford, they hunted wonderfully well under Shaker and they are in good flesh. Very handsome hounds." Sister smiled.

Clearing his throat he responded, "Thank you."

"What the hell?" Mercer exclaimed, then looked up. "Sorry."

"Well, what the hell?" Sister teased him.

"Justin Sautter, with the help of Meg and Alan, have gone through the family papers and found a note about the delivery of Benny Glitters's slate memorial. Roger Chetwynd"—Roger was old Tom Chetwynd's son—"Lucius Censa, the Chetwynd's stable manager, and a Negro worker accompanied the memorial. The Kentucky forensic people said the skeleton is that of an African American male, early forties, old break in the left leg. Anyway, they think the skeleton might be of the man who accompanied the slate memorial from here in Virginia to there. They also found a note in Lela's hand about the slate and the man escorting it, whom she described as a 'fine dark man with an adorable little dog.' I'll bet that was my grandfather!" Mercer said with excitement.

"I thought your grandfather walked into a whorehouse and never walked out," Phil remembered.

"Am I missing a good story?" Sister leaned toward Mercer.

"Grandpa Harlan did," said Mercer, "but I didn't mention that the whorehouse was in Lexington, Kentucky."

Phil calmly replied, "Mercer, even if it is your grandfather, why would he end up in a grave with a horse and a dog? It makes no sense."

"It makes sense to someone," Mercer's voice rose.

"I'm sure they are all dead," Phil replied.

"Well, they may be but that doesn't mean someone who is alive doesn't know," Sister stated as Crawford, Mercer, and Phil looked at her.

"If you all will excuse me, I'm going to concentrate on the living." Crawford withdrew.

"Me, too." Phil smiled.

Mercer drew close to Sister. "You're right. Someone might know. Wait until I tell Mother. I want to know who killed my grandfather and why. Mother's become very intrigued, too."

"I can understand that, Mercer, but you don't know for sure that this body was your grandfather's. As it was 1921, he must have had late children."

"He did and my father, his son, had me in his middle years. In my family, we stay, um, virile and healthy a long time."

"I hope so." She winked at him.

CHAPTER 7

Cold seeped into Uncle Yancy's bones. At ten, for a red fox he was old. Quick thinking and cleverness kept him alive when other foxes fell by the wayside. He wondered when his spouse would leave her earth, a spacious den. A nag, Aunt Netty had plucked his last nerve and he had moved out. She said she threw him out. Over the last three years Netty's expulsions became an annual event based, she said, on his messy ways. She prided herself on a clean den. His version was she didn't know what she wanted and had turned into an old crank.

Then spring would come, Aunt Netty would need help with one project or another, something usually involving killing rabbits, and she'd woo him back.

This night, twenty-two degrees outside but cozy in the mudroom at the Lorillard home place, Uncle Yancy swore he wouldn't fall for it this spring . . . if spring ever arrived.

Yancy had chewed a hole through the floorboards from underneath the mudroom to crawl up next to the tack trunk. A few of the floorboards were rotten, which made it easier. Sam Lorillard had thrown a pile of washed red rags in the corner, then forgot them. The fox, smelling crumbs and other tidbits would push the rags aside, enter through, then push them back. Once in the mudroom he had many places to hide, including jumping from shelf to shelf until he was on the highest one. To him, the mudroom was a little bit of heaven. The temperature inside hovered in the low fifties. The grasses and old towels in his den in the graveyard, another under the front porch, were all right if he curled up, but this was true luxury.

Uncle Yancy recognized the Lorillard brothers, Gray and Sam. The two kept the home place, having bought out their snotty sister, Nadine, who was now a leading light in Atlanta, wanting nothing to do with country life. She certainly wanted nothing to do with Sam.

Gray would stay home maybe two nights a week, less if he was called in for a consulting job in Washington where he retained a convenient small apartment. The rest of the time he stayed at Sister's.

Uncle Yancy knew many of the humans in his territory. The Bancrofts' farm touched the Lorillard farm on the Lorillards' western edge. He also knew Sister, Shaker, Betty, and Sybil and he even recognized some people in the hunt field. From time to time the hounds, all of whom he also knew, would pick up his scent and he'd lead them a merry chase until he tired of it. Usually he'd dump them at Hangman's Ridge, an eerie place. Too many ghosts and too many minks—those nasty little devils with their sharp teeth. He hated them. It was mutual, but their strong odor almost always threw off the hounds, and many's the time when Uncle Yancy walked down the backside of Hangman's Ridge. Just in case, he marked every gopher hole and abandoned fox den along the way. You never knew when you'd need it.

On the top shelf, he rested his head on his outstretched right arm.

The kitchen was next door, a wood-burning stove heating most of the wooden house with a little help from a newly installed heat pump. There Sam sat on a chair, bucket between his feet, bridle in his hands. Uncle Yancy could smell the special saddle conditioner, a type of saddle butter, that the wiry man always ordered from Grangeville, Idaho.

The men's voices carried into the mudroom and the fox found their deep timbre oddly soothing. He liked Sam, who he saw more than Gray. Something sad and lonely about the man affected the creature. Most all of the higher vertebrates can sense emotions in others. Humans deny this ability in animals, but then they also deny their own emotions. Uncle Yancy had nothing to hide, therefore he was open to all information.

"That stuff really is the best." Gray leaned back

in the wooden chair. "But it takes so long. First you have to strip down the leather, wash it good, use some saddle soap, then let it dry. Half the time I don't have the time."

"Brother, when do you clean your own tack? You pay Tootie to do it for you."

Sheepishly, Gray agreed. "Most times I do but, you know, those spring days, you smell the apple blossoms, then it's a joy to sit outside and clean tack or clean anything, really. The rest of the time, not so much."

"I never knew how beautiful this place was until I left for college. Harvard, well, it's in the city, grand as the place is, but I thought I would perish of homesickness."

"Me, too, not so much at college but all those years in D.C." Sam rose to start heating water on the stove. "I feel like hot chocolate. What about you?"

"Sounds good. I've been thinking about what you told me. What Sister told you after the Custis Hall meeting last night. Mercer's one brick shy of a load."

Gray smiled. "He's always been excitable."

"Excitable, hell, he's all over the map. Lorillard men aren't supposed to be, well, you know. Anyway, he treats me like a slug, a sea slug."

"Because you don't have any money. Sam, he's not that bad."

"Hell, he's not. The only reason he's nice to me

is when he nudges me a little to try to get business out of Crawford. Oh, how Mercer loves to make money and be around money."

"His side of the family has had money for a long time. While he's not exactly Crawford or Phil's equal, he's not poor by a long shot. And give him credit, he knows his business."

"He can recite bloodlines and sales figures. I told him once, forget blabbing about bloodlines. People don't care. Just talk about how much the sire won or the dam and what their progeny is doing on the track. But he keeps blabbing on, showing off."

Gray mixed the hot chocolate powder, the hot water releasing the enticing smell. "Here."

"Thanks. You taking a break from female companionship?"

"Sam, I usually spend Monday and Friday nights here if I can. Sometimes it is good to have one's little space."

"*A Room of One's Own*." Sam cited the Virginia Woolf book, as he was well educated.

"Something like that."

"I don't know if I will ever enjoy female companionship. Been a long dry spell." Sam started rubbing in the saddle butter using the warmth of his hands to help the waxes penetrate the leather. "Mostly I really do enjoy women but sometimes the way they think drives me over the cliff. Too emotional."

Gray shrugged. "That's painting with a broad brush."

"Yeah, but my experience is women notice the damnedest things. I mean stuff that just makes no sense. Kind of like Mercer." He burst out laughing.

Gray laughed, too. "The Laprade side of the family is given to emotional drama."

"They live for it. I'll bet you twenty Georges that if that body is our grandfather or great-grandfather or whoever the hell he is, some family relation, Mercer will be beside himself."

Gray touched his mustache, smoothing it outward. "Nero Wolfe. He'll have to solve the crime."

This set them both to laughing.

"I'm surprised Mercer hasn't driven to Lexington to offer up his saliva for a DNA test." Sam could hardly finish the sentence, he was laughing so hard.

"I don't get the science behind that but it must work." Gray finished his drink. "I wonder if we want to know too much. Maybe it's better not to know. Someday, someone will find Amelia Earhart or pieces of something that will solve her disappearance. What good does it do? She's gone. Same with the princes in the tower. Remember that, when the two little bodies were found under a stairwell in the Tower of London? Anyway, that was before DNA testing, but so many people are convinced these are the murdered sons of Edward the Fourth."

"Gives academics and novelists a field day. You know, did Richard the Third kill them, or did Henry Tudor once he became king after killing Richard at Bosworth Field? I'm curious I guess. Yeah, I am."

"You always liked history," said Gray. "I read some and I know we need to know what came before but Sam, I can't say as I care much. I care about now. I care about the future."

"But that's just it, the past is prologue."

"Teach you that at Harvard?" Gray smiled.

"Did. The guilt of throwing away that education haunts me. Christ, what a mess I made of my life, your life, anyone around me."

Gray had paid for two drying-out clinics. The second one took. As Sam had remained sober for nine years now, Gray began to relax, yet in the back of his mind was always the fear that somehow for some reason, Sam would relapse.

"It's all over, done. I don't know what was worse, not capitalizing on Harvard or losing your chance as a steeplechase jockey. You could have set up business after the competitive days were over but you're still in horses, you can still set up a sideline." He leaned down and picked up the saddle butter jar. "Build a better mousetrap."

"That saddle stuff really is the better mouse-trap." Gray wiped his hands on a cloth, then rose to wash them.

Gray took his cup over to the sink, looked out

the window. "Black as the ace of spades. Low cloud cover."

"Half moon tonight. The good thing about a low cloud cover is it keeps a little heat on the earth. Those cold clear nights make it hurt when you breathe."

"Tonight's cold even with the cloud cover," Gray remarked.

Sam opened the door to the mudroom, flinging two used towels toward the back door. "I swear I smell fox."

Uncle Yancy, flattened low on the shelf, watching with his glittering deep yellow eyes.

Gray joined Sam at the door. "Does. Probably the graveyard fox."

"Well, he has one hell of a signature if it's this strong in the mudroom." Sam closed the door.

Had the brothers walked into the mudroom, turned around and glanced upward, they would have seen the tip of a magnificent brush just falling over the shelf. Uncle Yancy was hiding in plain sight.

It would have been a good lesson for all to learn before it was too late.

CHAPTER 8

That same Friday night Sister's fountain pen glided over perfectly lovely cream stationery, the hunt club crest centered at the top. She sat at the graceful desk in her library, its smooth writing surface highly polished. This regal piece of furniture commanded the room. While Sister considered this her main desk she was one of those people who scribbled wherever she could. At the end of the day, after her shower, she would often troll through the house's rooms, picking up and reading through her notepads, finding much that could prove useful.

Golliwog, her insufferable long-haired cat, sprawled on the back of the leather sofa, her tail slightly swaying to and fro. Plopped on the sofa cushions the two house dogs snored; Raleigh, a beautiful male Doberman and Rooster, a harrier bequeathed to Sister at the death of an old lover, Peter Wheeler. He also willed her his estate, Mill Ruins, on which an enormous waterwheel, ever turning, could have been restored to grind grain should anyone be so inclined. Mill Ruins was rented for ninety-nine years by Sister's Joint Master, Walter Lungrun, M.D., a fellow in his prime, early forties. Peter had always sworn to Sister that he would leave her everything, but she'd thought he was joking. He wasn't and she found herself with two sizable farms to run, combined with the great good luck of owning desirable property.

Conscious of her wonderful luck, Sister realized there are people who resent anyone with resources. She accepted that blind hatred, and she had no real answer as to why the Wheel of Fortune had placed her on the upswing. She herself was not an envious person. She did, however, like very much that her position allowed her to be useful to others—specifically young people and animals. She cared little about anyone else's status or bank account. She either liked you or she didn't, and being Southern, if she knew you needed some financial help she often found a way to do that without embarrassing you. Many Virginians had a lot of pride and would not take what they considered a handout. She worried about so many people out of work, she worried about people sliding out of the middle classes into poverty, and she also was angered at those few who abused public trust whether on Wall Street, Silicon Valley, or Washington, D.C.—people who profited secretly or openly from the distress of others.

She was just one person. All she could do was to shoulder the load with people she knew. Sister was not one to write checks to organizations. She had to know to whom money was going and she had to respect them. If nothing else, she was consistent.

She'd written a check this Friday to Custis Hall for a scholarship for a fourteen-year-old whom Mercer sponsored. He wrote the other half of the check for the girl's first year.

Sister did not think of herself as a particularly loving or good person. She thought of herself as a clear-eyed responsible one. What others thought of her mattered precious little if at all. This quality above all others drove her enemies wild. Over the years, Crawford had dug, parried, and derided her, yet she never bothered to respond. Worse, she sought him out at the board meetings and remained friendly with his wife—or as friendly as she could under the circumstances.

Some of this impressive lady's supreme self-confidence was rubbing off on Tootie, who walked into the library.

"Bills?" asked the lovely young woman.

"You know, just when you think you're in the clear, the mailbox is filled with some more." Sister capped the pen, turning to view Tootie, who had recently turned twenty-one.

"Did you hear that Felicity got promoted?" Tootie mentioned a brilliant schoolmate of hers who had gotten pregnant. Unable to go off to college, Felicity took night courses toward a degree.

"Garvy Stokes knows talent when he sees it. I'm

behind on seeing Felicity. I haven't visited my godson in two weeks."

"He doesn't stop talking." Tootie smiled. "Not at all like his mother," she quipped.

"And how is your mother, speaking of mothers?"

Tootie shrugged. "Same as always."

"You haven't visited Chicago in over a year. Why don't you go once hunt season is over?"

Tootie sat on the couch next to Raleigh. The Doberman raised his head only to drop it in Tootie's lap, give her a loving gaze, then close his eyes.

Golly, on the other hand, opened her lustrous eyes. Far be it for the cat to miss anything.

"I don't want to," said Tootie. "It's always the same old thing. They make me miserable, angry, and finally bored."

"That's a harsh judgment on your mother and father."

"Sister, you've met them."

"I have, and I know your father doesn't much like me but he's still your father and he loves you the only way he knows how. And as for your mother, she does what most good wives do, she props him up, tries to get him to see reason or at least have some emotional understanding. She loves you, too."

"You know what, Sister? I don't care." A flash of defiance flared from that beautiful face.

Picking up the fountain pen, Sister twirled it.

"You've been with me one and a half years now and you've taken courses at UVA. You've kept your word about that. Things come so easily to you—riding, college courses. I don't know if that's good or bad."

"Not everything. I signed up for organic chem. That might not be easy."

"We'll see. You know Dr. Hinson will help." Sister named the veterinarian, a woman who liked Tootie.

"I'm trying to be like you." Tootie smiled. "I'm writing letters."

Sister beamed. "It's the only proper way to communicate, or at least to communicate some things. I was just writing O.J. to invite the Woodford group here in March. We've talked about it but a formal invitation is needed. Wouldn't it just be silly if they all get here and we have a storm?"

"What was it you called the storm in Lexington?"

"A pogonip, a freezing fog. The superstition is that it brings bad luck."

"Well, it did, didn't it?"

"I suppose it did."

"I found some old pictures of Benny Glitters."

"You did?" Sister asked, surprised and curious.

"Sure. I'll show you." Tootie rose, walked to a simple desk tucked in a corner, upon which was Sister's computer. The young woman sat down and quickly pulled up images from Google. "Look."

Sister stood behind her. "I keep promising to move the computer out of here to a better place, a bigger place, and move that little desk. Well, that's irrelevant, I fear. I'll never be able to use it like you do."

"You don't have to. You have me." Tootie clicked and sure enough there appeared an old sepia photograph of a petite woman in hacking attire, presumably Lela Harkness, astride a well-built bay.

"How about that? Don't you love that Lela looks like a magazine model? People dressed for the occasion in those days." Sister leaned forward, squinting a bit. "Benny Glitters looks like a handsome bay horse. Well, Thoroughbreds are usually some form of bay or chestnut with the occasional gray. Look how sturdy his forelegs are."

"I found other pictures, too." Tootie flipped through old photographs, some from the turn of the last century going up through the 1920s. "Here's one of Phil Chetwynd's grandfather, I guess."

"Roger was the grandfather. Old Tom, Phil's great-grandfather, started Broad Creek Stables. Both Phil and his brother—the one who lives in Charleston, West Virginia—resemble their father, also named Tom in honor of the original patriarch. I vaguely remember Roger. What I recall is that he was so competitive. When people had money in those days, they really had it."

"Look at this." Tootie filled the screen with

photographs of L.V. Harkness's daughters, and others of Walnut Hall through the years.

"Go back to Benny," said Sister.

"Sure."

"Okay, now can you find me a picture of Domino?"

"That's easy. He was so famous. There's lots of photographs." Tootie proved her point.

"Hmm. It's hard to tell how much Benny looks like his sire. Pull up one of Domino's most famous sons, Commando."

Tootie did. "He looks a little more like Domino. I mean, it's hard to tell bays apart."

" 'Tis. I'll tell you a secret. Always start at the hoof. Then go up the legs starting from the rear. Pause at the gaskin, the large muscle at the top of the hind legs often called the second thigh. Now look at the hip angle. Okay, go to the forelegs. Same trajectory. Right? Now look from the withers to the hindquarters. Okay, set that in your mind. Look at the shoulder angle, look at the angle of the neck from that shoulder, look at the chest. Finally, go to the head."

"I did that."

"Now pull up a photograph of Man o' War. He ought to be easy to find."

He was.

Tootie looked at the great horse as Sister had instructed her. "Well, they don't look alike but they are both really handsome horses."

"Yes, they are. A sharp eye can help you a lot, save mistakes." Sister paused lest she rattle on, although Tootie was a ravenous listener. "And after all the conformation talk, I tell you the most important thing about horses, hounds, and people: You can't put in what God left out."

Tootie quietly registered all this. "You mean the mind, the mind first."

"Indeed I do, especially for a hunting horse. You can get killed out there, Tootie. Sometimes I think people who foolishly ride a beautiful horse with a bad mind are just asking for it. I don't have but so much sympathy."

The two studied Man o' War, a delight for any horseman. Tootie clicked back to Domino, and they examined him again.

"Look at these photographs of Broad Creek Stables. This one is from 1902!" said Tootie.

"Old Tom Chetwynd. He had to be incredibly smart to found that coal business and then the stables, too. I often wonder why Phil doesn't leave for Lexington, but he's big beans in the Mid-Atlantic."

Tootie remarked, "Some people like my father have to be the big shot, you know?"

"I know, but Phil covers it up well." Sister watched as Tootie scrolled through more photographs.

"Stop." Sister pointed to a photograph of Roger Chetwynd and Lucius, the stable manager. Behind them stood some stable hands and a well-dressed African American. Farther back were horses in paddocks. "I'll be damned," said Sister.

Tootie studied the photograph. "I see it."

The natty African American had Mercer's chin and his high cheekbones. There was a resemblance but then again many people could have those features. Catching both their attention too was the adorable, bright-eyed Norwich terrier at his feet.

Tootie looked up at Sister. "Should we tell Mercer?"

Sister took a long time, leaned on the back of the sofa.

"I was here first," Golly complained.

Rooster opened one eye and regarded the cat. *"Shut up, Golly."*

"Methuselah's dog. Worthless old fart." Golly swished her tail.

Without rising, Rooster lifted his head, growling.

"That's enough," Sister commanded.

Golly eyed the harrier with malicious glee.

"No, we shouldn't tell Mercer about the resemblance," Sister finally declared.

"Why?"

"Mercer can be like a helium balloon. *Pfft.*" She moved her forefinger up in the air like a helicopter blade.

"I have a terrible feeling about those old bones. Mercer, well, I just think he could stir up a hornet's nest."

"But that could really be his grandfather." Tootie was confused.

"It was so long ago," Sister said. "The reverberations from violent crimes never quite stop. That's easy to see in the cases of"—she thought about earlier conversations with O.J.—"Lincoln's assassination, stuff like that. That's a significant political event but any murder is an event that touches others and can continue to do so. We should be careful."

"But we don't have anything to do with it."

"Tootie, if we are too interested or find some useful information, we *will* have something to do with it. That man was killed over money, a lot of money. You don't kill someone for a few bucks. Don't get me wrong. I want to find out what I can. Seeing that forefinger, the watch, and little dog skull really got me. But something tells me to be careful. That had to be murder."

"A woman. Men kill over women."

"He wouldn't be buried with a horse and his dog. He would have been shot in passion or stabbed. This is deliberate. You know how I told you to look at a horse from the hoof up, well, look at this from the ground up, so to speak."

"Didn't Mercer say his grandfather's clothes were found at a whorehouse?" Tootie was realizing that Sister was extremely practical when it came to emotions.

Mercer, on the other hand, was volatile and

emotional. Strangely enough, at the same time, he was shrewd and patient concerning business.

"Apparently, that was a ruse," said Sister. "Whoever murdered Harlan Laprade thought it through. People would be more than willing to believe a man would go to a house of ill repute, an expensive one, and fall into trouble. Especially if he's away from home. Men visit such places every day all over the world."

Young and idealistic, Tootie said, "That's horrible. Disgusting."

"Honey, most men, no matter where they are, high or low, Asia, Africa, the Americas, you name it, most men feel they are entitled to sex."

"Gross!"

"I can't judge. I can only tell you that if a fellow doesn't have a girl in every port, so to speak, he's happy to pay for a night of pleasure. In fact, it's easier. No strings. A straight cash transaction. Whoever left those clothes folded in the laundry room at the whorehouse was very, very clever and probably knew the victim would be there—or visit, then leave. How easy to kill him in an alley, take his clothes back to the whorehouse. Pretty easy, I think. First of all, no one would tell a wife her husband's clothes were found in an exclusive whorehouse. So there's one line of inquiry shut down."

"They would now." Tootie was incredulous.

"But not then. Remember the time. 1921.

Secondly, the murder victim probably had a reputation for chasing skirts. Those who knew him would be surprised at his disappearance but not really shocked. I mean it, Tootie, if a Laprade really is the victim, we need to be careful. Whoever killed him is long gone but the effects of that murder might not be, especially if it was over a boatload of money and it was done or conceived by someone highly intelligent." Sister put her hand on Tootie's shoulder. "Let's walk softly."

"Maybe we should hope Mercer doesn't find any photos," Tootie remarked. But he had.

CHAPTER 9

"Don't you have a brighter lamp?" Mercer fussed as he peered at old photographs.

"Use this little flashlight." Phil pulled open the narrow desk drawer, retrieved a small promotional LED light, and handed it to him.

Looking at the light, Mercer remembered. "This thing has to be four years old."

"It is. Gave them out at Keeneland back at the stables." Phil sat shoulder to shoulder with Mercer at his office desk in the old main barn.

"Last really good sale anyone had. This economy has to get better," Mercer grumbled.

"It will. Always does. The secret is to pare down and hang on. I forgot that Daddy saved all this stuff. Fortunately, he kept it in a metal box up at the house. Glad you made me look for old family photos."

"We don't have any that go that far back. That's my granddad Harlan," Mercer said, squinting at the sepia photograph. "Can't be anyone else." He flipped it over, and along with the filly's name, Topsail, was Harlan Laprade.

Shirtsleeves rolled up, bowtie, what looked like summer flannel pants and a snappy boater, Harlan stood next to the filly. Both stared straight at the camera.

"Knew how to show a horse," Phil said admiringly.

Mercer carefully sifted through more photographs in the pile from the metal box. A few were of back barns and run-in sheds being built, the main barns in front. Others cataloged mares, colts, fillies, and four standing stallions.

"Navigator. 1923. Bone." Mercer appreciated the bay stallion. "He had some age on him in this photo but he looks incredible. Just incredible." Mercer remarked on the heavier denser bone the horse displayed compared to so many of today's horses, who are more fragile.

"Had to have bone then. Still should. But so many races were a mile, a mile and a quarter. Few seven furlong runs then, I think." Phil tidied up the photographs. "Dad said that was the biggest change he'd seen in his lifetime, the jigging of race conditions to favor weaker horses."

A furlong is one-eighth of a mile.

"Mmm," Mercer half listened, his eye again drawn to his grandfather. "Good clothes run in the family."

"Seems so. Funny, I didn't know Dad kept so many photos."

"Mother advised me to ransack the old barn for photographs, files. I think my dear mama lost some things like photographs between moves and husbands back in the day."

Phil took the photograph of Navigator from

Mercer's hand. "Would you like me to make a copy of this?"

"Mother would like that," said Mercer. He was a bachelor and lived just next door to Daniella Laprade, which most folks would think was too close by.

"Looking at these photos, I wonder if they were happier then. Was life really simpler?"

"No. Nothing changes, Phil. I'm convinced of that. Technology changes how fast we can travel, communicate. Medicine changes, but people, no. People don't change."

"Yeah, I guess. You know, maybe I'll make two copies of this and send one to the Lexington Police Department."

"What can they tell from a photograph? All they have are bones, but now I'm sure they are my grandfather's. Did anyone at the farm keep records? Not breeding records and accounts but, you know, a diary?"

"Not that I know about but, Mercer, even if my great-grandfather Old Tom did or his son, my grandfather, did, no one would record the clothing being found in a house of ill repute, then send it on to the family. One didn't talk about stuff like that, especially if a woman might find the records and Dad always said that Grandpa and Great-grandpa were circumspect, especially where women were concerned. A trait I'm trying to pass on to my boys, but maybe they're too young."

"Ten and twelve, that's not too young."

"If whoever was in that grave had his throat slit, any kind of flesh wound, there won't be a trace. The only way to know how he was killed is if a bone was shattered or lead pressed into it." Phil switched back to the unidentified bones in the equine grave.

"Maybe our dentist has records. Worth a try. We've gone to the same family dentist since Christ went to Chicago," Mercer replied.

The old Southern expression made Phil chuckle. "A long time and I don't know as the Good Lord was able to reach the Chicago heathen."

"O ye of little faith," Mercer chided him. "Thanks for finding this stuff. It's not like you don't have other things to do."

"We all do," said Phil. "Overcommittment is the great American vice." He smiled. "Anyway, I enjoyed looking at the photographs. I think both our grandfathers were driven men—had to be, to be successful. People like that usually accomplish a lot but they miss a lot, too. Dad said he hardly ever saw his dad and when he did, the old man paid little attention to him. Maybe that's why he was such a good father to me."

"Different times." Mercer shook his head. "Look, I know in *my* bones that was my grand-father, Harlan, in that grave. He didn't return to Virginia, obviously, from delivering the slate memorial. Has to be him that was under it."

127

"It's a good guess but don't jump the gun, Mercer. All that does is create confusion."

"It's Mother that worries me. She wants to know. She's looking for dental records. She wants to know now."

"Mercer, no one can handle your mother and you aren't going to learn now. If you find Harlan's dental records and if they match the corpse's, what then? There's only so much you can do."

"If they match, Mother will not rest until the story is told. Who murdered him and why."

"Even if it leads to the whorehouse?"

"Even so. This is a different day. That won't embarrass her. I think it probably offends me more."

Phil closed the metal box, looked at his old friend with surprise. "Why?"

"I really believe prostitution harms women."

Phil turned his chair to face Mercer more directly as they'd been sitting side by side at the big desk. "Not if a woman chooses the profession."

"If they had equal opportunity, would any woman?"

"Hell, yes." Phil slightly raised his voice. "It's fast money and you know the Sims sisters from central Virginia? They opened and ran the most elite whorehouse in Chicago, The Everleigh Club, at the turn of the last century. Those two girls made millions, millions."

That gave Mercer pause. "Millions?"

"Millions before income tax!"

"Well, maybe the Sims sisters chose running a house but what about the women who worked for them?"

"Mercer, I don't know. People make choices in life and some are made for you. If I were a young, poor woman, had beauty, I'd rather do that than flip burgers. It's one way to work your way through college, as well."

"Maybe," Mercer said, unconvinced. "How did we get on prostitution?"

"Harlan's clothes being found in a house of prostitution."

"Oh, right."

"Mercer, are you all right?"

"I am. I am." He breathed deeply. "It's Mother."

"Sorry." Phil, having grown up with the Laprades around him, knew how demanding and imperious Daniella could be on her good days. The bad days were hell.

Daniella's sister, Graziella—Gray and Sam's mother—exhibited a totally different personality. Diplomatic, polite, reserved, you never knew what the older sister was thinking. With Daniella, the world knew. Both women had been smashingly beautiful as had their mother, Andrea. Suspicion lingered that Phil's father, Roger Chetwynd, flourished in Andrea's company. Knowing winks, nods, whispers behind hands, fueled the suspicions. The boys, when boys, had no idea and both their parents shielded them from loose talk. As they grew to manhood, of course, they heard. Neither one discussed it with the other. Nor did Gray or Sam ever bring it up with their cousin.

Many were the beautiful women, nowhere near prostitution, who made the most of their beauty. Then and now. Mercer's mother and grandmother were no exception, as Phil now pointed out.

"Andrea and Daniella received a monthly stipend from my grandfather as long as he lived. Mother said when Roger would visit she'd be sent to Graziella's. I learned early to not ask questions about that." Mercer rose, rolled his chair back to the wall. "You know, I want to know and I don't. Part of me wants to know if my mother is your grandfather's daughter. Part of me doesn't. Part of me feels if those bones are Harlan's, I should give him a respectable funeral." He shrugged. "I really won't have a choice." Then he returned to Phil's desk, snatched the little LED flashlight off the top. "I need one of these. 'Broad Creek Stables' green and gold. Easy to find. Anything black is hard to find."

"Chiseler." Phil smiled at him.

Mercer pocketed the flashlight, made in China. "I'm just recognizing your marketing skills."

"Get out of here." Phil laughed at him. "See you in the morning."

CHAPTER 10

A light shone in Daniella Laprade's living room window at six-thirty that same evening. Mercer pulled into his mother's driveway, stepped out of his Lexus SUV, glad for the lamppost at the walkway to the front door, for darkness enveloped everything. A stream of cold breath gave evidence to the plunging mercury. Hurrying to the red front door, he knocked, then opened it.

"Mother."

Daniella looked up from *By the Light of Other Suns*, which she was reading with intense interest. "Where's your coat, son?"

"Left it in the car."

"Well, it won't do you any good there. Are you trying to die before I do?" She closed the heavy book, carefully marking her place with a satin ribbon.

"You'll outlive us all, Mother." He leaned over, kissed the 94-year-old on her rouged cheek, then sat opposite her in a chintz-covered comfortable chair. "Good book?"

"Remarkable. It's about the diaspora of our people after 1865. Of course, we never left."

Mercer smiled. "Better the devil you know than the devil you don't."

"Indeed. Laprades and Lorillards live by that." Her diamond earrings, bracelet to match, long wool navy skirt, and cowl-necked sweater marked Daniella as a proper woman of a former generation.

Smartly turned out even at home, Daniella was always presentable, should an unannounced caller arrive. A lady can never be too careful about her appearance, age be damned.

Tapping her finger on the volume, she ordered, "Fetch me a drink. Make one for yourself. We could both use a lift."

Mercer repaired to the well-stocked bar tucked into a corner of an equally well-stocked pantry with wooden folding doors to hide the cans. He quickly returned, a stiff bourbon in one hand and a cut crystal glass filled with ice cubes and locally made ginger ale in the other. Then he returned, poured himself a thimble of scotch with his own ginger ale chaser. The ginger ale sometimes seemed to pack more punch than the liquor. That stuff could pucker your lips. The Laprades regarded clear spirits as inferior. If you were going to drink, it had better be bourbon, whiskey, scotch, or rye.

Sinking in the chair as his mother drank half her bourbon with one smooth draw, he held up his scotch, stuck his tongue in first, then took a tiny sip. A wonderful warm sensation traveled down his throat.

Daniella raised her glass, "God bless the state of Kentucky."

He nodded, holding up his shot glass. Then he said, "Mother, how are you feeling?"

"Now? Good." She placed her glass on the coaster. "Good, all things considered. I haven't been idle today. I called Dr. Zazakos about my father's dental records. As you know our family has used the Zazakos family since the earth was cooling and they keep records. Well, they keep everything, don't they?" She referred to each generation's habit of collecting something. "I swear they never see a piece of paper they don't want to save. Naturally, the wives throughout the years are far more intelligent. They collect diamonds." She half smiled.

"Well, Mother, you didn't do so bad yourself."

"I had many admirers. In my day, men showed their appreciation in useful fashion. Don't you want to know what I found out?"

"I expect you'll tell me."

"They have Harlan's records and Peter Zazakos promised to e-mail them to the Lexington authorities. This should hasten the identification of those bones which I know, I know in my own bones, are my father's."

"Indeed, you haven't been idle," Mercer said admiringly.

"Did you and Phil find anything?"

"Let's say that the Chetwynds are not like the

Zazakos family but we found some things that Old Tom, then Roger saved: old photographs."

"Well?"

"A few, the old sepia kind, showed Harlan standing horses."

"You'd think the Chetwynds would have saved more things. They have every trophy they ever won."

"Silver," Mercer replied simply.

"I used to have scrapbooks but when I left my first husband, a worthless worm if ever there was one but handsome, oh so very handsome, he burned everything before I could come back to move them. Even burned my hats. Spiteful and silly."

"Mother, that is the most I've ever heard you say about your first husband."

She half laughed. "I married in haste and repented at leisure. Back then, son, if a woman wasn't married by twenty she was an old maid."

"You were and remain beautiful. I bet you were besieged."

She loved hearing that and recalled, "Graziella and I had our gentlemen callers and I must admit, Graziella married better than I. More sensible. But I learned." She inhaled. "How I learned. Your father, my third husband, like you, was a good, responsible man. My second husband was, too, but World War Two claimed him like so many." She held up her glass. "Might you fetch me another?"

He did as he was told, then settled again opposite her, flicking a speck of dust from his cashmere sweater.

"Son, how much did that cost?"

"The sweater?"

"I'm not looking at your shoes."

He stalled, then confessed. "Four hundred and twenty-five dollars."

"Mercer." Her voice rose.

"Mother, I deal with ultrawealthy people. I can't look unsuccessful. Failure has a scent, you know, and so does success."

"True." She nestled more deeply in her chair. "Tomorrow you will call the Lexington authorities, I have the number by the phone, and inquire about the dental records. If they have had time to compare. They need to hear from more than me and you have a voice that can get attention."

Mercer did not think he had such a voice but he knew an order when he heard one. "Yes, Mother."

She sat upright. "I want to know and I want to know what happened. I put this out of my mind and then it rushes back again like a swarm of hornets circling, or maybe a wind. I don't know." She waved her hand. "I can usually express myself but I find I become overwhelmed. Daddy died while I was so very young."

"I'll do my best."

Finishing her drink she lowered her voice. "A

restless soul, painful and never good. We must lay those bones and that soul to rest."

He believed as did his mother and he, too, lowered his voice. "I wonder sometimes, I wonder about all those people killed in wars throughout time. Never properly buried if they were buried at all. Are they out there wandering? There's so much we don't know, Mother, spiritual things, things that so many people would ignore today or think we were unintelligent for feeling this way."

"Son, the truly stupid people are the ones who think they know everything."

CHAPTER 11

Water sprayed off Mill Ruins's water wheel, thousands of rainbows flying with it. Saturday, February 8, welcomed The Jefferson Hunt Club members, hounds and horses, with pale sunshine and a temperature of 36°F by 9:30 A.M. This tempered by nine-to-ten-hour winds from the north northwest.

Her senses keen from having hunted since childhood, Sister knew the mercury would rise, but not dramatically. Desirable as that was, a tricky wind could bump up quickly. You never knew about winds cascading from the north northwest, sliding down the mountains, which at Mill Ruins lay twelve miles west. The view always delighted people the first time they beheld the old mill and the clapboard house, some of which dated back to 1730. This had been Peter Wheeler's home. Evidence of Peter's unique personality lingered among his beloved box-woods, his curving paths laid out to "alleviate the boredom of symmetry," as he would counsel Sister. Peter had believed his tall paramour was overfond of straight lines, squares, and quadrangles. She was.

Presently, her Joint Master could be glimpsed in the stable, below tremendous oak beams holding it all together for close to three hundred years plus a few. Walter babied Clemson, his hunter, even though Sister would chide him, "You spoil that horse."

"Look who's talking" would come his swift reply.

Sister was a woman who couldn't live without close relationships to men. A few, especially when younger, were sexual but most unfolded like Peter's roses, revealing surprising depth of color. Men trusted her and loved her. She felt the same.

Fortunately, she also loved her girlfriends like Betty, Tedi Bancroft, and young women like Tootie, but for whatever reason she gravitated toward men.

As a Joint Master, Walter dealt with Sister almost every day, usually on the phone or texting. He'd traveled so much this hunt season from one medical conference to another that he'd missed a lot of the season. His specialty was cardiology and every day something new transpired in his field. He wanted to keep current so that his patients benefited from the latest procedures, as well as Walter's deep concern. Walter was called to medicine the same way that Sister was called to hounds and horses.

She always told him his life was worth more than hers: He saved people. Walter would reply that she saved them in a different way.

"Oh, this will take fifteen minutes." Atop her

former steeplechaser, Matador, Sister laughed as she saw Walter run up Clemson's girth.

Walter needed to walk Clemson around for five minutes, slide the girth two holes higher, and this would go on until the girth was tight enough for him to mount. But Clemson knew the trick of blowing out his stomach so once Walter—tall, with long legs—was tight in the tack, the horse would exhale. His stable boy would crank it one more time and, of course, Clemson would shy away from the side being worked on, usually the left. He was a stinker.

He was also plated in gold in the hunt field so one endured the horsey hijinks.

Betty, driving the rig, pulled on the long side of the barn, where Shaker had preceded them with the hound trailer.

With a minimum of drama, staff mounted. Betty, Sybil, and today, Tootie, remained behind at the hound trailer with Shaker.

At least once a week Sister put Tootie out with a whipper-in. If a visitor or one of the hunt members needed a buddy in the hunt field, then Tootie was assigned to ride near them. The young woman also worked young horses for others when time permitted. They paid her for this so she earned more pocket money. At the moment, Sister had no youngsters but when she found some, Tootie would be perfect to bring them along.

As Sister rode Matador toward those already

mounted, a riderless Clemson hurried up to her.

"What have you done?" She grabbed his reins, leading him back to the stable.

"Nothing" came the unconvincing reply.

Sam Lorillard with his coworker, Rory, hurried out to take Clemson.

"Did Walter fall off?" asked a concerned Sister.

"No." Sam smiled. "Dismounted for one more bathroom run. Clemson took off before I could grab his bridle."

"How come you're here today? I would have thought Crawford would be out."

"He's in Connecticut at Westover," said Sam. "He wanted to talk to someone face-to-face about curriculum. He's going to Miss Porter's, a lot of those expensive schools out of state. He's also contacting Andover, Exeter, Taft, Choate, St. Paul's."

"Got the bit between his teeth." She paused. "Good."

"Edgy took sick, called me so I came over. Walter needs someone in the stable." Sam smiled.

"As do we all."

Edgy, the stableboy, had gotten his name for his bad haircuts, which the young man declared were "edgy" so he was ahead of the curve.

Sister rode back to the ever-growing crowd. All were in their formal turnout, as Saturday's rides were formal.

Vicki Van Mater and Joe Kasputys, in perfect

turnout, waited with the others. Sister smiled and called to them as they had hauled their horses down from Middleburg, two and a half hours north.

The wind kept the pines rustling. Sister looked up to see the treetops bending. Just no telling what the day would bring. Like any day, she supposed.

Finally, everyone was up in the saddle. She used to just take the hounds and leave, but so many laggards created havoc trying to catch up that Sister now used the tactic of waiting while staring at them. Somewhat helped.

Henry Xavier, always called Xavier, Ronnie's best friend, was present today. Sister noted he had lost one hundred pounds since undergoing the operation to shrink his stomach. He looked almost as he did when he was a boy, when he and Ronnie and RayRay, her son, would ride out in high spirits. Xavier never lost his baby face, which everyone had attributed to the fat, but his face remained youthful without the fat.

Looking over these people, some of whom she had known since they were born, others for at least forty years, others just a year or two, she thought Fate had brought them together. This touch of philosophy or superstition evaporated when Parker, a young hound, looked up at her and howled.

She laughed. "Well then, folks, we have our marching orders." To Shaker, "Hounds, please."

"Come along," he called and hounds followed him over the arched bridge, past the huge turning water wheel that always startled horses unaccustomed to it, the *slap, slap* as well as the sight unnerving them. They headed past the mill, curved left on the wide farm road, patches of shimmering ice in the low potholes.

On other side of the road, two fenced fields beckoned. The original dry laid stone walls, rehabilitated by Walter, stretched a half mile down to the woods at the end of the pastures. At that point the fencing became three-board fencing, for who could afford new stone fences? Walter used what stone he could find to make jumps, but for keeping stock penned in, it was three-board— which was expensive enough. Those locust posts, if one could find them, cost a pretty penny. The left pasture ran easterly while the right was westerly and longer.

Sometimes hounds would pick up a fox behind the mill but not today.

"My feet are already cold," Mercer grumbled.

Phil counseled, "A hard run will take care of that."

"No, it won't."

"Okay, they'll still be cold but you won't notice."

As he said that, Pookah, Parker's sister, nose down, started trotting. Pansy, another hound from Sister's "P" lineage, followed right behind her.

Within a few minutes the whole pack, twenty-five-couple strong this weekend, kept moving—but silently.

Hounds are always counted in couples, a practice going back thousands of years to ancient Egypt.

Sybil, on the left, picked up the pace as did Betty, on the other pasture.

Ardent, a hound with a deep voice, one of Asa's get, boomed out, *"Hot, hot, hot!"*

All at once it was as though someone put a blowtorch to the earth, for the scent lifted right off, filling those hound nostrils. Everyone spoke in unison.

On the road, Sister trotted, then galloped. She wouldn't jump in at the coop in the middle of the field until she knew where the pack would head. It was just as easy to make the wrong decision as the right on a day like this but she made the right one today, for hounds took the coop instead. Flying over in tandem, one by one, they jumped the facing coop into the right field to fly straight for Betty and Tootie, who adjusted in hopes they didn't cross the line of the scent. If they did, two sets of hoofprints could only do but so much damage.

Hounds headed due west to the edge of the pasture where two jumps formed a right angle. Betty took the western one, landing on a well-cleared path. Tootie followed. Shaker was soon over, then the entire field.

Mostly hickory and oak, with branches bare, these woods provided good views. The occasional oak had the old leaves, dried out, still attached. A steady wind, about nine miles an hour, kept up a light rattling sound. In a few dry places sheltered by rock outcroppings, the leaves underfoot crunched, but by February all the exposed places had the leaves squashed down, turning into the beginnings of soil.

The fox, a gray called Grenville, led them to a steep incline down to a narrow but deep creek. Hounds clambered down, then swam the few yards across to the other side and struggled up. Old tree limbs hanging out of the creek bed gave the place a sinister air. Sister picked her way along the edge to the crossing, walked across, then moved out.

A true February run lasted one hour and twenty minutes until Grenville returned to his den not far from the old mill and not far from a red fox's den. Try as they might, the hounds had lost the scent.

As the trailers were nearby, a few people, winded, decided to retire.

Sister rode up to Shaker. "Let's go to Shootrough."

A twenty-minute hack down that same farm road took them all the way to the back of Mill Ruins, where there was once a large shooting preserve. Walter dutifully kept it planted with millet, Alamo Switchgrass, and stands of corn here and there. He himself didn't shoot but he liked feeding the birds and, of course, the foxes, too.

The minute the hounds cast into the millet, they roared through. For two more hours, hounds would find a fox, run it, lose it, find another. Many days in hunting, especially in November, are trying. Once out of the November doldrums, however, one can expect a good run or two. Usually the great runs are from mid-January to mid-March, with February holding pride of place.

Sister had no proof of this other than her own memory and the memory of other old foxhunters. Maybe they told themselves that to make up for the bitterness of February, but she swore by it, and now she hadn't enough breath to swear because she and Matador, her former steeplechaser, had just jumped a wide ditch, and took two long strides on the other side to clear a long line of boxwoods. Peter had planned these jumps and, of course, during his lifetime the boxwoods had grown. Being American boxwoods, they were looser than the English variety. She could hear the *swish, swish, swish* behind her.

A long, long expanse of pasture confronted her, and she could just see her whipper-in and the huntsman and pack. Everyone was flying and Sister thanked her lucky stars for riding a great horse. Other riders were pulling up. The pace had been too fast for too long for many riders. Sister thundered on, the panorama in front of her swerved right. A storage shed, a formidable seventy by forty, was on her right along a deeply rutted farm road. She stayed in the pasture, even as the pack was now out on the farm road, for Sister thought she knew this fox. She figured he would duck right into the shed, where Walter stored some seed as well as old pallets—always useful.

He did. Hounds dug at the side of the metal shed. They sang out in both triumph and frustration. Even though they couldn't get to the den, they had put their fox to ground.

Shaker slid off Gunpowder, a Thoroughbred he loved, walked up to the entrance dug by the fox and blew "Gone to Ground." Hounds hearing this distinctive call, not like any other, wriggled in delight. He praised them. Betty and Sybil, now alongside the hounds, remained mounted.

Shaker swung back up in the saddle effort-lessly, which Sister envied as it was no longer that easy for her. Tootie stood on the other side of the shed, just in case the fox popped out.

Walter had just ridden up to the scene. Clemson lacked the speed of Sister's Thoroughbreds, but what the horse lacked in speed he made up in good sense.

"Hell of a run," Walter breathed heavily.

"The best. Just the best." Sister looked down at those glorious hounds, full of themselves.

"We can do more," Trooper promised.

His brother, Tattoo, agreed. *"We can run all day. Really."*

Sister asked Betty, on one side of the pack, "Where's Tootie?"

"Behind the shed, just in case."

"Let's call her to us. Shaker, I think we'd best head for the trailers. What do you think, Walter?"

"I think if we continue I'll wind up with some new patients."

They laughed and headed for the mill, walking along slowly. Took a half hour, and the wind came up, as did an unexpected rain; light though it was, it was steady and cold. Snow can be warmer than a rain in the high 30°Fs or low 40°Fs. By the time everyone reached their trailers, they were happy to dismount. After wiping them down and then throwing on a sweat sheet, most put their horses on the trailer. The heavier blanket would be thrown over soon enough when the sweat sheet was taken off.

Phil said to Mercer as they walked to Walter's house, "Think there's any food left?"

"If not, we'll make those that came in early go to Kentucky Fried Chicken."

"That will take an hour." Phil knew how far the franchise was—too far when one is hungry.

Fortunately, the table was filled with hot meats, salads, corn bread, macaroni and cheese, jams, and far too many desserts. It did not disappoint.

Too tired to stand, people found places to sit, some even repairing to the old country kitchen. The bar got a good workout, too.

Mercer, Ronnie, Xavier, Phil, and Freddie Thomas, a very attractive female CPA, sat at the kitchen table.

Phil leaned toward the voluptuous Freddie. "May I get you another drink?"

"Phil, if I have another drink you'll need to carry me out of here."

"That's the general idea."

Xavier raised his eyebrows.

"I am shocked. Truly and deeply shocked." Freddie never was averse to male attention but then what woman is?

"Did you view?" Mercer asked everyone in general.

Seeing the fox, always a thrill, was believed to bring good luck.

"No, I was too far back. Halfway through the hunt, I knew Diva and I"—Freddie named her mare—"needed to rate ourselves."

"Yeah, me, too." Ronnie nodded. "We started out with a great run, and then it just never stopped except for the hack to Shootrough. What a day!"

They replayed the hunt. Kasmir stuck his head into the kitchen and smiled. Someone called his name and he closed the door.

"You know, I don't think anyone viewed because I never heard a 'Tallyho,'" Mercer said.

"You're right," Phil agreed. "I didn't either."

As the food settled a bit, warmth crept into their toes, and the liquor added to the high spirits. They chattered away, people coming in and out of the kitchen, some sitting for a spell. The breakfast would be remembered as fondly as the hunt itself.

Freddie had a question for Mercer. "I know you're a bloodstock agent, but I don't really know what you do. I mean, do you sit and study bloodlines on the computer?"

"I do, but I'm fortunate in being able to see so many horses now and over the years. I go to Kentucky about once every two months and I've added Pennsylvania and New York to the list. About once every two years I'll head down to Louisiana, too. You'd be surprised at how many good horses are down there. Florida, of course. Florida horses around Ocala have the advantage of limestone soils but no one has the advantage like Kentucky."

"Really?" she asked, interested.

"Don't get me wrong. Virginia can still breed great Thoroughbreds, along with some of our neighbors. You're sitting next to one of the best."

Phil slightly tilted his head to one side in acknowledgment. "Freddie, we now have so many supplements that we can give growing foals an advantage similar to Kentucky, but there they just turn them out. We have to spend extra money on supplements. You only get one chance to ensure a horse has strong, strong bones."

"I never thought about that," she said. "I just hop up on Diva and well, like I said, I never thought about it." Freddie smiled, then added, "What did people do before supplements?"

Phil leaned in closer. "Broad Creek Stables was started by my great-grandfather back in the 1870s in a state wrecked by the war, no young men, no money, amputees in the streets. It must have been awful, win or lose, too many damaged people. Well, I'm off the track, literally." He laughed. "But I think about Old Tom and then his son, Roger; they had to have had it really tough. But what they did and what Broad Creek did was to haul mares to Kentucky by train to foal. This way they got the same head start that a Kentucky horse did. We often used our own stallions and we built our reputations on them. Navigator being the first really great one. We'd bring the boarders back as yearlings or two-year-olds and so we got great bone in them."

"And my family was part of that, my great-grandfather and grandfather," Mercer interjected. "They loaded horses on the boxcars with stalls, traveled with them. Grandpa studied what was in Kentucky. He made suggestions to the Chetwynds that put Broad Creek Stables on the map, so to speak. My grandfather got Old Tom to purchase Navigator. I think Roger was studying at the

University of Virginia then. Grandpa bought a few horses for himself. You know, a good horseman can usually survive. He might not always make money but that's the thing about bloodline research, I don't need to buy horses. My job, let's say you want to get into the game and you tell me you have twenty thousand to spend on a yearling. That's nothing, but I can set you up. Anyway, for a percentage, small, I will find you the best twenty-thousand-dollar yearling possible and since I have so many contacts, a lot of times I can get you a really good horse right out of the pastures. Avoid the auction. All I need is gas money, my computer, and my notebook. My overhead is low. Phil's skyrockets but his profits are greater when it all works. I can put you in a syndicate, too, but that's another story."

Freddie listened intently to Mercer. "You love what you do, don't you?"

"I do. My fear is that Kentucky will just blow itself up with this gambling mess." He then explained to her how one could only wager on horses at the tracks, nothing else.

"But why would that hurt you?" She reached for a napkin.

"Freddie, people will go out of business. Horses will be dispersed to states where the legislature invites horsemen and gamblers alike. That means a lot more travel for me and having to make more contacts. Not to brag, but I know just about everyone in Kentucky. You have a mare who was bred to a son of A.P. Indy, take your pick, she delivers a foal and I call and ask about the foal or I send an e-mail. I know who I'm talking to and they know me. Besides, I can read between the lines. And remember, Kentucky is the heart of the Thoroughbred business. Destroy that business and you really take something from America. It's part of our history."

"True enough." Phil agreed.

Feeling a bit sleepy, Xavier murmured, "Mercer can put you in a syndicate, too, like he said. You know, where a group of people own a horse together? This defrays expenses but allows people from all kinds of jobs to play. Some people love racing like we love foxhunting, but it's costly. Syndicates open the door for more people."

On and on they chattered until finally Freddie looked at the wall clock. "It's four o'clock!"

They all turned around to look at the big round wall clock. "Time flies when you're having fun." Ronnie smiled, rose from the table, clearing everyone's plates.

Once home, Sister, Gray, and Tootie took showers, then collapsed in the living room, fire crackling in the large fireplace.

Gray sipped his scotch while Sister and Tootie stuck to hot tea. They also replayed the day.

As though out of the blue, Sister said to Gray,

"Honey, does your family keep scrapbooks?"

"No. Why?"

"Just wondered."

He swirled the scotch around in the heavy glass. "We weren't really a close family. My sister spent more time with Daniella, her aunt, my mother's sister. Dad worked all the time. Mom basically turned us out of the house to do whatever while she did whatever she did. A lot of housework, I think. We were glad to get out of that. One of us would come back bloodied. Sam and I fought like roosters. I don't know how we lived."

"Worked out." Sister smiled.

"Daniella might have family pictures but I don't think any of them were too close, except for her and my sister. Also Daniella had too many marriages. High drama. My sister's just like Aunt D." Gray still could be irritated by his sister. "I will admit my mother, Graziella, could get just as uppity about our dash of Italian blood but Aunt D can outsnob everybody. She met Eleanor Roosevelt once and ever after referred to her as 'My dear friend, Mrs. Roosevelt.' You get the picture." He rolled his eyes.

"I guess Mercer's a bit of a snob," Tootie blurted out. "He's fun, though."

"Yes, Aunt Daniella still casts her spell." Gray laughed.

Sister looked at Tootie. "Gray, let Tootie show you something."

Ten minutes later, in the den, Tootie showed him the Broad Creek Stable photo of Roger Chetwynd and the man who might have been Mercer's grandfather.

"What do you think?" Sister asked him.

"Could be. It's hard to tell from an old photo and sometimes we see what we want to see."

"Gray, why would Tootie and I want to see a family resemblance to Mercer?"

"You're right." He bent over to study the photo more closely. "Snappy fellow. No names on the photo. Well, yes, it could be Grandpa Harlan Laprade but"—he shrugged—"doesn't mean the bones with Benny Glitters or the watch belonged to him."

Curious about Gray's feelings, Tootie asked, "What if those bones do belong to your grand-father? You and Mercer have the same maternal grandfather."

"Like I said, we weren't close. I never knew him. He was long gone before I came into the world. And I hate to admit it but I am a little superstitious. I think you let the dead alone. I don't believe they should be disturbed. Whatever Harlan Laprade did, however he wound up underground with a horse and a dog, I figure he went into the afterlife with at least one friend, his dog. Just don't disturb the dead."

"Well, it's too late now," Sister replied sensibly.

CHAPTER 12

Kneeling in the birthing stall, Dr. Penny Hinson examined the newborn foal, male, who had struggled to his feet. At that moment, he looked as though he was on ice, with each leg in danger of sliding in the opposite direction. Didn't take the little guy too long before he pulled himself together.

Tootie Harris traveled with Penny on Mondays as the vet realized Tootie truly loved horses as did she. Hard to be a good equine vet without a bond of strong emotion for the animal. Sister gave her Mondays and Wednesdays off, sometimes Sunday and Monday, depending on what needed to be done in the stables or kennels.

Tootie hoped to become an equine vet and Penny, a good one, happily took the young woman along as a sidekick. Both stood in the stall while Phil Chetwynd stood outside.

"He's fine." Covered in blood, water, and manure, Penny stripped off her long, thin rubber gloves. Tootie wore them as well, along with heavy overalls, for the day was frosty. Penny tried to keep from introducing anything potentially infectious to a newborn. As it was, the little fellow would be breathing in air for the first time, along with some of the dust. Broad Creek Stables had immaculate birthing stalls, a ten-stall barn dedicated to this. Clean as it was, tiny particles of dust floated through the air.

With the newborn still wet from his journey, Penny looked him over carefully. "Phil, I think when he dries he'll be a blood bay, a true blood bay. Been a long time since I've seen one."

"You don't see them often," Phil agreed. "When sunlight hits that coat it's something, isn't it?"

Picking up gear, tossing gloves into a bucket, both women left the stall.

"How many mares are in foal this year?" asked Penny. "You had four foals last month and now this fellow. You're on your way to a full house."

"We're back up again, Penny," Phil said proudly. "When we last spoke I'd bred seven of my mares, three to my own stallions and four out of state. Sales prices are better, as you know, but the real issue is consumer confidence. If people think the economy is improving, they make it improve, know what I mean? Anyway, clients sent me five mares. Ignatius and I rejuvenated the old barn back on the northeastern quadrant. So far, it's been a good year, no problem births, no crooked legs either." He smiled, then glanced back in the stall. "That fellow is by Curlin. We paid good money for that stud fee. My fingers are crossed. 'Course the mare is topnotch, just topnotch. She raced sound for five years. Sound."

Penny remembered horses better than people. "I

remember seeing her at Colonial Downs and then you took her up to Maryland for some races."

"Just a wonderful horse." Phil beamed.

They walked outside the foaling barn, a steeply pitched roof with a cupola, and a large copper weathervane of a mother and foal.

Broad Creek, like Walnut Hall and so many of the old glory establishments—whether they were in Kentucky, Maryland, New York, Virginia, or South Carolina—had grown over the years. The various barns at Broad Creek with their building dates over the main doors, announced the years when the money was good. Anyone in the horse business or any business knows change is the one constant. Up, down, flat years, everything will happen to you sooner or later, but the difference with the equine world was the drama. Maybe this was because animals were concerned, creating a lot of emotion, or because the people who get into the business are gamblers by nature. Someone who wants a placid life doesn't breed Thoroughbreds. The lows can bring a man or woman to their knees. The highs make one feel as though they are soaring in Apollo's chariot.

From the 1870s to today, the Chetwynds had experienced it all.

Tootie noticed that the gorgeous Victorian main barn had the date in gold: 1877. The numbers had the flourish of those years. She looked around, seeing that two of the smaller barns also had that date. She made a note to check dates when she and Penny drove out, passing other structures.

Phil ushered the two women into his office. "Can I get you all anything to drink? A sandwich?"

"No thanks," Penny responded.

"No, thank you, Mr. Chetwynd." Tootie sat where he beckoned her to do so.

Phil took papers off his desk, along with some high-gloss announcements concerning stallions. He sat in a wing chair opposite the ladies, who perched on an old leather sofa. Decorated in 1877, the office maintained the ambience of that time. The two wing chairs and sofa had been re-covered once in excellent cowhide back in the 1930s. The walls, jammed with photographs of horses—horses even before Navigator—bore proof to the success of Broad Creek Stables. One wall held silver trophies and even silver Christmas balls, inscribed with horse names. The silver glistened; someone polished it regularly.

Tootie thought the task must take an entire day, which it did.

Phil rummaged through papers from The Jockey Club, handed a few to Penny. "Mercer and I go over this all the time. If you look at the pedigrees of our standing stallions—and I've run them back to the 1870s—you'll see, especially in those early years, many of the same horse names, which makes sense. There were not as many standing stallions in the country. At least I don't think there were. Hell, there weren't as many people."

Penny read the sire line on each certificate, the dam line going back three generations. She recognized names like Teddy, an early one, Rock Sand from 1900, Spearmint from Great Britain, 1903. Moving forward, she read the great Count Fleet's name, coming much closer to now. Lots of Forty Niner blood in 1987, Danzig, 1977, Lyphard, 1969 and, of course, Northern Dancer, 1961 and Mr. Prospector, 1970. She handed the papers to Tootie, who—while not as well versed in bloodlines—did recognize the names Northern Dancer and Mr. Prospector.

"Great ones," the vet said. "The mares are great, too. I always loved Toll Booth, just loved her name."

Toll Booth was a mare who was Broodmare of the Year in Canada in 1989. The Canadians breed some great horses, but then most all of the former British colonies do, whether you look at South Africa, Australia, you name it.

He laughed. "Penny, me too. I'm supposed to be a hard-nosed horseman, but I can be won over by a great name or a lovely soft eye. But, hey, I know you have calls to make. I'm curious. What I know about DNA is what the public knows: the double helix and all that. But is it really possible to determine ancestry from DNA? Equine ancestry?"

"That depends on what you really want to

know." Penny folded her hands together. "If you're talking purely about genetics, yes. Mitochondrial DNA called mtDNA is inherited only through the female line and it doesn't change from mother to daughter unless there's a rare mutation. So it's reliable. You can trace the Y chromosome too but not nearly as far back as mtDNA; mtDNA is pretty amazing."

"What's the disclaimer?"

"Records are notoriously unreliable. *The General Stud Book* was published first in 1791, in England. We imported our blooded horses from England so it matters to us, as well. Anyway, sometimes people would change the name of a horse when it changed owners. Hence the unreliability."

"It is a mess." Phil nodded. "But even with that, if I know the mother of a horse, say Rock Sand, whose mother was Roquebrune, an English mare born 1893, then we would know, right?"

"Right," Penny said. "You're probably aware of the study at the MacDonald Institute for Archaeological Research at the University of Cambridge, which gets us closer to the true origins of the Thoroughbred."

"That's why I sat you down here and am taking up your time," Phil explained. "The conclusion of the study was that Thoroughbred foundation mares were not all Arabs, or what were called Turks in the eighteenth century. Turns out they

160

were cosmopolitan in origin, with British and Irish native horses playing a big part in those foundation mares' bloodlines. As more work is done, and it certainly will be, could this throw our bloodlines into question?" He slouched back in his chair.

Penny smiled. "Not a chance, Phil. Don't worry. This is about foundation mares. Once we move into the middle of the eighteenth century, going forward into the late eighteenth century, blood representation is pretty solid. We have track records, literally, for those horses, as well as the records of their get."

Phil smiled in relief. "Well, I am a little too sensitive maybe, but Penny, people are so crazy now. I had a bad dream of someone suing Broad Creek Stables over a bloodline misrepresentation."

"Hopefully, you've had better clients than that over the years," Penny's mellow voice soothed.

"For the most part, but every now and then. I remember Dad found out a fellow he did business with was a crook. That's not exactly the same. But people are so quick to find wrong-doing or imagine it, and as more and more new people come to us—and of course, I hope they will—I feel Broad Creek has to protect itself more. Our country is run and ruined by lawyers, I swear it."

Penny burst out laughing. "I'll tell that to my husband."

Phil blushed slightly. "I didn't mean Julian, of course."

"Phil, put your mind at rest." Penny stood up. "You get more beautiful babies on the ground like the one I just delivered and you won't have a worry in the world."

Back in the big vet truck with Tootie, Penny headed toward Greg Schmidt's house out in Keswick. A highly respected equine veterinarian, sought after on many levels, he'd sold his business, thinking he would retire. Well, in a sense he had, but practitioners like Penny often asked for his advice.

"Dr. Hinson, that foal's eyes wandered," said Tootie.

"No, he doesn't have strabismus, which is a deviation of the eyeball's positioning. People can have it, too. But often a newborn's eyes aren't settled yet, so there's asymmetrical movement. This usually corrects itself in a few hours or at the most a few days." She slowed as a car pulled out in front of her without looking. "Idiot! Sorry."

"Does make you wonder." Tootie smiled.

"Nobody pays attention anymore. How's that for a sweeping statement? Oh, yes, while I'm thinking about it, foals are like human babies. The eye detects the information but the brain doesn't know what it is. A foal has to learn to understand what it's seeing, just as a baby does. It's a big world out there." Penny laughed.

"The thing that amazes me is how a horse remembers everything," said the younger woman, gazing at the beautiful pastures going by. "Once they see something, say an overturned bucket in front of the barn, they're going to look for that overturned bucket."

"Memory is fascinating. I was reading somewhere that memory evolves, at least for humans. It isn't set in stone. I'm willing to bet equine memory is more complicated than we now know."

Tootie perceptively remarked, "People remember what they want to remember."

"And forget what they want to forget." She turned left onto Dr. Schmidt's road. "And then something happens or they hear a song and boom, so much for forgetting."

CHAPTER 13

Lime green. Good silk." Mercer in Brooks Brothers placed the tie back on the store's display, an eye-catching tie-wheel on a round imitation Hepplewhite table. "I like a little color." He looked at Gray. "You, on the other hand, have no imagination. You don't need one more regimental tie."

Gray held in his hands a lovely tie of olive with regimental stripes of thin gold next to wide maroon. "Mercer, I work in Washington in a conservative business. No one wants an accountant in a paisley tie, especially if that client is a senator."

"How'd you stand it when you worked full-time? I couldn't abide the boredom!"

"Same way you stand talking to people about breeding, people who don't know a thing. That's got to be boring, repetitious. It's part of the business, educating the client."

"Yeah." Mercer pounced on a gorgeous raspberry tie with small embroidered rampant lions in pale blue. "This would do well."

Gray reached over, taking it from his cousin's hands. "Would."

As Gray held the tie, Mercer stared at it. "Are you going to buy it?"

"Not if you are."

"No, I need something bold. Anyway, we couldn't both buy the same tie."

"Like two women buying the same dress." Gray laughed.

Mercer rolled his eyes. "Never." He checked his thin watch. "Where's Sam?"

"He'll be along. Crawford always seems to come down to the stables just as Sam's ready to leave."

"Tough nut, that Crawford."

"I steer clear. Actually my worst fear is that someday Janie will snap and kill him."

"We'd all cover for her," Mercer replied. "This salmon color, great for spring."

"Mercer, it's the middle of February."

"Spring is just around the corner."

Both men dressed well if a little differently. Their mothers, the sisters, drummed into them that you had only one chance to make a good first impression. And both women were clotheshorses themselves, loving the opportunity to dress husbands and sons. For them, it was having two fashion lives, male and female.

Gray walked over to a wall with square shelves, all of equal size, like a big bookcase. Shirts filled the squares, each one having a brass plate at the bottom, indicating neck circumference and sleeve length. Gray found the square with spread collars.

Mercer joined him. "Go ahead, buy a pink shirt."

Gray turned to him. "Mercer, I'm not afraid to

wear pink or peach or sea green. But only for casual wear. There is no way I can wear a shirt like that with a suit in D.C. Now stop sounding like my mother or your mother."

"I could never sound like your mother," said Mercer, imitating Graziella's intonation, making Gray laugh.

Sam walked through the store's entrance, looked around, spotted them and walked over.

"Get hit up by Crawford as you were leaving?" Mercer asked.

"No. Tootie and Dr. Hinson swung by. Marty's horse has an abscess. I told Crawford I soaked Tonie." He named the horse. "As I've been doing for the last three days. It will pop soon enough. But Crawford has to have an expert's opinion, so he called Penny Hinson. He just came back from dragging himself all over the northeast to check curriculums. I'll give him one thing, he is indefatigable and, of course, it helps to have your own jet."

Gray and Mercer smiled.

Mercer appraised Sam. "You need a new jacket."

"No, I don't. I don't go out at night."

"Because you don't have any clothes." Mercer was half right.

The other half of the reason was that although Sam had stayed sober for years, nighttime carried the whiff of temptation.

"What I really need is a new pair of boots. Crawford says he'll buy them if I go up to Horse Country for the February Dehner sale."

Dehner, a boot company in Omaha, Nebraska, sent a representative to measure one's foot, calf, instep. The customer then picked the type of leather, the color, the cut, and type of sole. A new pair could run $1,000 plus with the extras and, of course, everyone wanted the Spanish cut, which was a bit more leather on the outside knee, making one's leg appear longer. Very elegant. Bespoke boots lasted for decades if one cared for them, which somewhat justified the price. When you're in boots for most of the day, comfort becomes important.

"Go on up, then," Mercer counseled.

"Guess I'd better."

Gray and Mercer bought their ties and Mercer bought two shirts he liked.

In the parking lot, Mercer slid behind the wheel of his Lexus SUV and said to the brothers standing nearby, "Follow me. Lunch is on me."

The two brothers drove behind their cousin a very short way to a nice restaurant near Brooks Brothers.

Once seated at a booth, the two brothers waited for Mercer to speak as he had asked them to lunch, a rare occurrence.

"You all are quiet," the dapper fellow remarked.

"We're waiting for you," Gray replied.

Mercer launched in: "The funny thing about the body in Benny Glitters's grave is the little dog elicited more sympathy than the human. The story got a lot of play in the media in Kentucky but it received a mention on national media, too."

Sam was surprised. "It did?"

"You never watch the news," Mercer chided him.

"Well, I missed it, too," Gray confessed.

"It was there for one day, a brief splash. Anyway, I called the detective in charge. Granted this isn't a red-hot case, but because of all the attention they make a stab at it. I asked if I find any of my grandfather's dental records, will they compare them to the skeleton's teeth? He said yes."

"Mercer, do you have Harlan Laprade's records?" Gray asked.

"I wasn't half-assed about this." Mercer paused dramatically. "Mother called Peter Zazakos, whose father, grandfather, and great-grandfather were dentists. *Mirabile dictu*, they kept all the records." Mercer was almost jubilant.

For a moment, Gray and Sam said nothing, then Sam said, "I guess we should give him a decent burial in the Lorillard graveyard. That's where we're always planted. I know that's Grandpa Laprade. They should know shortly in Kentucky. There can't be that many murders in Lexington in February."

"One hopes not," Gray replied.

"Where's Auntie D in all this?" Sam asked, about Mercer's mother Daniella.

"Lashing me on. She's quite caught up in the drama." This was an unexpected comment from her son on Daniella Laprade, who at ninety-four retained most of her good qualities and all of her bad ones.

"She's used to getting her way." Gray's eyebrows flickered for a second.

"We can solve this murder." Mercer sounded so confident. "Mother says she knows in her bones. Those bones are her father and he was killed."

"Mercer, you've fallen off your perch." Sam used the old country expression. "Her, too!"

"No, I haven't. I can't say about Mother." He smiled. "Sam, you've got good research skills. Think of all those term papers you wrote at Harvard."

Sam got to the point. "Mercer, just what do you want?"

"I want you to research whorehouses in Lexington, especially the high-class ones. Lot of men with money to spend in Lexington. Times were good." He paused. "We know that the fancy houses of prostitution for the white boys often had a few drop-dead gorgeous ladies of color, Chinese girls, other women considered exotics. International trade." Mercer could always see the business angle of any transaction. "Might even be exciting. You know, his clothes were left folded in the laundry room."

"Maybe the killer was in a hurry," Sam suggested.

"Then why take off his clothes?" Mercer pointed a fork at Sam.

"That is a puzzle." Gray took a swig of his hot coffee.

"Well, I guess I could do it." Sam was a little intrigued.

"Gray, you investigate gambling parties," his cousin ordered. "Poker. Dice. Horses. I've got a hunch a wide net of gambling was part of this."

"Mercer, I think the dead should be left alone," Gray interjected quietly.

Quick to seize on something he could use, Mercer agreed warmly. "Right, but Harlan Laprade is disturbed, so we might as well find out what happened. It would mean so much to Mother and to your mother, too, were she here."

Hard to argue against this. Graziella died five years earlier of an aneurism. She rested in the Lorillard graveyard.

Gray sighed deeply. "I'll see what I can do."

"Given our business, Gray, I expect you know every trick in the book, how to make money illegally, how to hide gambling wins and losses. That sort of thing. And people keep records, even if it's chits. They have to remember who owes what to whom."

"I'll try."

"Oh, the dog. It was a Norwich terrier. A vet looked at the skeleton. Didn't need DNA."

To change the subject, Gray asked, "You hunting tomorrow?"

"I am. After All is one of my favorite fixtures. It's perfect, really." He mentioned the Bancroft farm, everything arranged for foxhunting. Trails, jumps, creek crossings, all were maintained by the Bancrofts. People always liked driving through the covered bridge to arrive at the stables and thence up to the house.

"I'll be with Crawford," said Sam. "He's hunting down in Buckingham County tomorrow, a huge fixture, about fifteen thousand acres of pine."

"But Buckingham is Oak Ridge's territory," said Gray, referring to the hunt club that had the right to hunt there.

"Crawford is happy to spread his brand of contempt for others all around. Rules be damned. Sooner or later, the chickens will come home to roost." Mercer hoped Crawford would get his comeuppance.

Sam was envious. "You all should have a good hunt." Tuesday's hunt in what was known as The Jefferson Hunt's home territory would prove just that. For those who believe in prophecy, it would prove haunting.

CHAPTER 14

Comet, hunting on the Bancroft property, heard the trailers rumbling down the long gravel drive, then they rattled through the covered bridge at After All Farm. The covered bridge amplified the sound.

Comet, like all The Jefferson Hunt foxes, knew when a hunt was to occur. Not that he kept a fixture card in his den. He didn't need one. Every time Sister's trailers left the stables and the kennels, it was hunt day away from the farm. When humans wore their kit, hounds yipped with excitement in the kennels, and Sister's trailers stayed put. The hunt would be at the farm.

The only days that confused this healthy gray fox were when the trailers left the farm to go all the way around to Foxglove Farm on the other side of Soldier Road. If they had ridden up over Hangman's Ridge, then down into the often swampy meadow below, they'd cross Soldier Road and wind up at lovely Foxglove Farm, owned by Cindy Chandler. Sometimes they'd strike a line and then the red Foxglove fox would cross Soldier Road, the meadow, Hangman's Ridge, and shoot to Sister's house. So he was on Comet's territory. For whatever reason that fellow loved her house and had various ways to wiggle under it. Once the Foxglove fox leapt into an open window of the gardening shed. What a mess. The red fox was just thrilled with the damage he'd caused. Comet was less thrilled. What if it made Sister mad at all the foxes? He liked his treats she left out.

On this Tuesday, February 11, Comet felt confident he would be far ahead of hounds should Shaker cast down Broad Creek. He was three-quarters of a mile from the bridge. He listened intently. Human babble fascinated him. They uttered so many sounds; some high, some low, and their laughter especially fascinated him. Big bellow laughs, little titters; some people laughed like woodpeckers, *rat ta tat tat*. While Comet was too far away now to detect the titters, the low guffaws, he could hear big laughs and he could always hear a high-pitched sound. Thank God for the horn. He always knew where Shaker was.

Comet, full, for hunting had been successful, sat until no more trailers passed through the covered bridge. The youngsters in the pack, once scent was found, usually ran right up front. While this was not a blindingly fast pack, it was fast enough so that Comet, who owed much of his health to Sister's feeding and worming program, plus the fact that as a youngster he'd been trapped and given his seven-in-one shots, headed for Pattypan Forge. He, too, was fast, also having the advantage of more nimbleness. If they did pick up his line once the pack reached Pattypan Forge, they would become confused for a time.

Aunt Netty kept an immaculate den in the old forge. Occasionally, Uncle Yancy would visit. The old stone building—the stones square-cut, quite large—held scent inside on a moist day. Today, at nine-thirty, the mercury had just nudged up to 34°F and clouds hung low, ranging in color from dove gray to charcoal. The rawness in the air promised snow flurries. Scenting would be pretty good, so why not throw them off early?

Pattypan, abandoned for close to a century, had the additional advantage of being overgrown. The place was full of rabbits, always a plus in a fox's mind, and other foxes did come around thinking the same as Comet: game. Crows would hang around and a medium-sized barn owl lived up in the rafters, keeping to himself. He loathed commotion and if Aunt Netty and Uncle Yancy screamed at each other, this foxy fellow would tell Bitsy, the screech owl who nested in a tree hollow at Sister's farm. This was like telling the town crier as Bitsy, believing in a free press, more or less kept every animal current with the latest gossip.

Shaker blew two short toots that meant "Pay attention." This was really for the humans. Comet knew it was time to move on. He trotted along Broad Creek while a downy woodpecker clinging to a tree trunk swiveled his head to see the gray ghost below.

"Morning," the bird called.

"Morning," Comet called out. *"Good eats?"*

"Tree's a supermarket." The downy pecked to prove his point, extracting a cocoon that Comet could see in his beak.

As Comet moved on, Shaker moved out with twelve couple of hounds, a decent number, although Sister especially loved those days when she'd ride out with thirty couple. The sound remained in one's memory forever. But twelve couple allowed youngsters—and he had half his pack as young entry and second-year entry—to step up to the plate. One must develop future leadership among hounds the same as among humans. Both the Senior Master and the huntsman believed this and planned for it.

Betty, per usual, rode on the right, Sybil on the left, while Tootie rode in the field with Felicity, who took Tuesdays off. The two had been classmates at Custis Hall, the prep school. Felicity needed a break from her curious, active child. The two school friends had ridden together all four years at Custis Hall. Felicity became pregnant, graduated, then married, a surprise to all. Gray, Ronnie, Xavier, Phil, Mercer, Kasmir, his old school chum, High Vijay, the Bancrofts, Walter, Ben Sidell, Ed Bancroft, the Sheriff, and Freddie rode out, along with a guest this Tuesday. The guest, a drop-dead gorgeous lady in her early thirties, perfectly turned out in ratcatcher, was visiting from North Carolina. The clothes for informal days were usually a tweed jacket, a tie, or colored stock tie. One had more room for personal expression wearing ratcatcher. Many men in the field fervently hoped this would be the first of many visits from Alida Dalzell. Plus she rode a stunning, 16H flea-bitten gray Thoroughbred/ Quarter Horse cross. They were a vision.

Shaker headed down Broad Creek. The draw intensified the moisture. Even during one of those awful Virginia dry spells, awful when they occur during hunt season and not especially wonderful during hay season either, the scenting along creeks or around ponds and lakes might hold, if ever so briefly. Today a carpet of enticing odors curled into hound nostrils: rabbits, two bobcats, a gopher, a few minks, turkeys, turkeys, turkeys, and the lovely powdery scent of a woodcock.

"Oh, this is sweet." Giorgio closed his eyes.

"Bobcat. We'll get a fox soon enough," Cora counseled.

Dragon, who would jostle to take the lead, only to be put in his place by bared fangs and a snarl from Cora, smarted off. *"Giorgio, you wouldn't know a bobcat if he bit you in the ass."*

"No, but you'd know if I tore into yours." Cora shot him a dirty look, which the other hounds called *"the freeze."*

Dreamboat, emboldened with each hunt now,

nose to the ground, concentration intense, moved faster. Then he trotted. Finally, sure, he lifted his head, let out a deep call, *"Gray fox."*

As though someone tossed a match into a tinderbox, *whoosh,* everyone spoke at once, everyone on.

Shaker blew "Gone Away." He and Hojo negotiated thick tree roots that had risen out of the ground with the freezing and thawing.

Some of those roots were best to jump, which the horses determined to do, to the surprise of some of their riders.

Many people in the hunt field like to set up for a jump, always a good idea, but terrain in central Virginia throws curveballs. Sit deep and take what comes. If you're tight in the tack, you'll be fine. Easier said than done, of course, and already two people popped off their mounts like toast.

Bobby Franklin, very glad he had Ben Sidell back there who took care of stragglers, kept the last horse in First Flight clearly in sight.

A light snow now fell like a lace curtain, adding to the extraordinary beauty of the wide creek, ice edging the sides, the conifers dusted with white.

Well ahead, Comet had taken the wide right path through the woods to Pattypan Forge. Hounds followed and just as the wise fox planned, hounds threw up at the forge. There were too many smells, including fox.

Threw up is the proper term for losing scent and literally throwing their heads up.

Aunt Netty, in her den inside, suffered no worries.

The pack blasted into the forge.

"Over here. Over here." Tattoo dug so fast at Netty's den that two rooster tails of dirt flew behind his front paws.

Diana stopped for a moment. *"Tattoo, she's an old nag. Let's find someone who's running."*

From the anteroom of her den, Aunt Netty cursed, sounding like a wail from a sepulchre. *"How dare you, you domesticated toad poop!"*

This so shocked Tattoo that his jaw dropped open. He stopped digging.

"Come on, Tattoo," Twist, his littermate, advised.

Shaker and the field held up outside as hounds worked inside. The riders sported a mantle of light snow.

"I've got the line," Pansy cried.

"I've got a hot one, red, red hot," Dreamboat bellowed.

Cora checked first Pansy's line, then Dreamboat's. Hounds knew, thanks to all their schoolwork, that one should stay on the hunted fox but a red-hot line is a red-hot line. Cora thought to hell with it. They'd chase the hotter line.

"Come on!" The fabulous hound rallied the others, for the pack was just about to split.

Already flying out of the back of Pattypan Forge, Dreamboat was now followed by the entire pack. The underbrush made the going rough and the humans had to run upwind, southerly, that day, on a narrow deer trail until it intersected with a somewhat wider riding trail, not very wide but wide enough to gallop without smashing your kneecaps.

Sister, on her beloved Rickyroo, eleven years old, almost twelve, knew that sure-footed though he was, the snow could be slippery and it was falling faster. Hunting in a falling snow, one of life's great pleasures, made her glad to be alive.

Most hunts wouldn't go out in a deep snow because it's not sporting. The fox can't run well should he be out. While hounds have to surf a deep snow, they plow faster than the fox. Hard on the horses, too. On the other hand, if a crisp coating lays on even a deep snow, a fox can fly along, whereas hounds slip and slide, break through, cutting their pads. But this snow, flakes large, twirling medium to fast, ground now covered with a thin sheet, this was perfection.

Ducking a few low limbs, Sister lost sight of Shaker but thanks to a blast on the horn every now and then, she knew where he was headed. In a quarter of a mile, the bridle path intersected two roads making a turkey's foot. Right, left, or center, those were your choices.

Which one would the fox make? Uncle Yancy,

ever so clever, didn't bother with the path. He slid under thick brambles, and catapulted onto the ruins of an old stone wall to run atop that for a bit. Hounds struggled in the nasty undergrowth but once they reached the stone wall they hopped up, as had Uncle Yancy. All twelve couple tried to get atop the stones, but some had to settle for walking beside it.

Walking frustrated them because they knew the older codger was gaining ground.

Betty, on the right, could no more get into that thick cover than anyone else. Tempted though she was to dismount, she knew better. Unless someone is in trouble, stay up, always stay up. Sybil, on the left side, had a little bit easier time as she was on a deer trail with fallen trees. Fortunately the crowns of the blown-over trees had smashed into other trees so she jumped tree trunks, easy to do on Kingston, bold and smooth.

Sister emerged onto the turkey-foot intersection. Shaker to her left headed fast toward the Lorillard place. Hounds, all on, hit the "hallelujah chorus."

Edward and Tedi rode in Sister's pocket with Kasmir not far behind. They allowed a decent distance but were right up there. Sister had offered the guest, Alida Dalzell, the honor of riding up with her but the beautiful woman demurred, saying she didn't want to slow down the Master.

As it was, Alida wouldn't have slowed down anyone but she didn't want to seem to take advantage and the only person she knew in the field was Freddie Thomas. As she had invited her, Alida rode with Freddie. As some riders were slowed a bit by the snow, the two women began to creep forward. This was not a violation of protocol. For those men whom they passed, this was a delicious experience; Alida, up in the irons, rode at such pace, her rear end well out of the saddle.

Little by little, Sister and First Flight were closing the gap between themselves and the hounds, whom they couldn't see but could sure hear. Ahead of them, Shaker could now see his tail hounds. Betty, finally able to move along, had crossed the turkey foot, taking the straight road where she knew a narrow trail would cut off toward the Lorillard place. Sybil wove through the debris-strewn path to emerge at an old, still-sturdy shed. If she kept going, she would shortly reach the edge of the front pasture at Sam's farm.

Just as Sybil galloped to the front pasture, Uncle Yancy shot into it, going straight for the graveyard, which rested a distance from the house.

Sybil took her hat off, pointed Kingston in the direction of the fox, and as the pack and then Shaker came into sight, she shouted "Tallyho!" That done, she quickly hopped the fence into the pasture, veering wide left, hoping to get up to the side of the pack as she, like Shaker, ran behind.

Jumping a tiger trap into the pasture, Betty had heard the "tallyho" so she kept to the right with extra vigilance. The last thing she wanted to do was turn the fox, nor did she want to lose the pack.

Shaker, on the road side, flew around to the right, jumping the same tiger trap that Betty had just cleared. Seeing this from a distance, Sister headed straight for it once she, too, got off the road.

By now Uncle Yancy had glided over the neat graveyard stone enclosure, reached his den, and ducked in. No one saw him duck out to creep to the Lorillard house, where he slipped under the back mudroom, climbed up into it, pushed back the rags, and jumped from one thing to another until he was on the top shelf, warm, a bit winded, and quite happy. Really happy, since he could hear the hounds blabbing outside.

The pack leapt into the old graveyard and found the den. Not wanting to jump into what he considered sacred ground, Shaker dismounted, throwing the reins over Hojo's neck. Perfect gentleman that he was, Hojo watched the proceedings inside the graveyard.

"Leave it. Leave it," Shaker ordered.

One doesn't want hounds digging at graves, even if there is a den there. The huntsman blew "Gone to Ground." As he did so, Mercer—unable to control his excited horse, Dixie Do, who pulled like a freight train—passed the Master. Sister and the field watched the show.

Dixie headed straight for Hojo, came close to the patient huntsman's horse, swerved for a moment, and took the low stone wall to stop hard in front of Shaker. That Mercer stayed on was a miracle.

"I do so apologize, Shaker." Mercer couldn't say much else.

"Happens to us all one time or another. Best you apologize to the Master."

One never passes the Master.

Mercer turned the now tractable Dixie Do toward the field, Sister in front, the whippers-in to the left, removed his cap, and bowed his head.

A moment's silence followed, then Mercer quipped, "Sooner or later we'll all end up here."

CHAPTER 15

N o one could quite believe it." Diana talked to Inky through the kennel chain-link fence. Hound and fox were quite comfortable conversing this way. Good fences make good neighbors.

"We were too astonished to speak," the hound continued. "We looked at him, looked at Shaker. Everyone shut up. Mercer apologized."

"Bet Uncle Yancy is still laughing." Inky admired the old red fox and his wily ways.

"What a setup he has." Diana knew the old boy could get into places, then disappear.

"Getting cold again." The beautiful black fox looked up at the cloudless night sky. "When it's clear, the stars seem bigger, don't they?"

"They do." Diana fluffed her fur.

The two canines—one wild, one domesticated—chatted a little bit about other creatures, and celebrated the seasonal lack of bugs, one advantage of the cold.

"I'm going back to my den," said Inky. "I built up a lip on the northwestern side and it's even warmer than before." Inky paused. "Do you know where you're hunting from on Thursday?"

"No, but it won't be around here. Sister never likes to overhunt a fixture if she can help it."

Diana headed back to the kennels to curl up with her roommates, warm with all those bodies and deep bedding.

Inky hurried to her den in the apple orchard, happy to go home after eating the treats left for her in the barn. She liked talking to Diana—a most sensible animal, in Inky's estimation.

Inside, Tootie, tired after the day's run, checked her e-mails on Sister's computer. Felicity loved the hunt as did Parson, her horse. Val, Tootie's old Custis Hall roommate, had e-mailed her from Princeton, decrying the lack of good men to date, a common theme with Val.

The next message she read, then re-read. Within a minute she was furiously scrolling through information online. After, she walked down the stairs, stopped in the library, then headed to the kitchen.

"Sister."

"Yes, madam," Sister teased her as she sat at the table, polishing her boots. "If I don't do this after hunting, I wait until I really resent it because I need clean and shining boots."

"I cleaned mine, too." Tootie took one of Sister's boots, polish evenly applied, and began brushing the well-worn leather.

"Thanks, sweetie."

"Dr. Hinson e-mailed me about bloodlines. Actually, she started with the Przewalski horse from seven hundred thousand years ago. We know the animal's DNA, isn't that something?"

"It is."

"Anyway, she said I should investigate the Turn-To line, especially the mares of El Prado, Sadler's Wells, and go back to Turn-To. She said I can never know enough. If I want to be an equine vet I should know the most important sires and mares for a lot of different breeds. She said start with Thoroughbreds as the records are good."

"Be specific. What do you mean about mares?"

"I mean the mothers of those great stallions."

"And did Dr. Hinson tell you those Turn-To mares, out of his line, have real toughness, can go long and hard without injury?"

Turn-To lived from 1951 to 1973.

"She did." Tootie smiled at Sister, always admiring of how much she knew about horse and hound bloodlines. It was people's bloodlines that the Master didn't care to study although by now, at 73, she's seen, in some cases, up to five generations of humans from one family.

"Dr. Hinson knows her stuff. She's right to get you to study more than, say, the skeletal system," Sister said.

Tootie then told her about the call at Broad Creek Stables, how lovely the foal was and then the discussion with Phil.

"Never thought of that, I mean lawsuits over

bloodlines. Once the Jockey Club started having Thoroughbreds tattooed in 1947 I should think that would have cut down on unethical representatives of Thoroughbreds."

"Some letters and numbers can be altered," said Tootie. "A *T* can be made to look like an *F*."

"Well, yes. I would think Phil has few worries. His stallions and mares have produced good foals, good runners, for close to a century. The Chetwynds are both lucky and smart. Takes both in the horse business."

Though tired, Tootie polished with energy. A slick shine gleamed on the old black boots.

"Did you know that Hail to Reason's dam?" Tootie named one of the great horses of the twentieth century. "Nothirdchance raced ninety-three times in six years and went on to breed?"

The mother of Hail to Reason clearly evidenced stamina and soundness.

"Well, I didn't know that name but I did know that Turn-To bred a lot of tough mares to compensate for his unsoundness. From his line we got Hail to Reason in 1958, Sir Gaylord, so many great horses."

"How do you remember all that?"

"Honey, it's easy to remember what you lived through, and I was a horse-crazy kid. Still am. If you want an interesting project, given that you were over at Broad Creek Stables, check the pedigree on Navigator, the horse that put Broad

Creek on the map long before even I was born."
She laughed. "Hey, that's a good shine."

"So Turn-To bred tough mares and produced tough mares who then produced tough foals, regardless of sex?" Tootie asked.

"When it all went right, yes, and luckily it went more right than wrong. You know breeding higher vertebrates isn't exactly like breeding Mendel's pea. Seems to me there's a lot more variety."

"I guess. Oh, Dr. Hinson sent all the research stuff to Phil Chetwynd. I mean since he asked her about DNA and stuff. Does that ever happen to you?"

"What? I don't know but so much about genomes and DNA."

"Sorry. I meant sometimes do you get obsessed about something and you can't let it go? You have to find everything about it?"

"I do. I only wish that when I was young I had done more research about some of the men I was attracted to. Would have saved a world of trouble."

They both laughed.

Then Sister said, "Actually, Tootie, physical attraction isn't logical so I don't know if the research would have prevented my mistakes, and wisdom comes if you learn from your mistakes. You'll notice some people make the same mistake over and over."

"Kind of like they've got one foot nailed to the floor and spin in circles."

"One way to put it."

"Sister, is Mercer gay?"

Sister looked up from her boot. "No, why?"

"Well, he's never married. He's kind of emotional."

"I'm not sure emotional stuff has anything to do with it. No, Mercer never married because his mother never released her claws. Daniella would have destroyed any woman he did marry. No one was ever good enough."

Sister picked up the boots, putting them in the mudroom. The two house dogs and Golly slept on the floor, the kitchen being warm.

"You know, I think that's the best shine my boots have ever had. Thank you." She looked down at the threesome. Raleigh the Doberman let out a long sigh.

"You'd think they'd hunted today." Sister laughed.

"What a day." Tootie smiled.

It was and it wasn't over yet.

The Chetwynds, Phil and Cheri, hosted a small dinner party for seven people: Kasmir, Alida Dalzell, Freddie Thomas, High and Mandy Vijay, and Sybil Fawkes. Mercer's account of his disgrace added to the high spirits. This followed his story about his presumably murdered grandfather; he was certain it was his grandfather, given the history: Harlan's horse transport by train in the old days, the slate memorial, Mercer's mother's many axioms for a happy life, which could be reduced to "Have a bad memory."

Mercer was at his best. As another round of after-dinner drinks enlivened the proceedings in the high-ceilinged living room, Mercer piped up again. "Phil, can I go through Broad Creek's account book and files from the twenties? Just in case I find something?"

Phil thought for a moment. "What you'll find is mildew, but sure. Just put everything back where you found it."

Next to Mercer on the sofa, Alida said, "What a fascinating story, your trip to Kentucky, the freezing fog and sleet storm and then finding a body."

Phil smiled. "It was an unforgettable hunt, pretty much as today's was."

Sybil leaned toward Mercer. "You got off lightly."

"Sister was in a good mood." He sighed happily.

Thinking out loud, Alida said, "Maybe there's some kind of symbolism about your grandfather and his dog being buried with Benny Glitters."

Phil was curious. "Symbolism?"

"He rode to heaven on a horse," Alida responded.

"Or the other place." Mercer shrugged.

"No, Mercer, that will be you." Phil lifted his glass to Mercer. They all laughed, lifting their glasses, too.

CHAPTER 16

A stiff breeze swept across the front of the main Broad Creek Stables barn. Patches of snow dotted pastures facing north. Otherwise, the mud-brown landscape offered no promise of spring, not even an early crocus.

Phil stood next to Sister and Tootie while Phil's manager, Ignatius, trotted a yearling.

"Let-down hocks aren't going to be a problem foxhunting and they might not even be a problem racing." Phil pushed his gloved hands into the pockets of his down jacket, as he focused on the hind legs. "But racing, as you know, can be hard. I'd rather not see him end up there." He broke into a smile. "He'll have a wonderful life as a hunter."

Sister replied, "Conformation is always worth studying. We've all seen horses with less than perfect conformation who were fabulous winners. Seattle Slew for starters. Ignatius"—she smiled at him—"hold him up a minute."

Sister walked over to the colt with Tootie. Phil stayed put. The older woman touched the youngster on the neck, ran her fingers down his neck, then over the muscles on both sides of his spine. He didn't flinch, nor did he move away from her. She continued over his hindquarters, felt his stifle, then stepped back. She returned to his front, knelt down and ran her hands, gloves off, down each leg, then picked up a hoof. The colt stood calmly. She moved to the rear, picked up the hind hooves.

Coming back to his head, she reached into her pocket and pulled out a delicious peppermint, which he happily ate off her palm. She liked that he had been handled, had ground manners. Quality was already there: bone, a wonderful sloping shoulder, a good frame. He would muscle up naturally if he came to Roughneck Farm, and with no steroids.

She never asked Phil if he used steroids or doses of growth hormone. They were illegal but not that hard to get. Walking up and down hills, running around the huge pastures, gave youngsters a solid foundation. At three, a horse would begin to learn his trade. Sister rarely hunted a horse until the animal was four. She preferred five. Like people, some mature more quickly than others, but she believed in bringing a horse along slowly, no drugs. Usually the horse told her when he was ready, and she listened.

This handsome one looked at her with a large soft eye, nickered, and was rewarded with another peppermint.

"What's his name?"

"Midshipman."

"Your Navigator line then?"

Phil nodded. "Yes, so you know he has stamina."

"I do." She patted him on the neck, offered one more peppermint.

Ignatius returned Midshipman to his field.

The horses at pasture had large three-sided run-in sheds, backs to the wind. They were warm enough. Phil always had them deep in straw. Once in work, they would get their own stall, plus plenty of turn-out in the pastures.

After Midshipman thundered across his large paddock to join his friends, Phil waited as Ignatius brought out another three-year-old. Sister carefully watched the colt move. He was fluid.

"Okay," Phil called. "Trot him right toward the Master."

Ignatius did, then turned and trotted the horse about 16.1 hands away from her.

"Tracks well," Tootie said low.

By this she meant his legs didn't flay out to the side, nor did he have an odd way of moving. As Sister would say, "Has a hitch in his giddy-up."

Then Ignatius slowly trotted the horse in a circle in each direction.

After this, Sister checked out the colt just as she had with Midshipman.

"So, Phil, you gelded him."

"I did. He's sort of a number-two guy, you know? I figured he'd be better off gelded with other geldings. We broke him, worked him on the track, and truthfully, he's slow."

She laughed. "Your slow isn't my slow."

"Exactly." He laughed, too. "Both of these boys have good minds, manners. No one is afraid, rolling their eyes, avoiding people. They're curious. When I mentioned these fellows to you I was way wrong about their ages. Both are three years old."

"What do you want for them?" asked Sister.

"Come on into my office, get out of this cold and we'll talk."

Sister glanced at Tootie. They briskly followed Phil through the stable and into his wood-paneled office. How good it felt to be warm.

"Sit down, ladies. Anything to drink?"

"No. Don't butter me up, Phil. Oh, what's the three-year-old's name?"

"How do you know I wasn't offering you coffee or tea? I know liquor won't work." He smiled genially as he peeled off his coat. "The three-year-old's name is Matchplay. He's got that Wimbledon blood if you go back a bit. He's pretty easygoing."

"Okay. How much?"

"Well, I've put time and money into the boys. They're sweet guys. I'll send them over. You live with them for a month. If you like, Sister, how about two thousand dollars apiece?"

"Phil, that's generous."

"Not so generous, Sister. With the economy the way it is, you can't give away horses. I try to help out the Thoroughbred Retirement Fund, as I know you do, too. It's depressing but I figured you'd hit it off with these two. They're your kind of horses. Mostly I'm trying to get back what I put in. I'll never recoup the stud fees but two thousand dollars covers food, trimming, and shots."

"I appreciate that. Let me think it over. I'll call you tomorrow."

Before she could rise, she heard a heavy thud from the secretary's office next door.

"Dammit!" Mercer's voice grumbled.

A woman's voice could be heard, Phil's secretary. "Mercer, sit down. I'll pick it up."

Phil rose. "Excuse me a minute." Opening the door between the two offices, Phil stuck his head in the other one. "Are you mistreating Georgia?"

Georgia's voice carried. "Mistreating me. He's a pain in the ass. Look what he's done to my office."

"Oh, Georgia, I have books spread out," said Mercer. "It's not that bad. I'll put everything away."

"Phil, why did you tell him he could go through records from the early years? I could strangle you."

Phil laughed. Mercer and Georgia could be heard laughing, too.

Sister couldn't stand it so she got up to position herself in the opened door. "Georgia, strangling is too good for him. Did you hear what he did on the hunt yesterday?"

"I did and Sister, you were too kind to him.

195

Should have thrashed him with your whip. Or tied him to a tree."

"We could still do that," Phil offered.

"Yeah, yeah." Mercer sat down at the small second desk. "Well, Sister, I've been busy, so before you all sit in judgment of me"—he stared hard at Georgia—"I found the cost of Benny Glitters's slate slab, the bill for the engraving, and the bill for shipping. And, best of all, the cost of Harlan Laprade's travel to Lexington, Kentucky, with the memorial slab."

Phil folded his arms across his chest. "Anything else?"

"I was looking for lodging."

"Mercer, obviously Harlan went to the house of ill repute," said Phil. "I really doubt my grandfather would note that in the official records. He wouldn't put in a rate for lodging, I just know it."

"Oh, hell, Phil, none of us know what our grandfathers would countenance. I just wanted to see what the slate cost. For giggles, I went to the old studbooks—on the computer, of course—and pulled up Benny Glitters's pedigree. Blue chip. Too bad he washed out at the track."

"A lot do."

"Yeah, but Domino for a sire?"

Phil listened. "Mercer, you'd better put everything back in its place. If you don't, I have to hear about it from Georgia."

"You can hear about it now." She threw a paper clip at Mercer.

"Oh, Georgia, you just want my attention."

"I've got it."

Phil closed the door. "I must have been out of my mind to let him root through the old account books and files."

"Phil, Mercer can talk a dog off a meatwagon." Sister laughed.

"Yes, and I had imbibed entirely too much wine." He sighed. "I suppose I hoped he would wear himself out with this research stuff; 1921 was a long time ago and he isn't going to find anything to help him solve what happened. And for all we know," Phil whispered, "Harlan Laprade may have deserved it. He inflamed someone's anger. I'm not going to say that to Mercer, and I sure won't say it to Daniella. She orders him about. She orders me about."

Sister couldn't help but laugh, which made Phil laugh, too. "There are people who leave an indelible impression."

Phil's eyes brightened. "She used to swing a cricket paddle at us. Oh, yes, she'd come to the barns because we'd usually be here after school and she was ready for any manner of boyish wrongdoing. Neither of us liked school. We went to different ones, of course. I don't know whose was worse, mine, which was private and cost Dad an arm and a leg or his, public." He frowned.

"Another trip down Memory Lane. I've heard so much about Mercer's family, now I'm doing it. Hey, let me get Georgia to run off the pedigrees of Midshipman and Matchplay."

Phil opened the office door again and Sister and Tootie heard, "I haven't done a thing. Stop checking up on me."

"This has nothing to do with you. Georgia, run off the pedigrees of Midshipman and Matchplay."

The sound of a chair being rolled could be heard, then Mercer appeared in the door frame.

"Sister, aren't those two good-looking horses?" he asked.

"Yes, they are."

"I admire you for looking at young horses. Means you think you'll live a long time." He ducked back into the office before she could say something.

Driving to the farm, Sister smiled as Tootie read the pedigrees. "I hope I'll live a long time."

CHAPTER 17

A lone red-tailed hawk watched from high up in a pin oak. Hounds worked diligently below, scuffling and snuffling. High winds postponed Tuesday's hunt to this Saturday. They were glad to be out. No fool, the hawk knew hounds might stir a mouse, who'd zip out from under leaves. Presto, lunch.

Dragon moved ahead of the pack. The wet leaves had packed down but an enticing delicate hoof stuck out from under a deep layer of decaying leaves. The large, powerful hound nosed over, inhaled deeply, yanked the deer leg out from under. The foreleg, still jointed, dangled from his jaws. Tail upright, he circled the pack, tempting them with his treasure.

Sister fretted over anything that brought a hound's head up when working. Deer carcasses, what was left of them, lay in all the fixtures, although some more than others.

This fixture, Mousehold Heath, had more than others because the Jardines, a young couple, both worked during the day. Poachers made good use of their absence. The terrible thing about poachers is sometimes they would wound a deer but not be able to track it and kill it, for fear of getting caught. The poor animal suffered for days, weeks even. In other cases poachers were trophy hunters, would take the antlered head, leaving the remains. Of all the misdeeds of irresponsible hunters, this enraged Sister the most. When so many are hungry, to waste food, to not share, to her it was an unforgivable sin.

Well, Dragon's prancing wasn't unforgivable, but she hoped he'd pay for it soon and he did. Sybil swept up upon him.

"Leave it," the strong rider ordered.

He slunk away and that did it. She popped her lash, catching him right on the rump.

Ever the dramatist, Dragon howled. *"I'm being murdered!"*

His sister, disgusted, walked right by him, nose down. Didn't look up.

Nor did any other hound. At one time or another, Dragon had offended every four-legged creature out there. He did, however, get back to business.

Rain started. Even with your tie tight around your neck, water would slide down your back. The mercury, hanging at 43°F, intensified the effect.

As it was a Saturday hunt, February 15, everyone endured it.

"We've been out here a long time," complained Twist, one of the second T litter, a year younger than the first.

"Keep trying," Cora encouraged her. *"Sometimes in bad conditions, you'll hit a line."*

200

"In this stuff?" wondered Thimble, Twist's littermate.

"Oh, come on now, Thimble, you've hunted in the rain before," Ardent, older, teased her.

"I don't remember it raining this hard," the elegant tricolor replied.

Within five minutes, the rain bumped up from a light steady patter to a barely-can-see-your-hand-in-front-of-your-face downpour.

Sister would hunt through any weather but she knew few people felt as she did. She was ready to turn back to the trailers when Pickens, a young entry, spoke.

The older hounds checked it out and within a flash, every hound in the pack roared.

Sister was on Lafayette, who surged. He was one of her best horses and best friends. Between them, they had twelve years of friendship, as she had bought him when he was a two-year-old.

The footing would deteriorate rapidly but at this moment it wasn't too bad. As the rain soaked in, it would get ugly.

She couldn't see Betty or Sybil. The only reason she could see Shaker at all was his scarlet jacket. If anyone behind her had a mind to turn back, the incredible music changed their mind.

"Whoeee!" Shaker called out. He then blew "Gone Away," which is a bit different than calling hounds to a line. However, the rain rolled into the bell of the horn so this call sputtered.

He kept calling. Hounds kept speaking. An obstacle would loom in the rain just in time for one to see it. The pack, then the people, threaded through an old wooded patch—huge trees whose bark turned dark with the rain. The sight would frighten anyone with an active imagination.

The red-tailed hawk returned to his nest. Most animals had the brains to seek cover. Not the foxhunters. Even Thimble—running hard, scent strong—became oblivious to the lashing rain.

Way ahead, the fox ducked down into a creek with deep banks. A tree, half its huge root system hanging out over the creek, contained a half-hidden entrance to the den. Within a minute, she was snug in the back of this cavern. Plus she had other entrances and exits.

Hounds reached the creekbed, threw up for a moment.

"You can do it," Shaker urged them.

Much as they didn't really like each other, Diana and her brother worked well together. In tandem, the two worked past the line, returned to where the scent last held.

"She jumped in." Dragon looked down and as he did so, his sister had launched herself into the swiftly running creek.

He followed her, both of them swimming against the current. The entire rest of the pack poured over the bank. The drumming of the rain now had the counterpoint of the separate splashes of hounds.

Diana reached the thick tree roots. She could hold on with both front legs, her nose pressed to the roots. *"She's in here!"*

Other hounds joined her but when the current would carry them downstream, they'd swim back. Cora wisely found a place where she could scramble up. Everyone but Diana followed. They all worked around the wide trunk at its base.

"Found another den opening!" Twist cried out.

Thimble, Twist, Taz, Pookah rushed to it. Digging wasn't much use, so Trooper stuck his head into the small opening.

"Do you know how stupid you are?" a squeaky voice sassed.

"Huh?" Trooper was surprised.

"Stupid. Stupid. Stupid. Do I need to repeat myself?"

Diana finally gave up her post, clambering up with the others. She, too, cocked her head at the den opening.

"The vixen sassed me," Trooper informed her. *"Rude. So rude."*

"Stupid!" The fox was now enjoying this. *"I'm high and dry and you all are wetter than muskrats."*

On the opposite side of the bank, Shaker put his horn to his lips, playing the three long notes. "Come on. Come on. Well done."

"Nothing much we can do," Cora counseled.

Last to follow the others back into the creek,

Trooper threatened, *"You're lucky we're leaving."*

"Don't let me keep you." She emitted that foxy puff of air, a laugh.

Trooper now felt insult added to injury. He did join the others though, and Shaker turned back.

It took everyone twenty minutes to pick their way back to the trailers because the surface on some of the hillsides began to give way, and horses slipped. Other spots proved fine—better drainage perhaps.

Back at the trailers, as always, people wiped down their horses. Because of the unremitting downpour, they put them on the trailers, haybags in place.

"This is so heavy," Sister said as Betty helped pull off the Master's sodden jacket, heavy even when dry.

Sister grabbed one of the terry-cloth towels she kept in the trailer tack room where the three women crowded together, tried to dry off. Tootie shivered.

Betty, ever maternal, ordered, "Honey, take off what you can. I always bring a gear bag with extra clothes in our sizes. I even have a pair of jeans."

Through chattering teeth, Tootie began to peel off layers of soaked clothes. "I didn't think it was supposed to get this cold."

"Rain in the low forties. Always a killer." Sister wiped down her torso, grabbed a sweater from her gear bag, slipping it over her head.

"You're not going to keep your breeches and boots on, are you?" Betty sternly intoned.

"Well," said Sister.

"Take them off," Betty ordered. "You have jeans in your bag. Just put them on. The Jardines aren't going to care that the Senior Master shows up for the breakfast in jeans. Come on, you'll catch your death."

Tootie took the clothes that Betty handed to her as she was fussing at Sister. "Catch your death," said Tootie. "A strange phrase. Makes death sound like a baseball."

Sister sat on the little carpet covering the lower ledge in the cramped quarters, taking the socks Betty offered her. "Warm socks. Listen to that rain!"

The aluminum trailer amplified the hard rain.

"Maybe we need water wings." Now in dry clothing, Betty inspected Tootie. "Umm, the jeans are a tiny bit big on you, but not so bad that you could fit another person in there." She rummaged around in her bag. "Here, use this belt."

Finally dry, warming up thanks to dry tweed jackets, the trio looked at one another.

Sister thought for a moment. "Rain comes from Zeus, right?"

"Lightning bolts and thunder sure do." Betty pulled down Big Ray's old golf umbrella from a ledge above the hanger rod. "Sister, this thing has to be thirty years old."

"If it keeps us reasonably dry while we make a run for it, fine. I never saw any reason to throw it out."

"All these years, I never really paid attention. Just looked like an umbrella tucked up there with your helmets." Betty then burst out laughing. "Ray was a terrible golfer."

"If he'd changed his pants, he would have improved his game." Sister could still hear her first husband cursing after a misdirected shot.

Tootie hugged herself; her tweed jacket was thin.

"He wore these corduroy pants with embroidered crossed golf clubs," Sister reminisced with the others. "I swear that ruined his game."

Sister and Betty laughed, remembering Ray. Betty opened the door to peek out, then quickly shut it when rain blew into her face.

"Can you see anything?" Tootie asked.

"Obviously not."

"Well, we have to try. Everyone else is in the same boat." Sister pushed open the door but the wind pushed it back.

Putting her shoulder to the door, she forced it open, nearly tumbling out onto the now soaked ground. With difficulty, she held the door as the other two hopped down. Betty quickly put the umbrella over their heads as the wind slammed the door shut and Sister made sure the latch caught. She was already wet.

The huge umbrella blew inside out as they hurried toward the Jardines' small house, other people also braving the mess to get there. Once inside, everyone sighed, shook water off. Betty didn't leave the umbrella open but leaned it against the umbrella stand, more or less ruffled.

Bobby greeted his wife; everyone was talking. The Jardines—young, happy with each other and their tight little house—buzzed everywhere at once. Jim put more logs on the fire in the kitchen and in the living room.

Everyone gravitated toward anything hot.

After a half hour, the food worked its magic, as did the drinks. Scattered throughout the living room on furniture, on the floor, chat filled the entire house.

Back to back on a large hassock, Phil and Mercer talked to those close to them. Sister, being Senior Master and a lady of some years, was offered a seat on the sofa by Walter, who stood up.

Walter said to Sister, Phil, and Mercer, "Shaker was smart to stuff the hound trailer with straw. They're as warm as we are."

Sister nodded, then said to Phil, "How about if I get those two horses Monday, weather permitting?"

"Sure."

Leaning against Phil's large frame, Mercer bragged to Sybil, Tedi, and Edward how he had written a letter to *The Blood Horse* about the gambling issue in Kentucky and how he squarely placed the blame on unscrupulous Indiana people paying off equally unscrupulous folks in Kentucky.

Phil turned his head. "Mercer, those boys play rough. Like the hound with the deer leg, leave it."

Mercer didn't reply but shrugged.

Sister remarked to Mercer, "Phil has a point. Excuse me while I find my whipper-in."

"See you next hunt." Phil smiled as Sister walked through the people, many slightly damp as she was herself.

"Betty."

"Mmm." Betty swallowed quickly. "Got me with my mouth full. These biscuits are light as feathers."

Sister held up her hands palms outward. "Don't tempt me. You know breads are my downfall."

"You've been the same weight since I've known you and that's over thirty years. I'm the one that has to worry." Cheerfully Betty picked on herself because she had once gotten heavy and worked hard to lose it.

"Will you drive the rig back to the farm?"

"Yeah, sure. Where are you going?"

"Riding with Shaker and the party wagon." She cited the hound conveyance. "Need to review some things with him. Breeding ideas. Stuff like that."

Once back at Roughneck Farm, Sister in the kennels with Shaker, Betty and Tootie in the stable checked everyone over, as did Sister and Shaker. After finishing chores in the kennel, Sister ran to the stable for the rain continued.

"Hey. Everyone okay?" Sister called as she slid through the small opening in the big double doors.

The swirling rain even managed to fly through that small opening.

Betty noticed. "If this keeps up there will be flooding."

"You're right about that and then tonight it will all freeze. Boy, I hate that." Sister watched Tootie put a heavy blanket on Lafayette. She noticed Tootie checking the big clock inside the barn. "Date?"

Tootie smiled. "No, but I wanted to drop off my paper for Dr. Hinson and she said she'd be working a little late today, but it is already five-thirty."

Sister looked into each stall, water buckets were filled, and a nighttime flake of hay had been tossed in just in case someone got the mid-night munchies. "Come on, we'll take you over. Everything looks fine in here."

"Good idea," Betty agreed. "I can pick up that wonderful paste she mixes up. Stuff heals surface wounds in no time. I put it on those thorn scratches I got a week ago and all gone." She held up her hand. "Thorns cut right through my glove, too."

Sister inspected. "Penny never stops thinking of ways to make life better for horses. As for you, well, she'll be happy about that, too, but not as happy as if it were a horse."

The three of them laughing, they shut off the lights, walked through the tack room and paused for a moment.

"Let's go in my old yellow Bronco. A lot easier to see in this weather," Betty suggested sensibly.

Making a dash for it they scrambled into the large SUV, Tootie in the second row of seats.

The clinic, about twelve miles from Roughneck Farm, would take longer to reach in this weather. Betty, a conservative driver, sometimes drove Sister crazy because she always thought Betty drove too slowly. Today, she was glad of it and actually kept her mouth shut.

Twenty-five minutes later the large curved Westlake Equine Clinic sign appeared in the Bronco's headlights.

Pulling into the parking lot, Tootie exclaimed, "Good. She's still here. The truck's here and the lights are on."

"We'll wait for you." Sister, damp for half the day, was beginning to feel it.

"I need my magic cream," Betty said as she cut the motor.

Sighing, Sister replied, "Well, if you two are going to get wet again I might as well join you."

Even though the three of them wore Barbour

coats, best for horsemen, the lashing rain found its way down the back of the collar, hit their faces, and a bit dribbled onto their fronts, a trickle sliding down their hunt shirts. And the rain was so cold, a few degrees above sleet.

Tootie, the fastest, reached the door, holding it open for the others.

The front office was empty, tidy and clean as always. A light shone out of an office in the hallway, polished except for some muddy boot-prints that looked as though the wearer had slid on the floor.

"Dr. Hinson," Tootie called, pulling her paper from under her coat.

"Are you writing a term paper?" Betty asked.

"I'm practicing." Tootie smiled. "It's my bloodline research on the Turn-To line."

"Penny," Sister called, then said in a lowered voice, "Maybe she's in the bathroom."

After waiting five minutes, Tootie pushed open the low door separating the public space from the large receptionist's area, her desk, computer, files on the other side of the divider. That area, too, was neat and clean.

Tootie walked down the hall and entered the door with the light—Dr. Hinson's own office.

"Dr. Hinson?"

Sister and Betty, each of whom had gratefully sunk into a waiting-room chair, stood up as they heard Tootie running down the hall.

The young woman's face registered shock. "She's dead!"

Both Sister and Betty shot down the hall behind Tootie. As they entered the roomy office, Sister noticed nothing amiss except for Penny Hinson, head on the computer keyboard, arms reaching toward her computer.

A single hole in her back, slight powder burns on her shirt, bore testimony to how she was killed.

Hands on her face, Tootie sobbed.

Sister put her arms around the young woman, as did Betty. The two older women looked at each other and Sister released Tootie. She picked up the office phone and dialed 911.

After reporting this dreadful discovery, Betty walked Tootie out to the lobby. Sister followed.

Sheriff Ben Sidell was close by, as he kept his horse at After All Farm. He reached them in fifteen minutes. He'd called his team immediately, but upon opening the clinic door he was glad they'd be behind him. He wanted to get statements as quickly as possible, so Sister and Betty could get the distraught Tootie home.

They each recounted what had transpired.

Tootie cried, "She never hurt anyone."

In a gentle voice, the sheriff counseled her. "Tootie, sometimes terrible things happen to very good people. This could be a robbery. My team and I will have to go over everything. She was a special person with a gift for healing, and you made her happy because you hoped to follow in her footsteps."

Tootie nodded as Ben touched her shoulder.

Sister leaned toward him. "I used the phone in her office. If you take fingerprints mine will be on it. The papers on the floor are an exercise Penny wanted Tootie to do. She dropped them when she saw the body. Betty and I left everything as we found it."

Betty added, "There were muddy prints into her office and in the office. We walked all over them adding our muddy prints."

Ben smiled tightly and nodded. "I'll take that into account. You all can go now. I know where to find you."

Tootie, face puffy from crying, whispered, "I will follow in her footsteps, Sheriff. I will."

"I know you will," he replied with feeling.

CHAPTER 18

The constant drumming on the roof of Westlake Equine Clinic added to Sheriff Ben Sidell's dismal task. Three hours after arriving, Ben, along with his best officer, Eli Mason, stood at Penny's desk one more time.

Eli reviewed what they found. "The force of the shot rolled it forward just a bit." He kneeled down to point out the tracks in the rug.

"Right." Ben stood beside the chair. "She was working at her computer, not worried, *bam,* she slides forward slightly, slumps over, head on the keyboard. Since the bullet wound was in her back, she had to have been forward a bit in her seat. Whoever killed her had a clear shot, stood close to her."

"The bullet didn't exit, so my guess is it's flattened on a rib."

Penny's body had been removed but both men had been able to intensely focus on the scene and the victim before the ambulance took her away.

"Save your guesses, Eli. The autopsy will tell us that. And I guarantee you the gun isn't registered."

"Everything in here is neat. No drawers rifled through. The petty cash is undisturbed." Sporting a fashionable three-day-old stubble, Eli rubbed his cheek. "Her guard wasn't up. She knew her killer."

"Most likely. The question is, what else did she know?"

"Vets cast a wide net. She works on horses, sees the barns and owners everywhere. No telling what she stumbled into if she did."

"There's always that, the odd moment when the wrong person notices something at the wrong time, but veterinarians deal in drugs. There is a black market for equine drugs, just as there is for human drugs."

Knowing next to nothing about horses, Eli raised his eyebrows.

"There are the obvious drugs," explained Ben. "The painkillers, some of which people take, but there are also far more lucrative drugs for an enterprising person: steroids, any performance enhancing drug, even growth hormone. Some of these substances can be cooked up in labs here, some in other countries and smuggled into the U.S. like any other contraband. It's an enormous market."

"But surely there are ways to detect illegal substances, just like for human athletes," Eli asked.

"A clever distributor, someone who comes and goes without attracting attention, could easily sell, deliver the goods. Could be a vet, a trainer, anyone others are used to seeing. There isn't the societal pressure to test animals that there is for people, with some exceptions."

"What exceptions?" Eli cracked his knuckles.

"Show jumping. Racing, especially racing. A crooked track vet could be useful. I can't imagine Penny being part of a drug ring, distributing stuff. Then again, Eli, you never really know, do you?"

"That's the truth. So let me get this straight. You pay for the drugs. They are delivered. But there has to be someone on the take who does the testing at the track."

"Pretty much, but there's a market besides the track. Anyone breeding horses who wants them to muscle up early might use steroids or growth hormone—both of them controlled substances. The horse looks mature, looks well muscled and impressive early. The muscle gains stick but the downside is the joints aren't fully developed. Easier to sell a well-muscled youngster. Many kinds of equine discipline might benefit from steroid use. Rodeos don't perform drug testing. Nor do most jumper shows or cross-country shows. Now some of those have vet checks, like endurance rides, to make sure the animal is okay, but that's not the same as testing for steroids. There's money to be made, a lot of money, but especially on the tracks."

"Would a clinic legally carry them?"

"Most will have some controlled substances because they do have useful applications. Just like for people."

"So this clinic would have, say, steroids?"

"Yes. When we talk to her senior partner, we'll ask him to unlock cabinets, show us their supply and the tracking system." Ben crossed his arms over his chest and looked out the window. "This rain just won't let up." Then he focused on Eli, now standing on the other side of the chair. "Westlake serves a few breeding Thoroughbred barns, dressage, jumper barns—everything from a big operation like Broad Creek Stables to someone like me, who owns one horse and loves that horse like crazy."

"So your horse might be prescribed steroids?"

Ben nodded. "Maybe for an unusual illness. Foxhunters wind up with leg injuries, a tendon problem, an abscess in the hoof, maybe even an abscess in a tooth. Or we might see West Nile virus, things that call for specific medicines. Unfortunately, there are many problems for which there really aren't good medicines. But a hunt horse would rarely be put on a controlled substance. Penny gave me joint supplements for Nonni, a little equine aspirin when Nonni needed it."

Eli smiled. "I have a lot to learn."

"We all do," said Ben. "Like you, I have my hunches. I leave the medical investigation to those with that skill, but you and I have to think of all manner of things, no matter how odd. The only clue we have right now is that Penny probably knew her killer and trusted him or her."

"We have her computer." Eli cocked his head in its direction. It was still turned on, a letter to a magazine on the screen.

"She'd been reading *The Blood Horse*, Mercer Laprade's letter. When our team goes through the computer, they'll find accounts, all manner of barn calls, patient notes, magazines, professional newsletters. Getting back to hunches, my hunch is that Penny stumbled onto something."

"Could be it has nothing to do with being a vet."

"True." Ben sighed deeply. "She was a good woman and a good vet. You didn't know her but those of us who did trusted her with the lives of our horses, which is like trusting someone with the life of a family member." He held up his hand. "I know that sounds silly to someone who doesn't own a horse."

"I have Joker, that counts." Eli smiled.

Joker was a cat so fat he should have been named Two Ton.

"Counts." Ben looked around. "Let's go through each room one more time. We could have over-looked something, especially me, since I know the victim. No matter how experienced you are, when someone you like is murdered, it gets you."

They opened the closet door in Penny's office. Clean overalls hung on a hook, along with two lab coats. A pair of work boots and a pair of Wellies sat on newspaper, caked with mud. Leaving her personal office, the two men walked down the hall, turning into each partner's room. There were three, counting Penny. They opened a supply room. The drug closet was locked. When her senior partner arrived, they'd tackle that.

Penny's unlocked truck had been searched by the first team on the scene. Very neat, Penny even had a tray in her truck where small items like pens, notepads, and Scotch tape were organized in the center console. The large medicine cabinet on the back of the truck was locked, but the keys were in the truck so that was investigated, too. Pretty much, she carried what every equine vet would carry on a call: lots of elbow-length, thin rubber gloves, syringes, clenbuterol, magnesium-based drugs for joints, horse tranquilizer, and a metal box with scalpel and other tools. Occasionally, Penny had to operate on the spot. For this she carried a large canvas sheet and a plastic one, also. She had items for bacterial infections, vials with antiviral meds, many of them new to the market. She had thread to sew up wounds, needles for same, and she even carried a small steamer, which she used before she would operate. She'd wipe her scalpel with antibacterial fluid, then steam it for a second. Penny was nothing if not thorough. Her X-ray equipment, plates, and heavy lead-lined gloves—all very, very expensive equipment—were neatly tucked into the truckbed medicine cabinet.

Establishing a veterinary practice wasn't cheap,

nor was maintaining it to the highest standards. To Ben, it was clear that Penny cut no corners.

The two men walked back down the hall to the inviting lobby and receptionist's long desk.

As they watched the deluge, waiting for Westlake's senior partner, Ben softly said, "Had she lived, I think she might have gotten elected to national office in her profession. She was so bright, so forward thinking and she truly cared about horses. You know, Eli, the media harps on all the bad actors out there regardless of profession. There are so many good people doing their job, helping others, helping animals. Educators, doctors, carpenters, you name it. Good people. She was one of them."

Eli thought. "You are, too, Sheriff."

Sister, Gray, and Tootie, along with Raleigh, Rooster, and Golly, felt the warmth from the library's fire. Sister's favorite room, the library always felt peaceful, but especially on a difficult day. Photographs, some from the 1880s, reposed in polished silver frames. Sister was surrounded by her family, most gone. Sometimes she'd look at a photo of herself at thirty and wonder, "Was I ever that young?"

A wonderful photo of Sister—in a white evening gown dancing with Gray in his evening scarlet— sat on the corner of the desk, a testimony to the present.

They'd eaten a light dinner, discussing what had happened to Penny with surprise and sorrow. Now they listened to the crackle of the fire, inhaled the fragrance of the applewood burning with seasoned oak.

Gray read the paper: "The western bypass is like malaria. It keeps returning with exaggerated symptoms."

A proposal for a western bypass around the heavily traveled north/south 29 corridor had been batted about for thirty years plus. With it came studies, meetings, outrage, presentations from those in charge at the state level, and innumerable environmental studies. It went on and on. So far, the public had been able to stop the bypass from being constructed.

"Gray, this will be going on into the twenty-second century, I swear. Tootie, your grand-children will be fighting it."

Tootie looked up from her book and smiled, but tears filled her eyes.

Gray noticed, rose, going over to her. He sat on the edge of her chair. "Honey, I'm so sorry. It was just a terrible shock."

Tootie cried harder now, so Sister fetched a box of tissues and sat on the other chair arm.

"How could something like this happen?" the young woman sputtered.

"I don't know." Sister handed her a tissue.

"I expect Ben Sidell will eventually root it all

out," said Gray. "He adored her. Well, we all did." His voice carried his own sorrow.

"Is it always like this?" Tootie's voice wavered.

"Like what?" Sister asked.

"Is life so sad?"

"Sometimes, yes, but you get through it," Sister said.

Raleigh came over, putting his head under Tootie's hand.

"They know. Animals always know." Tootie cried a bit more.

"They do," Gray agreed.

"I bet there's an animal that knows who killed Dr. Hinson." Tootie dabbed her nose.

The rain streaked across the windowpanes.

"Maybe so." Sister put her palm on Tootie's smooth cheek.

Tootie looked up. "Maybe this is about an animal."

Gray and Sister looked at each other, then Tootie.

Sister said, "It's possible. Let a little time pass, perhaps things will fall into place."

CHAPTER 19

U ncle Yancy watched the somber group of humans make their way to the Lorillard cemetery. Yesterday two men had dug a neat rectangular grave, flinging mud over their shoulders. Sitting on the back stoop they had not noticed him, but today, the thirty-two people arrived. Uncle Yancy needed to hide. From under the front porch, the view was clear. Human behavior interested the older fox. Sometimes he thought he understood it, other times he found it very mysterious.

Mercer pushed his mother's wheelchair, sending specks of mud onto his trousers. At the front of the stone-walled cemetery, the wooden gate with a cross cut into it was open. Plain yet aesthetically perfect for the place, the tombstones, some over two hundred years old, worn smooth, stood in neat rows. No tombstone was huge or gaudy. Some graves were covered with slate like Benny Glitters's grave. Harlan Laprade's grave would rest at the end of the middle row, next to his wife. Graziella Lorillard, sleeping forever, would be next to her sister when that time came.

Gray and Sam's sister, Nadine, walked on the left side of Daniella Laprade. Both women, wrapped in furs against the cold, emitted streams of breath from their mouths. The ground, frozen since last night, forced people to take care where they put their feet.

After Kentucky authorities had confirmed the skeleton as Harlan Laprade's, Mercer, his mother, and Nadine—who now insisted upon being called Chantal—had chosen Friday for the bones' interment.

Most of the mourners were hunt club members who had taken off work. Phil Chetwynd walked to the right of Aunt D, as he called Daniella Laprade, thanks to the long association of the Laprades with the Chetwynds.

The service included a reading from the Old Testament, one from the New Testament, an invocation, and a prayer for the peace of the soul.

Sister thought Friday a bad day to bury anyone. In some parts of the United States and Europe, executions were held on Friday, considered to be the Devil's day. Of course, she kept this to herself. Gray had enough on his hands. Gray and Sam's sister had flown up from Atlanta to be with Aunt D, who she loved more than she had her own mother. Nadine also intruded into decisions her male relatives had made without her.

Mercer had picked a funeral director to receive Harlan's bones, plus the dog's bones sent from Kentucky. The authorities saw no reason to keep what was left of the fellow. This was an old crime. Like any urban area Lexington had more pressing

224

ones, not that Lexington considered itself urban. Cincinnati was urban, Louisville was urban, Lexington was beautiful. They had a point.

Nadine wanted a regular casket. Mercer, Sam, and Gray balked. A child's casket would do, for there wasn't enough to put into a large casket. The savings would be considerable.

She screamed, "You are rearranging your grandfather's bones to save money?"

So Mercer and Gray had then split the normal-sized casket costs. Sam had driven to Arvonia, Virginia, in Buckingham County to pick up a beautiful piece of slate donated by Bill and Carolyn Yancy from their slate quarry. Then Sam, who barely had two nickels to rub together, paid to have the thick slate engraved with name, date of birth, and date of death—or, as close as they could approximate Harlan's date of death. Ever sensitive, Sam also added under Harlan's name, "His beloved dog sleeps at his feet."

Nadine was one step ahead of a running fit. This in front of Daniella, ninety-four, whom Nadine had supposedly come to comfort. Earlier, the screaming, tears, and outpourings had taken place in Daniella's living room, with the old lady present.

After twenty minutes of prime-time emotion, Daniella bellowed, her voice strong, "Shut up, Chantal. The boys have paid for everything. You haven't paid a red cent. Furthermore, Phil has arranged for a catered lunch in the home place and the hunt club has paid for all the liquor. Shut your big flannel mouth."

In a plaintive voice, Nadine warbled, "I paid for my plane ticket."

Now, Harlan's remaining daughter and grand-children stood beside his grave. The men bowed their heads. Not one of them looked at Nadine while she dabbed at her eyes with a lace hand-kerchief. She handed one to Daniella, who clutched it in her begloved hand.

After the service, the assembled trod back to the house, spotlessly clean, as Gray had hired a cleaning service for their place. Not that it was so bad, but Sam worked long hours and Gray shuttled between D.C. and central Virginia. Also, they were two men—enough said.

At the front steps, Sister paused, sniffed. Eau de *Vulpes vulpes*. Ah, yes, the graveyard fox, which was how she thought of Uncle Yancy. Filling her lungs, a small smile at the corners of her lips, she stepped into the center hall.

After having been lifted up the stairs by all three of "the boys," as she thought of them, Daniella reposed by the living room's roaring fireplace, fruitwood lending a wonderful aroma to the gathering.

Nadine helped the nonagenarian out of her coat. The elderly well-dressed lady could walk with two canes, but the wheelchair was more reliable.

She was loath to give it up. Nadine wasn't the only drama queen in the family.

As Nadine hurried upstairs to hang her aunt's coat, Daniella, hair white, close-cropped, crooked a finger at her son. "Bourbon," she ordered.

"Yes, Mother."

"A double."

"Yes, Mother."

"No cheap stuff, you hear me?"

"Yes, Mother." Mercer sped to the kitchen, where Gray and Sam had set up a makeshift bar the night before.

Behind the bar, Xavier said, "Nice service. The slate was impressive. A lot of people here."

The last act of the burial had the two grave-diggers, in black suits, lift up the slate to lay it exactly right over the freshly dug grave. It was still to be filled in but the slate covered it for the mourners. Mercer had wanted people to see it. With the help of the generous Yancys, Sam had done a good job.

"If slate was good enough for Benny Glitters, it should be good enough for him. Thanks." Mercer took the drink, hastening back to his mother.

Without a word, she grasped the offered libation and tossed it back. Handing him the empty, she ordered, "Another double with a chaser of ginger ale. I want old-fashioned ginger ale. The stuff that bites your tongue. I need more than a water chaser today."

The boys knew her habits and her favorite brand rested under the bar with her name written on it.

Mercer reappeared in the kitchen. "Another double. A ginger ale chaser," he told Xavier.

"Mercer, there's not a lot of your mother to absorb this. Want me to lighten it?"

"Hell no. I would wheel her back here, drop a siphon in the Woodford Reserve, and she'd suck it right up. You'd never know the difference."

"I don't remember her drinking so much when we were kids."

"Because we were drinking too much ourselves. Didn't notice." Mercer laughed, taking the drinks, one in each hand, to again attend to Mother.

Sister was talking—well, listening actually—to Daniella. She smiled weakly as Mercer approached.

"I tell you, that man could do anything with a horse. Had an eye, could calm the most fractious." The crotchety old woman paused, then said loud enough for Phil, standing near her, to hear, "And our family built the business with the Chetwynds."

On cue, Phil turned. "Good luck for both families."

"Not for my father, ultimately." She swallowed half the bourbon, then downed the ginger ale.

Mercer watched wordlessly. "Mother, I'll be right back but I need a drink myself."

Chin jutting upward, she appraised him. "I'll expect you back here shortly."

"Yes, ma'am."

Turning her face up to Sister, voice low, Daniella said, "I told my nephews to make Artillery Punch. Just knock people out. You need it after a funeral."

"Excellent advice, Daniella."

And indeed, an enormous punch bowl borrowed from the Bancrofts contained a lethal concoction.

With Phil kneeling to chat with Daniella, Sister walked over to Mercer.

"You are very good to your mother." She recounted Daniella's description of Harlan as an expert horseman.

Mercer burst out laughing as they reached the bar. "She has a vivid imagination. She was small. I doubt she remembered much of Harlan. No way. I expect she listened to her own mother. Me, I just nod my head."

This made Sister envision a bobblehead doll in Mercer's image. She put her arm through his for a moment. "You have much to bear."

He shrugged. "We all do in our own way, don't we?" Xavier handed Sister a tonic water with a lime wedge and a stiff bourbon for Mercer, who, eager to change the subject, said, "The attorney general for Kentucky ruled that Instant-Racing is a pari-mutuel game. Good. But the Kentucky Supreme Court passed the buck, excuse the pun, and wouldn't make a ruling on the legal status of Instant-Racing. So it's been bounced to the Franklin Circuit Court. That will be a circus, all the pros and cons argued before the bench." He looked straight into her light hazel eyes. "You know, Sister, it's the same old, same old. Doesn't matter the issue."

"There's a lot of truth to that," she agreed.

A brief interlude at the bar allowed Xavier to listen. "Mercer, what's Instant-Racing?"

"An electronic racing game that the race-tracks will run and they set the take-out. See, it's gambling but it's not casino. Indiana, as you know, has really put the hurt on Kentucky and the Kentucky legislature—well, don't get me started. You all read my letter to *The Blood Horse.* Anyway, it will put money in the coffers." Mercer wished he hadn't used that word—too close to coffin.

"If it gets through the Franklin Circuit Court," Xavier remarked.

"Yeah, there is that. But it's not a bad idea, you know?" He heard his mother bellow out his name. "Back to it."

Sister and Xavier glanced at each other just as Kasmir walked in.

"Master, I can only wonder what's next," he said.

"Kasmir, we're on the same page there. First the discovery of Mercer's grandfather. The watch. I will forever see that finger in the dirt and the hint of gold from the watch. Mercer was determined to prove it was his grandfather and he did."

Xavier chimed in, "And now Penny Hinson."

"A supreme shock," Kasmir murmured quietly.

"These events are unrelated, of course, but still, two murders almost a century apart," Xavier said, then they all paused, for Nadine's voice from the living room was so loud even Uncle Yancy under the front porch heard her.

"Don't you call me that! Don't you dare call me that, you worthless drunk!" Nadine spit into Sam's face.

Gray stepped between them as Mercer tried to shield his mother, who observed with disdain.

"Our mother named you Nadine," Sam shouted back. "What is this Chantal shit? Everyone in this room knows who you are."

"Sam, come on. It's the wrong place, the wrong time." Gray grabbed his brother's elbow, hauling him back, whispering in his ear, "The bitch isn't worth it. Don't give her the satisfaction of getting under your skin."

Mercer bent down. "Mother, I see your glass is empty."

She handed it to him with one hand, but held him with the other. "Don't go just yet." Then she looked up at Nadine. "Chantal, comport yourself. Today is a day to honor my father, your grandfather. I don't want to hear another cross word."

With that, she nodded to Mercer, who headed for the kitchen.

Nadine burst into tears, left the room, and could be heard thumping up the stairs.

In the kitchen, Xavier, having gotten the drink ready just in case, handed it to Mercer.

Mercer wordlessly took it, hurrying back to the living room. He feared what his cousins might do next, especially Nadine, who trouped down the stairs again.

All eyes upon her, Daniella handed the immediately empty glass back to her son, and hoisted herself up on her canes. Phil hurried over to help steady her. No one made a peep.

"Mom?" Mercer whispered.

Ignoring him, she addressed the gathering. "This has been a disturbing time for our family. My father is at peace but we are not." Taking a long pause, she, too, raised her voice, "Revenge. I want my father avenged."

Mercer said nothing. Then Phil gently lowered her back into the wheelchair. He whispered to Mercer, "Let sleeping dogs lie."

A shiver crept down Sister's spine. On the contrary, she thought: Give the Devil his due.

CHAPTER 20

The day after the proper burial of Mercer's grandfather, The Jefferson Hunt met at Orchard Hill, the farm on the northeast corner of Chapel Cross. Sister and Walter had recently secured an additional farm, also large, which abutted Orchard Hill to the east. Named Tollgate, as before the railroad came through there was a tollgate there, it now had new, more sporting ownership. The club could hunt through first Orchard Hill, then Mud Fence, then Tollgate. Put together, the fox and hounds could run over three thousand, five hundred acres, not an enormously large fixture but certainly an ample one for Virginia.

As always, Saturdays drew the largest number of riders, this February 22 being no exception.

George Washington, one of the best riders of his generation, a passionate foxhunter with his own pack of hounds, was born February 22, 1732, so this was always a special day. Washington's huntsman was a slave whom he respected greatly. General Washington was the only Founding Father, and indeed one of the few men of his generation, who freed his slaves upon his death. Men, both North and South, owned other human beings then. Sport brings people together no matter what the century and in many ways, no matter the circumstances of those who pursue it. In Washington's day, the chance for hard riding, beautiful vistas, and catching up on all the news afterward at a breakfast created closeness. No phones, radio, television, Internet—back then, you learned what was afoot from your neighbor or perhaps a broadside. Newspapers were few and far between in our country's early days. People always want to know the latest news. Then as now, spicy scandal is cayenne for conversation. And again, then as now, foxhunting enlivened the blood, causing some people to forget the restraints of monogamy.

Sister noticed Alida Dalzell, again Freddie Thomas's guest, in the field. Sooner or later, a Jefferson Hunt man would lose his head over that woman.

Addressing the group before taking off, she cited our Founding Father's birthday and simply encouraged them, "When you drink the water, don't forget the people who dug the well." With that, a nod to Shaker, and "Hounds, please," they headed due east.

Cora with Diana led the pack. Twenty-two couple hunted today, for the temperature promised good scenting. The clouds covered them like a gray blanket, the frost was melting, and the mercury at 36°F promised to climb into the low forties. The breeze was tolerable but shifty. In central Virginia the winds usually come down from the northwest. If wind blows from the south, often it brings moisture from the Gulf of Mexico. Rarely does it blow steadily from the east, a slashing easterly wind meant a storm off the sea, the true nor'easter.

A little gust bent over broom sage. The untended fields at Orchard Hill were reverting back to the yellowish-tan broom sage. Bad for pasture but good for cover.

A gray fox named Gris heard and saw the trailers so he prudently moved toward his den, about four miles east. A young fellow, he had not yet found a mate, so he had roamed a bit out of his territory. Earl, the red fox on Old Paradise, secured one vixen, but Gris knew there was a girl out there just for him.

Right now there was a pack of foxhounds looking just for him. They trotted through Orchard Hill briskly, no scent, not even feathering. Crossing the railroad tracks, they climbed a small bank into Mud Fence.

"How about if I steer toward the right?" Diana suggested. *"The tree line ought to yield something."*

Cora, nose down, said, *"I'll move that way, too, but you be furtherest out. We don't want Shaker to think we're skirting."*

Huntsmen from the British Isles, often strict about skirting, will call a hound or have a whipper-in push them back. They want the pack more tightly together. Often huntsmen from the old countries aren't familiar with American hounds when they first arrive on our shores. They want to hunt them like an English pack. But American hounds exhibit independence just like American humans. If they trust you, even if they go into woods and you can't see them, they will come back. Some English and Irish learn this lesson, others do not, but most of our cousins on the other side of the Atlantic learn how very, very good those American noses are. Golden.

Highly intelligent and driven, Diana put her nose down, following the line of the woods. She could detect woodcock scent and squirrels, which were everywhere. She passed over a bobcat line and wasn't interested. Then she picked up rabbit, promising because often rabbit scent or the rabbit himself can lead to fox scent. Same with turkeys. The only thing better would be a cornfield with lots of leavings or blackberry bushes in late fall. In February food becomes more scarce and all animals forage in wider circles unless humans feed them. She passed over deer scent, keeping on the rabbit line that faded, it being a very light odor. Disappointed but determined, she continued on, then stopped at a large fallen tree trunk. She leapt onto it, following a definite fox scent.

"He's been here and not long ago!" Diana sang with excitement.

The entire pack trotted her way, many of them following as she walked on the tree trunk. What a sight!

Then Diana jumped off, barreling straight into the woods. Everyone followed, hounds beginning to open.

Long snaky vines dangled from trees and the underbrush. These slowed the horses but the hounds found ways under or through them.

Betty, per usual, on the right, had ridden down to the east/west tertiary road to run along the grassy strip. Behind her and across the road, the fire station receded quickly as she clipped along.

Sybil rode along the edge of the woods as Shaker went straight in along the field. Sybil, a complete whipper-in, possessed game sense, which she was well rewarded for as Gris popped out fifty yards in front of her. She counted to twenty, for one must always give the fox a sporting chance, and then called at the top of her lungs, "Tallyho!"

Shaker didn't hear her but hounds sure did. They trusted Sybil but also knew to keep on the line. Field members could tallyho golden retrievers, cats, sundry animals. With Dreamboat alongside, Diana did not rush to Sybil. They kept on the line, which veered to the north and intensified.

Within two minutes of Sybil's sighting, the pack burst out of the woods, followed by Shaker, then the First Flight.

Shaker called, encouraging them on. Hounds lived to hear their huntsman's excitement. So did the horses and humans. Next, Bobby Franklin blew out of the woods, with Ben Sidell close to him.

A bystander would see the panorama unfold with human riders in the same dress they donned during the reign of William and Mary. For some viewers this was a step back in time. And if they could overlook the attire, they could even step all the way back to Homer's time. Hunting on horseback has been consistent for millennia whether the quarry is chased by sight hounds or scent hounds.

Scarlet coats dotted the subdued winter landscape. The horses added more color: bays, chestnuts, a few grays, cream-colored horses, and even a paint or two. Each animal was groomed to perfection, coat shining, tack clean but not for long, as a bog lay straight ahead on both sides of a quirky little stream that widened, then narrowed.

Gris knew scent better than hounds. Naturally, he dashed through the swamp—not so difficult for him as he weighed about seven pounds. He could hop from fallen branch to moss-covered tree trunks, usually avoiding the water. Hounds blew in and sank right up to their bellies.

"My coat is a mess!" Twist grumbled.

"Stop being a priss!" ordered her littermate, Thimble. *"Next you'll want your nails painted."*

Hounds knew about canine beautification from

the TV in the kennel office. Occasionally Shaker or Sister would allow small groups in while they did chores. The hounds especially like advertisements featuring animals. A certain Pedigree food ad was their current favorite.

The struggle of the hounds to slog through the bog was nothing compared to the horses. They had to blast off their hindquarters, leaping up, then drooping down—tiring work. They crossed the stream only to hit the bog on the other side. Everyone emerged with slick gray hindquarters, for the gray muck flew upward. People wore mud on their faces, coats, and, of course, every pair of boots in the field was now slimed up.

Once out of this, they flew straight into Tollgate with its new fences, new gravel on the farm road, and new equipment sheds.

Sister saw an unfamiliar figure fly by riding a gorgeous steel gray Thoroughbred. The horse made Sister recall Buddha, a gray racing Thoroughbred some years back.

"What the hell?" She couldn't help herself and then she saw over the rise Crawford's pack of hounds in front of this woman. The black and tans were in front of her but out of sight until they charged up over the swale.

The woman had the sense not to blow her horn. She would only spoil a good run. Sister noted that. Whoever this was, she knew hunting and was a lovely rider.

The interloper sailed over a seven-board coop. Sister soon followed. She always thought a jump existed to keep stock out or stock in and you only needed one big enough to fulfill that function. The new owners of Tollgate—three-day eventers —built big jumps for training. She thought they were at a show this weekend. Sister was grateful, for she didn't know how they would take this impromptu joint meet on their land.

Hounds stopped. Cast themselves. The woman, perhaps midthirties, her face already a bit weather-beaten, but she had good features, rode up to Shaker.

"I'm terribly sorry, sir. They came to your horn."

He nodded. "You must have just been hired by Crawford Howard."

"Yes, sir. I'm new, but Sam Lorillard went over maps with me. I know this is off-limits. I truly apologize."

"God help you." He smiled. "Come on, girl. Stick with me. Your hounds will hunt with mine."

As hounds, now forty couple strong, all opened, she had little choice. Crawford's Dumfriesshires, not as racy as the Jefferson hounds, nonetheless hung right in the middle of the pack. What a vision, black and tans with Jefferson's tricolors.

Hounds circled in the front meadow and hurried behind the spruced-up house. Sister did not follow too closely because she didn't want to tear up what was lawn. She circled at the edge just as the pack dove back into more woods.

This run lasted for an hour and a half, but the pack had switched from Gris, who dropped them. Hounds knew. The humans did not, but the gray, clever fellow had ducked into a den where a red fox had been while that fellow had also been out courting.

Now both packs, screaming, headed back through Mud Fence, back through Orchard Hill, past Chapel Cross itself, and crossed the road west of the Gulf station to tear through Old Paradise.

As the two huntsmen reached the old tobacco barn, far away from the main barn and the ruins of Old Paradise, Crawford Howard, his wife, Marty, and Sam rode toward them. When their pack had flown out of their hearing, they had been trying to find it again. Sam had followed Shaker's horn but the huge loop somewhat confused them.

Beet-faced, Crawford rode toward the two huntsmen now calling hounds back.

Marty spurred her horse to come alongside him. "Honey, don't fire that girl. Please don't. It was her first time out and our pack heard the other hounds. We couldn't, but they did."

"Goddammit!"

"Crawford." Her voice became stern. "It takes a long time for a pack to trust and know its huntsman. She needs the summer to work with them

241

and don't you dare embarrass me by cussing her out. Do you hear me? Gentlemen don't cuss women in Virginia!"

Only Marty could speak to him like this.

His color began to fade. He slowed Czpaka.

Sam prudently rode behind.

Very close to him, Marty leaned over. "You be civil or you won't get any for a month."

This threat reached him. "All right."

"I love you. I will not let you make a fool of yourself. Give this girl time."

He took a deep breath, rode up to Shaker. "I see you've met my new huntsman, Cynthia Skiff Cane."

Shaker inclined his head toward the woman. "She rides like a Valkyrie."

Skiff blushed. "I'm sorry, sir." She addressed Crawford. "I—"

Crawford interrupted, Marty right by him. "No need. What I want to know is how did they hunt?"

"Well," she replied.

Mindful of the situation and having dealt with Crawford for years now, Shaker added, "You've done wonders with them, sir. They hunt as a team."

Marty inwardly sighed relief, grateful to Shaker.

A mud-splattered Sister rode up. "Good to see you, Marty, Crawford, Sam. How I wished you'd been with us. I think we picked up your main barn fox but somewhere on this hill we lost him. What a run."

Marty immediately replied, "One of these days we'll just put them together."

"Indeed." Sister said this in a welcoming voice. "Kasmir has put together a wonderful hunt breakfast at Tattenhall Station. Please come. We'd love to have you."

"We'll be there as soon as we get the hounds and horses up." Marty beamed. She missed her old Jefferson Hunt buddies.

Riding back to Old Paradise, Jefferson turned in the opposite direction toward the train station, and Crawford knew he was outnumbered.

Marty said, "Honey, I'm proud of you and you know I'm proud of our hounds."

"They did sound great coming up the hill, didn't they?" He felt somewhat vindicated.

"Did, and I think this girl will work out. She's a gentle soul and the hounds like her, as does Sam. I trust his judgment." Marty smiled at him.

True to their word, Crawford and Marty came to the breakfast. Sam and Skiff took the hounds and horses back to Beasley Hall, Crawford's estate.

Kasmir, warmth itself, greeted the Howards when they walked through the door at Tattenhall Station. Gray zipped to the bar along with Ronnie Haslip, who knew Crawford well. Actually many of them did, as he used to hunt regularly with The

Jefferson Hunt. Gray had a drink in Crawford's hand in about three minutes.

"Scotch on the rocks, as I remember."

"Thank you, Gray."

"Marty, your vodka tonic." Ronnie gave her a drink.

Kasmir clapped his hands. Gray whistled and the large noisy gathering fell silent. "Join me in a toast to our first joint meet with our neighbors."

"Hear! Hear!" Phil Chetwynd raised his glass.

After that, even Crawford enjoyed himself as everyone did their best to say something nice to him. They all liked Marty, so that part was easy.

Mercer, once he had Crawford's ear, wanted to know more about the Thoroughbred ridden by Skiff. "The gray?"

"Son of Holy Bull."

"Ah, Crawford, you do have an eye. I always wondered why you didn't get into the game."

"Mercer, I learned long ago the way you make a million dollars in racing is to start with ten million."

Although he'd heard that line, sadly true, for decades, Mercer laughed. Crawford relayed that he'd heard the burial was special and the slate memorial had a tribute to the dog. Mercer, of course, replayed every detail from the pogonip hunt. On his second scotch with a plateful of food, some of it Indian, Crawford listened.

Freddie came up as Mercer left. "Good to see

you and looking so well. May I introduce my friend from North Carolina, Alida Dalzell."

Of course she could.

Food, drink, and the company of a beautiful woman put Crawford in an excellent mood. Marty didn't mind a bit. She was in the middle of people she liked and had been terribly upset to leave when Crawford had yanked out his support when not chosen as Sister's Joint Master.

Younger, less egotistical, Walter had been the right choice. He would guide The Jefferson Hunt in the spirit unique to it. He lacked Crawford's fortune but his other qualities ensured careful leadership. Walter was also the outside son of Sister's late husband, Ray, which she didn't know until shortly before she had chosen Walter. Walter's father, if he knew, ignored this, and had raised Walter as his own, which emotionally, he was. Truly, let sleeping dogs lie.

Even as a boy Walter had reminded Sister of Big Ray in so many ways. She never thought about Walter being his son. Why would she? But it made her feel good to have part of Ray with her. Sister thought monogamy a good idea but difficult to achieve. Ray conducted his affairs with discretion as she did hers. The marriage had thrived. Everyone finds their own way.

Walter was now chatting with Crawford, good politics on the Joint Master's part.

Kasmir spoke with an animated, delighted

Alida. She laughed until the tears came to her eyes.

"I hope you are not returning to North Carolina soon," said Kasmir. "We have so little hunting left but the end of the season is often the best." His liquid dark eyes shone with kindness.

"I," she paused, "Mr. Barbhaiya—"

"Oh, please call me Kasmir. I insist."

"Kasmir," she pronounced his name with a lilt, "I'm on a leave of absence. I won't bore you with the details of my work but I'm thinking it through. Anyway, if Freddie will tolerate me for a bit more I would like to hunt, but I've only one wonderful horse."

"I have a stableful, all bombproof. Sister has taken very good care of me. You come take your pick."

"I can't impose upon you like that."

"You must. Dear lady, I have made a fortune. I lost my wife to cancer and she was my heart and soul. I moved here to be close to the Vijays; High and I went to college together." He abruptly stopped. "Here I am talking about myself. The point is, why have something if you don't share? To see you ride my horses would make me happy and I think it would make my horses happy, too. You'll do a better job than I do." He laughed.

She touched his hand. "You flatter me, but I would love to ride your horses and you aren't boring me."

With that they both sat down in a railway pew and couldn't stop talking.

High noticed his friend. Kasmir looked enchanted, enlivened even. Sister noticed, too.

Ben Sidell and Mercer discussed the old murder since Mercer couldn't distance himself from it. But then, having your mother cry for revenge in front of everyone kept it all front and center.

Gray handed Sister a brownie. "Sugar, chocolate. What more could you want?"

"Just you." She kissed him on the cheek. "Well, I'd better do my duty." With a deep breath, she walked over to Crawford, now talking to Betty and Bobby.

"It's good to have you here." Sister smiled at him. "And before I forget, I'll e-mail you my suggestions for natural science changes at Custis Hall."

Betty and Bobby left them alone.

Crawford recounted some of Mercer's tale.

"It was bizarre," she said.

"Well, Mercer feels sure he can find out the whole story." Crawford put down his plate on the long table. "Why bury a man with a horse and his dog?"

"Solve that and I suppose you solve the crime."

Crawford shrugged. "Obvious to me."

Sister leaned a bit forward, curious, for he had a unique mind. "What? Who killed him?"

"Why he was killed?" Crawford shrugged again. "The horse, of course."

CHAPTER 21

Pookah was a small weedy hound, a throwback, for her sister looked a proper American hound. She ate her kibble from the trough. Fortunately, the kennels had a small kitchen where Shaker and Sister could heat up foods and keep medicines in the refrigerator. The two humans had worked together for years. Given the cold and the long run, they decided to warm some chicken broth, along with gallon bottles of corn oil and canned food for hounds who needed a little help keeping on the pounds. A hound or horse can burn off weight quickly with hard hunting. So can people.

Master and huntsman watched the young gyps gobble everything. At the hunt breakfast, Sister hadn't gotten to eat much and was still hungry. She opened the fridge, pulling out a power bar.

"How can you eat those?" Shaker grimaced. "They taste like cardboard."

"Well, they do, but if I eat a candy bar it's too much sugar. Once we're finished here, I'll heat a little lasagna. Gray made some last night to soothe his nerves. He makes the best lasagna."

"Crazy days," Shaker acknowledged. "Hearing Daniella holler for revenge, I don't know. Does that sort of dramatics ever solve anything?"

"I don't know, but I guess for her it would." Sister peeled back the bar's foil wrapper, taking a small bite. It did taste like cardboard.

"Thimble," Sister admonished the dog as she had bumped her sister Twist to grab more food.

"She takes too long," complained Thimble, but she moved back to her spot. *"If she doesn't eat it fast, I will."*

"Chatty Cathy." Sister laughed. "You know, most times I'm glad I don't know what they're saying. It's probably something like 'Here comes that old dame again.'"

"I would never say that," said Twist, lifting up her elegant head. *"I love you."*

"Me, too," came the chorus from the youngsters.

This made both Sister and Shaker laugh.

"That huntsman can ride, can't she?" Sister admired competence in all pursuits.

"Yes. She seems nice enough. You were smart, well, you are smart, to invite Crawford and Marty to the breakfast."

"I will kill him with kindness," said Sister. "My mistake in the past was to let him anger me. I confess I should never have socked him at the Masters Ball in New York City. Even if he had it coming."

"Oh, that was years ago." Shaker wished he'd been there.

"He'll never forget."

"Sister, that man probably never forgot the first time his own mother insulted him. I call it injustice collecting."

She took another bite, hungry as she was. "Mmm. A big ego. As long as you tug your forelock, he's fine, and you know, Shaker, he earned that ego. The man built an empire, starting with strip malls in Indiana and branching out from there. Only Kasmir exceeds him in accomplishment. Sure, the Bancrofts are rich, but that's inherited wealth, and I hasten to add, they use it wisely. Edward managed the family company for decades so he didn't sit on his butt and collect dividends, yet it isn't the same as starting from scratch and building an empire. That takes guts, faith, and incredible energy."

"And luck." Shaker crossed his arms over his chest.

"You're right about that." She smiled, covering the bar with the foil wrapper.

Pookah watched every move. *"If you're done with that, would you mind if I chewed it up?"*

Noticing soulful eyes turned upward to her, Sister looked at the power bar. "Sweetie, if I give you this there will be a nasty fight. However"— she walked back into the kitchen, grabbed a handful of little meaty chews, returned, and sprinkled them all over the broth-drenched kibble—"More treats."

"You spoil those hounds."

"And you don't?" She poked him. "I can't eat this thing now, but maybe I will later."

Shaker half closed his eyes, shook his head. "Boss, how would you feel if I contacted what's-her-name?"

"Cynthia Skiff Cane, she goes by Skiff."

"Right. I have a hard time remembering names. Anyway, if she needs anything I'll do what I can. I like her. She must have whipped in somewhere. I don't recall hearing of her as a huntsman and I know pretty much who's who."

"Go ahead. I don't know who she is or where she learned her stuff either. Anyway, it is in our best interest and her best interest to try to get on even terms with Crawford. You know, he still hasn't named his outlaw pack. I would have thought that would have been the first thing he did when he broke away from us."

Hunts are forbidden to rent land but one hunt may lease a fixture or territory to another hunt. All the rules can get confusing.

"Don't know. But you all can't have the same territory. No way the MFHA will abide that and he doesn't rent territory from us."

"But if he did, that bugaboo might be laid to rest. I support the MFHA most times, and the times I think they've gone over the top, I just shut up."

"The truth is, Sister, Virginia can do whatever she wants. The entire state can walk away from the national organization, and the threat for others of being excommunicated if they hunt with us won't work. People will still come here. This is the center of hunting in the United States. No one can break that power."

"Give Maryland her due." Sister loved the Maryland hunts.

"I do, but Maryland would be neutral, just as she was during 1861 to 1865."

"Shaker, it's a small state. They have no choice." Sister did her best to keep things on an even keel.

"So you've thought about it?"

"A secession?" Sister laughed. "Well, I suppose any Master in Virginia has had it cross their mind if something upsets them, but I think we can always work things out, whether it be with the national organization or Crawford."

"He won't join the MFHA."

"I know. I'll consider that problem later. Right now I want, if not harmony, then accommodation. His pack has joined ours three times. Once, a fine mess, a couple of years ago, and twice this year. We need to think this through and your idea of getting to know Skiff is a good one. Right now, I just want to finish out the season on a happy note."

"Been a good season."

"It has, thanks to these children." She indicated the hounds.

"Wait, wait until we're in our prime like Diana," Pansy bragged.

"We can give everyone a rest tomorrow, then walk out Monday," said Sister. "I wish this cold would break. Going down into the teens again tonight. The electric and propane bills are thirty percent higher than last year. Thank God for wood-burning fireplaces and the stove in the basement. By the way, how's your stove doing?"

"Fine. Heats up the cottage and I can keep the thermostat at fifty-five degrees."

Shaker lived in a clapboard cottage not far from the kennels and stables. He could walk to both places, which saved gas. Living arrangements and often a vehicle were usually part of a huntsman's employment package. Every hunt differed to some degree, the richer ones able to offer more, but The Jefferson Hunt covered the basics. Also, Walter, thanks to his being a doctor, had a decent idea of the insurance coverage changes and how to adjust for Shaker.

"I'm going to head up to the house," Sister said. "You hunted the hounds beautifully today and you handled a strange woman riding up to you and Crawford's pack with your usual aplomb."

"He needs good whippers-in." Shaker identified one of Crawford's main problems, a problem for most hunts.

"That's just it," she said. "No one can work for him without jeopardizing their position with the

MFHA. You aren't supposed to hunt with outlaw packs any more than you are supposed to work for them. Which is why I like your idea of finding out a little bit more about Miss Cane," she said, taking her leave.

From the front office, she stepped into cold air and a setting sun.

Raleigh and Rooster greeted her as she neared the house.

"I've been so lonesome without you." Raleigh leaned on her.

"Me, too. I've been bored." Rooster jumped straight up.

Opening the door to the mudroom, bigger than the one at the Lorillard place, she hung up her barn coat and scarf. After taking off her lad's cap, she opened the door to the kitchen.

"What a heavenly smell." Gray had heated up the lasagna for her. She grabbed the bootjack by the mudroom door, pulling off her boots. "Oh, I do like taking my boots off in a warm room. Doesn't hurt as much."

Gray bent down to check the glass door on the oven. "Almost ready."

"Honey, have I told you I love you?"

He grinned. "I can never hear it enough."

"I saw you eating a big plate at Tattenhall Station." She removed her vest, tie, and titanium pin, which she fastened through a buttonhole.

"And I saw you didn't. People don't let you sit down and eat."

"Gray, it's always that way. I don't even notice anymore. At least I get a drink. Where's Tootie?"

"Reading *Handley Cross*." Gray named one of Robert Smith Surtees's novels from the nineteenth century. "She needs a distraction."

"I envy her reading it for the first time. Kind of like the first time you read *Gulliver's Travels* or *Huckleberry Finn*."

He placed the plate of lasagna before her, a drink, too, then sat across from her as Golly wove between the chairs. Golly operated on the principle that humans were clumsy. Be prepared. The dogs sat, ears up, hoping for a morsel. Not the cat. Trusting her lightning reflexes, she'd snare anything that fell from the table.

"Quite a day," said Gray. "Crawford and Marty actually enjoyed themselves."

"Marty especially." Sister savored the delicious pasta. "She's such a good person."

"She is," he agreed.

"Things settling down?" she asked, changing subjects.

"In the sense that neither Sam nor I have to deal with Nadine, yes. She's with Auntie D and flies back to Atlanta tomorrow. She doesn't want to see us any more than we want to see her. I'm glad it's over. Or almost over. Mercer's taken up his mother's cudgel, so to speak."

Sister told him what Crawford had said. "Preys on my mind."

Gray crossed his ankles under the table, leaned back in his chair. "You know, it does. Whoever killed Harlan knew about the memorial slate, knew the grounds of Walnut Hill, and obviously knew Harlan and his proclivities." He sat up, folding his hands on the table. "It's possible that someone also knew his schedule, argued with him, and a fight at the whorehouse did him in."

"Is. It's also possible that Benny Glitters knew something about Harlan."

"Vice versa." Gray now tapped his fingers on the old kitchen table.

Finishing up, she put her plate on the floor so the dogs could lick it, while handing a piece of lasagna to Golly. After this, she washed her hands and the dish.

"Gray, I'm about to abuse you."

"Really?" He started to unbutton his shirt.

Laughing, she put her hand on his shoulder. "That, too, but right now I need you at the computer. You can do anything."

Smiling, he replied, "If I can't there's a whiz kid upstairs who can."

In front of his big screen in the library, Sister asked, "Get Benny Glitters's breeding."

Didn't take Gray long. "Domino the sire, the mare was by Hastings."

Sitting next to him, she said, "Man o' War's

grandfather, Hastings. An excellent pedigree. See if you can get Benny Glitters's racing record."

That took a little longer but finally, "Here. He started out pretty good."

"He did, ran third in his first race, then two seconds, and then didn't place. So they retired him. You'd think he would have been learning, gotten better. As far as we know, based on what they knew at Walnut Hill, he retired sound."

"Maybe he just didn't like racing," Gray posited.

"Possible. Such a pity with that pedigree. Few if any would use him as a stud, given his race record."

"Anything else?"

"Not right now. Thank you, honey. Something doesn't ring true for me. I can't put my finger on it."

"Janie, horses wash out at the track all the time. Plenty of them have successful sires."

"I know, I know, and some like Secretariat sire okay sons but great daughters—great brood-mares, who in turn sire winners. But I'm going to call Ben Sidell. You can listen." She sat down at her desk and called. "Ben. Sister."

"Wonderful day," said the sheriff. "Wonderful breakfast."

"It was. Forgive me, but I'm going to intrude on your case. Sort of."

"I'm all ears."

"Do you have Penny's home computer?"

"We do. Her husband gave it to us. Didn't have to ask."

"Shall I assume there's nothing amiss?"

"It's what you would expect. Clients, ailments, treatments on the office computer and her personal computer is crammed with e-mails from friends and some research. Lots of stuff on wildlife but nothing that would set off an alarm."

"Will you do me and maybe Penny a favor?"

"Of course I will."

"Have your tech person sweep through for bloodline research. Before Penny's murder, she became interested in the Przewalski horse."

"Never heard of such a breed."

"Well, you won't see one in the hunt field. It's an ancient feral horse, one hundred percent wild, and it is at least seven hundred thousand years old. We have the genome, the oldest one we have up to now anyway. It's far older than any genome we have for humans."

"Where did they find this?"

"In the permafrost in the Yukon. Found a foot bone. This animal is the ancestor of horses, donkeys, zebras. Somewhere between 72,000 and 38,000 years ago the line split and one line became domesticated horses. The other remained feral."

"What do you think is the connection?"

"DNA. As an equine vet, Penny would be interested. But if you find she was looking at any pedigrees, especially of current horses or Benny Glitters, the horse in the tomb, maybe if I look at them I might be able to help discover why she was killed."

"You think her murder is related to the one in Kentucky? The one in 1921?"

A long, long pause and then Sister said with conviction, "Actually, I do. Something tells me this all goes back to Benny Glitters."

CHAPTER 22

In the distance, Sister saw Comet lounging on the foundation ruins of Roughneck Farm's original house built after the Revolutionary War. Although the air remained quite cool, the sun shone and the elegant gray fox, winter coat luxurious, warmed in its rays. Most mammals know enough to blunt wind, and Comet sprawled on a flat lintel stone that must have once graced the door of the small stone place. Over time, with more money, the original inhabitants—a husband and wife, both British subjects—built the summer kitchen, which still stood at the big house. They also built the core of the big house. Stones intact or fallen provide domiciles for foxes, skunks, minks if they felt like it, plus skinks, snakes, and other sharp-eyed creatures, although not all at once of course. With Comet in residence, no other medium-sized or small mammal would live there. He would make certain of that.

Walking hounds with Shaker and Tootie, Sister saw him about a football field away.

"Hold up," she said quietly, pointing out the reposing fox to Shaker and Tootie.

Shaker put his horn to his lips, blowing two sharp toots to get the attention of the hounds with them.

Comet lifted his head. *"Oh bother!"*

"Two toots?" Young Pickens sat wondering.

Dragon sat also. *"Listen, kid, I don't know why two toots, unless Shaker wants our attention for something or just to get us to stop. Don't worry about it."*

Worried, the youngster asked, *"But what if I hear two toots in the field? What do I do?"*

Cora put Pickens at ease. *"That's Shaker's way of telling you where he is if we can't see him, or he's fallen behind."*

"Oh." The satisfied hound rose as Shaker, Sister, and Tootie walked forward.

Shaker always loved viewing a fox. "I expect he would have heard us in plenty of time, but a sunbath might dull the senses. Every now and then he'll give us a merry chase, just like the black vixen in the apple orchard but I swear, if they see us walk down to the barn or the kennels in hunt kit, they repair to their dens. I find that so unsporting," he joked.

"Maybe they find us unsporting." Tootie smiled.

"I expect they find us crazy." Sister laughed, for she loved foxes, had spent a lifetime observing them. "We go out in most all weather, we run around, they are either running in front of us or watching us from a vantage point. They know every trick in the book and we keep falling for it."

They walked another half mile to the base of

Hangman's Ridge, turned back, puddles still frozen, strips of snow deep in crevices, lining the north side of any kind of rise. But it felt so good to be outside. A little slip and slide only added to the adventure.

Back home, hounds waited in front of the big draw pen to the side of the kennel office. Shaker called each one by name. When that hound came forward, he swung open the tall door to allow the hound inside.

Once inside, everyone received a treat. Again, each hound's name was called when boys were separated from girls. Tootie then walked the girls to their various runs while Shaker led the boys.

Like any hunt, The Jefferson Hunt divided animals by sex to ensure no fights because the boys could tell when a girl was coming into season long before a human. This made for a happy atmosphere and no kennel fights, plus there were no unintended pregnancies.

Shaker and Sister studied individual hounds, knew hound families, and when possible, tried to hunt with other hunts to observe their hounds in action. One of the glorious things about The Jefferson Hunt was that six excellent hunts fell within an hour or hour and a half radius. And if willing to travel longer, one could hunt with another fifteen crack hunts. Sister loved watching other hounds, closely observing staff work as well. Seventy-three she may have been, but she was always learning, and one thing she was sure of was that she would never know it all.

The rumble of a huge diesel engine caught their attention.

"Oh, it's the horses from Broad Creek," said Sister. "Shaker, do you need Tootie right now?"

"No. We're done."

"Come on, girl." Sister walked outside just as the stable's big rig turned in the large circle before her barn.

"Ignatius, how did they load?" she asked.

"Good. Phil's had us working on it, they've had some natural horsemanship lessons. Once they understand what you want, they are pretty willing."

"If you need a hand you tell me, but you know what you're doing." Sister appreciated a good horseman and thought it best always to get out of the way.

"Where'd you like these two?"

"Let's put them in this smaller paddock here. Stretch their legs a bit. Tootie and I will bring them in to their adjoining stalls in an hour."

Ignatius walked up the rubber-covered ramp, slipped the butt bar, and untied the slipknot, bringing Midshipman off first, which set Matchplay to screaming.

"Don't leave me! What's happening?" the flashy chestnut whinnied.

263

Midshipman neighed back, *"It's a pretty place. Don't worry."*

"Ignatius, I'll hold this fellow so you can get the other one," said Sister. "No point in more stress."

"Righto." He bounced back up, yanked the slipknot. It was a good thing he had the lead rope securely in hand because Matchplay didn't back off the trailer. The athletic gelding leapt backward, Ignatius hanging on.

Sister couldn't help but laugh. "Well, if I ever have to jump backward, I believe he can do it."

The sensitive horse quickly nuzzled his buddy, being instantly reassured.

"Tell you what, they are both athletes, but this guy . . ." He glanced up at Matchplay. "Quick, quick, quick. Once he's in work, I bet you he could turn under you in a skinny minute. Good you've got a long leg."

Sister led Midshipman, Ignatius took Matchplay, and she responded truthfully, "Ignatius, that long leg is attached to a seventy-three-year-old body."

"You ride like you've always ridden." He flattered her but it was mostly true. Sister was tough.

"You are kind." She changed the subject. "Tootie will be working with these fellows and Sybil Fawkes will come over."

"Sybil's good. I used to bug Phil to use her to catch ride but he wanted men." Ignatius mentioned the practice whereby young people or journeymen jockeys ride whatever is available at a stable. Often those horses were difficult.

"I can understand that since most jockeys, whether on the flat or over fences, are men. Some good girls get in the game now. I don't know what the percentage is but it's all to the good. I figure a good rider is a good rider."

"Me, too, but you know how Old Man Chetwynd used to grumble about a horse being woman-broke."

"Yeah, I know. He'd point the finger at me and complain, 'You're too soft on them. Too soft.'"

Tootie opened the gate to the paddock. Sister and Ignatius walked the two horses in, turned them to face them, then slipped off the halters. That fast, they wheeled around to run. Why walk when you can run? Same with children.

After five minutes of this, with the humans watching, the two snorted, slowed down, then stood and looked at the other horses in the larger paddocks and back pasture.

Lafayette, the senior horse, called out, *"You two listen to me. You are lucky to be here. No biting. No kicking. You are at the bottom of the totem pole. You hear? And furthermore, don't you dare hurt our Sister."*

"I'll take a chunk out of you if you do," warned Matador.

"They're fine." Sister put her hands in the

pockets of the old flight jacket. Even with gloves, her hands got cold fast.

"Phil's got all the paperwork—you know, all that stuff, transferring ownership from Broad Creek to you."

"I do."

He climbed back up in the cab, grabbed a folder already a little greasy, and handed it down to her as he stepped down.

"Jockey Club papers in there, too." Phil had registered the two horses with the national organization.

Sister flipped it open. "How about that? He went all the way back to the foundation stallions. Past breeding papers in here. That's helpful."

"Phil never does anything halfway." Ignatius grinned. "Plus those foundation stallions put Broad Creek on the map."

"Yes, they did. Well, Midshipman goes back to Navigator, which makes sense. Do you remember a 'chaser Broad Creek once ran, called Bosun's Mate?"

"Could jump the moon, turn on a dime, and give you a nickel's change." Ignatius grinned.

"By now, Broad Creek has to have used up every naval term imaginable." Sister smiled back.

Ignatius pointed to Midshipman's pedigree and his Jockey Club name, Nelson's Midshipman. "This is the sixth generation with a Midshipman in the name. Oh, the farm's gone through them all."

"Easy to remember." Sister handed the paper to Tootie, who read it.

Ignatius put his forefinger on Matchplay's papers. "Goes all the way back to Spendthrift."

"Becomes an addiction, studying bloodlines." Sister took the paper back from Tootie. "We can study these in the house. Ignatius, wait up a minute. I have the check for Phil."

As she trotted into the tack room, the place where years fell away and memories flooded in, Ignatius and Tootie chatted.

"How do you like it here?" he asked.

"Mr. Donaldson, I love it. I'm learning so much."

"Tootie, call me Ignatius. I think the last time I was called Mr. Donaldson was when I sat in the recruiter's office just out of high school. Navy." This was said with pride.

"My father was in the army. He always said it made a man out of him," Tootie responded.

"Sure did for me. And now women can go in and do something other than nursing and personnel. Even when I was young, I thought that was kind of narrow."

"How did you wind up with horses?"

"I grew up here. I learned a lot in the navy, saw a lot, but then I wanted to marry and see my kids grow up. So I came home and Phil hired me. I knew a little bit about horses. Learned a lot more. Ah, here comes the Master."

Sister handed him two envelopes, one with Phil's name on it and one with Ignatius's name. It is customary to tip anyone who shows a horse at a breeding establishment and customary to tip anyone who delivers a horse for you.

Ignatius, naturally, did not open his envelope. Sister had a blue chip reputation for doing right by people.

"Oh, hey, I almost forgot. I was standing here flapping my gums." He reached up, placing the envelopes on the seat of the truck, then dashed to the back of the trailer. "Present from Broad Creek."

"That Phil." Sister shook her head.

Phil had sent Matchplay's and Midshipman's winter blankets along. It is customary to send a halter with a sold horse but as blankets can cost upwards of $300, depending on make and style, this was quite a gift.

Ignatius smiled broadly. "He says nothing is too good for the Master."

As Ignatius drove off, the two new to-be-foxhunters watched the rig.

"I don't want to do that again," Matchplay declared.

"What, worm?" Aztec called over the fence.

"Get on that machine," the young Thorough-bred answered.

"Kid, you've got a lot to learn." Keepsake laughed.

Midshipman prudently said nothing.

Back in the house, the two women hung their coats in the mudroom, eagerly stepping into the warm kitchen.

"Some days I feel colder than others, even if the temperature is the same," said Tootie.

"Weird, isn't it?"

The two sat down to pore over the pedigrees. Gray came into the kitchen and Sister told him the two geldings had arrived. He sat down at the table with them.

"Would you all like anything hot to drink?" Tootie offered. "I'm still cold."

"Sure," Sister said. "Surprise me."

"Me, too." Gray allowed Golly to jump onto his lap. "Just got off the phone with Ben. He asked for you to call him."

"Ah. I will after"—she turned her head—"the hot chocolate."

"He asked me to recommend a forensic accountant. Not from the area."

"I suppose you can't mention the case."

"Actually, I can. Ben wants someone to go over Penny Hinson's books—anything relating to billing, accounts receivable, and cost of supplies."

"Someone not from here?"

"Well, it is better, and I recommend Toots

Wooten in South Carolina. She won't miss an errant comma." He smiled. "Being an accountant in some ways is consoling because you do find answers in black-and-white. The problem is when you start thinking life is black-and-white."

Tootie placed three mugs on the table. "Real milk."

"Perfect." Gray appreciated real hot chocolate.

Sister held the mug in her hands as Gray said to her, "I've been thinking about Benny Glitters, what you said the other night, and I don't think we should tell Mercer. For now."

"He'll run to his mother with it?" Sister's voice lifted up.

"Yes, then who else will he tell? And God only knows what Aunt D will do."

Sister spoke to Tootie, "While you were reading Surtees after the hunt, Gray and I pulled up Benny Glitters's pedigree. He is Domino's son. Then Gray got his race record. Started out pretty good, then back of the pack—pretty much what we'd heard his story was."

"Doesn't Mercer know all that?" Tootie inquired.

"He does, but Crawford said something at the breakfast, kind of an offhand remark. He said it wasn't the human in the tomb that mattered, it was the horse."

This startled Tootie. "That's strange."

"This is me—not Gray or anyone else—but I

have a feeling I can't shake. Penny Hinson's murder is somehow connected to all this."

Tootie said, "How?"

"Well, that's the question, isn't it? Let me call Ben back." Sister rose, walked into the library and dialed.

Whenever possible, Sister used a landline. If the government wanted to, they could put on a tap like in the old days, but all the new technology—cell phones and computers—attracted them more because more people used them. Also, they were easier to hack. Corporations could spy on one another, too. It wasn't that she had anything to hide, it was just that she was of a generation that valued privacy.

"Ben."

"Good of you to call," the sheriff said. "You asked for any bloodline research on Dr. Hinson's computers. She had the breeding for all of her patients—I guess I call them patients—who had breed registrations. In the case of a backyard horse, she listed the parents if the owners knew. But she did have all the breed registrations and she also did research as you mentioned concerning the, I can't pronounce it—"

"Przewalski, forget the Pr, say it like a Cz."

"I expect the only way to speak Polish right is to be born to it," he replied good-naturedly. "Penny had looked into that; she'd investigated gene splitting. Her research was what one would expect

271

of a woman of her intelligence and dedication. But nothing that shouts out 'danger.'"

"Ben, any signs of clients with a drug addiction? Not that she would be dishonest, but sometimes clients can order drugs they don't really need, even needles, and then they sell them."

"No. There are bills for needles and 'bute. But again, nothing that would indicate abuse. Let me get back to her DNA research for a minute. Again, I don't know about any of this, but is it possible to manipulate DNA?"

"In theory, yes. In practice, not so easy." Sister inhaled. "You're thinking, can someone duplicate the DNA of a great stallion and not pay the stud fee? Get DNA from a son or daughter? Well, it wouldn't be an exact duplication, but when you consider that some stud fees soar well over $100,000, the motive is there."

"It occurred to me."

"Again, in theory, yes. In practice, no. It's still too complicated. Too few veterinarians would be able to do this and ultimately, they could fall under suspicion."

"So one would need to be highly specialized for that sort of trickery?"

"For now. In time these things will be simplified, like using stem cells to cure some conditions in horses is specialized, but more and more veterinarians can now do it. Also, Ben, all this takes a fair amount of investing in the technology. But something's there. Something is right under our noses."

He breathed deeply. "If only I had a hint as to what she had or knew that was so valuable or dangerous. But then again, Sister, Penny's murder may not be related to her profession." He paused. "But I'm on your train. I think it is, too."

After that call, Sister walked back into the kitchen. "I have an idea. Let's find every photograph we can of Domino, his sons and daughters, and Benny Glitters."

CHAPTER 23

Aztec picked his way over timbered acres; an inviting snow-covered pasture beckoned the horse to the western side. Hounds drew through the slash. This last Tuesday in February proved that February was actually the longest month in the year, with grim, cold, sleety, snow-filled days. However, fox breeding was in full swing so frozen toes or not, a true foxhunter gladly mounted up.

Soldier Road ran east to west, with Hangman's Ridge on the south of that paved road. When Sister hunted from Cindy Chandler's farm, Foxglove, the ridge loomed as ominously as it did from her farm on the other side of the high, long, flat former execution ground. Driving toward Charlottesville on Soldier Road, one would arrive at Roger's Corner, a clapboard convenience store at the first crossroads going east from the Blue Ridge. Traveling west, if you drove a four-wheel vehicle you'd eventually come to dirt roads but you could snake your way up and over the Blue Ridge Mountains, finally reaching a two-lane paved state road between Waynesboro and Verona. A turnoff on the left side of Soldier Road would take you to Route 250, a much easier passage over the Rockfish Gap.

All along this Appalachian chain, rounded by

time, gaps allowed inhabitants before colonists to travel east to west and vice versa. However, the Native tribes on either side of the famous fall line engaged in killing, capturing, and harassing one another, so little traffic took place.

The fall line runs roughly southwest to northeast, traveling northward. The angle, not acute, allows a sense of direction even for those born without this sense. Then again, if you can see the mountains, you always know where you are. However, you can't see them from the fall line where the state of Virginia lowers to the Atlantic Ocean many miles away. There the soil changes, the land flattens out. The three great rivers—the Potomac, the Rappahannock, and the James— enriched those flat lands. Even heading west, the alluvial deposits were generous.

On the east side of the line lived the Algonquin-speaking tribes; to the west were Sioux speakers.

Sister often thought of different peoples colliding—be they Indian or European, and then the later importation of Africans. Somehow out of bloodshed, truces, broken truces, and the superior technology of the Europeans, Virginia became what she now saw, a state of breathtaking beauty laden with natural treasures.

Like Aztec, she peered over the slash to the pasture beyond, distinguished by snake fencing, an inviting yellow clapboard house circa 1816, a true white stable and a red barn in the distance.

She was excited. She had wanted to hunt this new fixture before the season ended mid-March. Close Shave was so named because survival there had been a close shave.

She'd hunted since childhood and had been a Master for close to four decades. She knew not to rush into a new fixture, throw up jumps everywhere. You needed at least a year to study the land and your foxes—or perhaps coyote—as Close Shave sat hard by the mountains. Once a Master and huntsman had a grasp of the fox's running patterns, jumps could be put in the best places to keep close to the fellow. Naturally, the foxes figured this out but by that time, the humans knew the territory well enough to compensate for the latest clever ruse.

Today's field, just fifteen people, did make it a bit easier. A large field on a first day can be as difficult for staff as it is for the field.

Mercer, Kasmir, Freddie, Alida, Phil, Tedi and Ed, Walter, Cindy Chandler, Sam Lorillard, Ronnie, Xavier, Tootie and Felicity, and Gray, all wore their heaviest coats, and were eager to see the new territory. Staff had ridden it at the end of the summer and once again mid-fall to get their bearings. Cindy Chandler had secured this place for the club, as it abutted the westernmost part of Foxglove. Like Tollgate, it was owned by new people; middle-aged, neither Derek or Mo Artinstall rode. Cindy, charm personified, shepherded them to social-club functions, sent a personal invitation to the panorama of Opening Hunt while giving them glorious coffee-table photograph books of foxhunting. They had such a good time, they gladly gave permission for the club to ride across their land.

Cora stopped at a large walnut. The timbering in these parts had been select cut, and were pine only. *"Damn, this is a tough day,"* said the hound.

Diana touched the same spot. *"Old. But if we fan out, maybe this line will heat up."*

Ardent, also in her prime, inhaled. *"A signature. A calling card. I say we'll get lucky. Come on, girls."*

Trident grumbled behind these three to Trooper. *"I really get sick of the girls thinking they are better than we are."*

"Me, too!" Trooper agreed.

Thimble, sweet but not always as astute as one would wish, piped up. *"We have more drive. Shaker and Sister always say that."*

The two males whirled toward her with angry faces, and the sweet girl dropped her ears and eyes. *"Sorry."*

Dasher, an older male, coming up behind this little knot, cheerfully said, *"Hey, who cares what anyone says? If there's a fox, we'll find him."*

Hounds spread out. Reaching the snake fencing, they jumped over, continuing to search through the pasture.

Dreamboat, right up with Diana and Cora now, pushed toward a brook, not really wide enough to be a creek. On the western side of this fast-running water were rock outcroppings. Blue ice frozen from the crevices stood like a wall. These deep gray rocks, a few two stories high, contained larger crevices, suitable for housing critters. The rocks continued on for forty yards, then abruptly stopped, giving way to firm ground in heavy woods.

Dreamboat flung himself into the brook.

Diana trotted to the edge of the brook as Dreamboat crawled out under the rocks. *"Cora, he's on a roll."*

He was, too. Dreamboat had finally come into his own, out from under the shadow of his aggressive brother, Dragon, who'd been left behind at the kennel that day.

Sister and Shaker found out the hard way that when you assemble your pack for the day's hunt, you had to select with care. Not every hound would hunt with Dragon. Maybe they should have drafted him out, but he was brilliant. Sister always thought of this as her batting lineup for the game. Dragon was Number 3 while Diana was Number 4 when together. Apart, they did better and both could be number 4s, no jostling for position.

Cora hit the water, too. Within two minutes, the twelve-couple pack worked on the rock side of the brook.

Tails feathered. Hounds moved faster. Noses touched the ground, lifted up a moment, then touched again.

"Let's boogie!" Trooper shouted with glee and off they ran.

From their exploratory rides, Shaker knew where a nice crossing was. He quickly got over. Betty and Sybil found the going a bit harder because once over the water, they needed to find some kind of deer trails. The undergrowth was almost impenetrable, easily as bad as Pattypan Forge.

Sister followed Shaker. That summer, the club had cut a big cross through the woods, a trail large enough for horses and one that terminated on each of the four sides of the large woods.

In front of the hounds ran twenty wild turkeys. Hounds ignored them. A few horses found the sharp-eyed birds unnerving.

The lead turkey, an old turkey hen, cast a hard, bright eye at Aztec, the imposing horse leading the field.

"Mind your manners. I can fly right up in your long face."

"Bother," exhaled Aztec, who saw turkeys in the pasture often.

"Pauline, don't start something," the turkey immediately behind the lead turkey advised.

"This is our territory. These creatures need to be put in their place." Pauline flickered her

long tail, but she did scurry away just a bit faster.

X-man, a green horse ridden by Sam Lorillard, snorted. *"What if they all fly up? I hate that sound."*

Sam would ride Crawford's green horses with The Jefferson Hunt to season them. As it was his day off, Crawford felt he was getting free labor although he was loath to admit a day with Sister helped a horse more than a day with him.

Nighthawk, Kasmir's beloved best mount, advised X-man, *"They have brains the size of a pea. Ignore them."*

"I resent that. You're the peabrain." The last turkey at the rear of the line clucked as she hurried to catch up.

As the line disappeared in tall grass their movements reminded Sister of that old dance the Turkey Trot, except that the turkeys did it better.

Right after the turkey parade, a confused squirrel paused for a moment, then prudently shot up a tree.

Far ahead of the field, hounds continued their cry, but the line was fading. They lost it at the edge of the woods.

"Dammit!" Trooper cursed.

The racket disturbed a barred owl, now awake and crabby. The golden-eyed bird looked down at them from her hole in the tree trunk.

"Vulgarians," she issued her verdict.

The vulgarians, confused and irritated, sought the line in a 360° radius. Finally reaching the hounds, Shaker held up to watch. Anyone can thrill to their pack in full cry but to watch them work was Shaker's joy, and Sister's as well. Given the narrowness of the passage she stopped fifty yards behind him, but some of the hounds worked back toward her.

The huntsman allowed them ten minutes, deemed it futile, and called them to her.

Sister looked behind her. "Huntsman."

Shaker yelled out before people tried to back into the mess. "Master, just turn around and go out. Let's get back in the pasture."

When they reached the pasture, hounds cast again. They tried for another hour but to no avail.

Not about to brave the cold, Close Shave's new owners waved from the kitchen windows when the field rode by. Shaker took off his hat and Sister tapped hers with her crop. The field followed suit.

A stiff wind rolled down the mountains. Clouds backed up on the crest.

Shaker blew hounds back to him and rode up to Sister. "I think we're done. This will be a very good fixture."

"Yes, it will. God bless Cindy Chandler. We've got some work to do, but that's hunting, isn't it?" Sister smiled, and turned Aztec as they walked back to the trailers.

A small tailgate marked the first hunt at Close Shave. Derek and Mo Artinstall allowed the club to tailgate in an old well-built, six-stall empty barn. Putting on a hunt breakfast was a great deal of work. Sister and Walter would never ask for such a gift from a landowner. In fact, they were happy to use the barn. Somehow it fit the spirit of the group. Out of the wind, director's chairs and card tables set up, people were warm enough in their coats, some changing to down jackets for the tailgate.

Taking Tuesdays off, Walter had bought a variety of Woodford Reserve bourbons, each having been aged in different casks. Ribbons in hunt green colors adorned the necks of the bottles. These stood open on one card table with a large card, hunt scene on the front.

"Everyone, sign the thank-you card to celebrate our first hunt at Close Shave," said Walter. "I'll drop this off at the Artinstalls when we're finished."

One by one people came up, removed their gloves, blew on cold fingers, signed their names.

"How did you like Mumtaz?" Sister asked Alida.

"Ravishing. The mare is one of the best horses I have ever ridden." Alida glowed.

Kasmir joined the two ladies, bearing two cups of bracing tea. "Would you all like a spike with that?"

Sister kissed him on the cheek. "You're spike enough, Kasmir. Alida gave Mumtaz a good ride."

"Ah, my girl needs a good rider. I bump along," he demurred modestly.

"Kasmir, you're a wonderful rider." Alida complimented him honestly, for he was.

"A wonderful man." Sister dearly loved Kasmir, praying as did everyone who was drawn to him that he would find happiness.

Mercer signed the card, then joined the others. As it was a small field, most everyone crowded around the Master and staff.

"Why don't we all sit?" Sister invited everyone. "I don't know why but my legs are tired."

Those who brought their director's chairs pulled them over. Always organized, Walter had carried bales of straw on the back of his truck, plus a few in his trailer. He'd placed them around the chairs and everyone gratefully sank onto canvas or straw.

Phil remarked, "It is funny how you can ride hard one day, no aches. Not much another day and you're shot."

"Low pressure," Freddie Thomas offered.

"Well, a nip of spirits should pick up everyone's pressure." Mercer held up his plastic cup. "Say, whatever happened to our stirrup cups, the ones with fox heads?"

"Mercer, no one is carrying stirrup cups to a meet unless it's a joint meet or a high holy day," said Tedi Bancroft, who always found Mercer amusing.

"We need more elegance," Mercer declared with conviction.

"Oh, Mercer." Sam shrugged. "You've been saying that since grade school. Since you discovered Hubert de Givenchy."

The crowd laughed.

Phil offered a toast. "To Mercer, first flight of sartorial splendor."

"Hear! Hear!" They all agreed.

People wanted to amuse Mercer, especially those who had been at his grandfather's somber reburial. No one could forget Daniella and most knew how demanding she was of Mercer.

They chattered among themselves.

Seated across from Phil, Sister smiled. "Remind me to carry a director's chair."

He wiggled on his straw bale, too. "Sticks right where it hurts, doesn't it?"

"By the way, thank you for the extensive pedigrees for Matchplay and Midshipman. I enjoy reading pedigrees. Going back through the names brings back memories."

"Yes, it does," Phil agreed enthusiastically. "I suppose most everyone measures their life by music, sports, books, movies, special occasions. For us, it's horses, great runs."

"That it is. Gray, Tootie, and I were looking at photographs of old horses. It's interesting how some sires leave a stamp, and others not so much. Given Midshipman's line, of course, we went back to Navigator. A very nice-looking horse with what was then thought of as a lackluster pedigree."

Mercer leaned forward. "Proved them wrong."

"I think it was the Ca Ira blood, the old French Thoroughbred who was Navigator's sire," Phil said. "No one knew much about him."

"Ca Ira." Kasmir popped up. "An eighty-gun frigate, French, that had the misfortune to battle Lord Nelson."

"How do you know such things?" Alida was impressed.

"Going to school in England helped." Kasmir smiled. "You do learn everything about Admiral Lord Nelson."

"You did. I bet the others all forgot it," Alida teased him.

Phil referred back to the photographs. "Hard to tell too much from those old pictures but you sure could see the good cannon bone on Ca Ira."

"One doesn't think of the French when one thinks of Thoroughbreds, or Germans either," mused Gray.

"Given that those people had been at war with one another for centuries, that makes sense. Never give the other country credit," Alida remarked, which made most of the others realize she was more than beautiful.

Phil asked Sister, "Must have been a scavenger hunt finding old photographs?"

"Anything is easy when you have Tootie

and Gray. Put them in front of a computer."

Tootie said, "It kind of started with Przewalski's horse. Dr. Hinson told me I needed to study the evolution of the horse. That led to DNA." She paused. "Dr. Hinson was so smart and she told me that one really breeds to families more than individuals. She said you needed the right mix. A horse like Benny Glitters from a great family is as rare as Mr. Chetwynd's Navigator. Dr. Hinson said horses usually breed true. Well, she said people do, too."

"She was right," Phil agreed. "I'll miss Penny. A terrible loss, both as a vet and someone who could see the big equine picture."

Mercer nodded in agreement. "No date set for her service?"

"Not that I know of," Sister confirmed.

"Medical Examiner. Takes time," Sam replied simply.

"Well, how many suspicious deaths can there be in February? They can't be that backed up." Mercer put an entire chocolate chip cookie into his mouth.

"Who knows?" Freddie raised her eyebrows. "But you do associate violent crime with hot weather. At least, I do."

"All the more reason to be a white-collar criminal." Sam laughed. "Not seasonal."

"Do you ever think that Crawford made his fortune illegally?" Phil asked.

"No. Not for one minute," Sam responded instantly.

"Umm." Phil changed course. "It's good of him to let you hunt with us on Tuesdays."

"It's usually my day off," said Sam, "but he is pretty good about it, especially if I bring along a green horse. Some learn more quickly than others. The trick is to be consistent."

"Sam, I still say Crawford needs to get into racing." Mercer ate another cookie, a pang of guilt accompanying the pleasure.

"He's not going to hear that from me." Sam tired of Mercer nudging him, always nudging him.

Phil stood up to look out the large glass windows in the closed barn door. "Windier."

Cindy Chandler got up, too. "This is the winter that refuses to end, isn't it?"

Sam and Gray talked to Mercer a bit more as the group started to break up.

"I'll fold up the tables, put the bales back on your truck so you can go drop off the bottles," Phil offered. "Otherwise, you'll be here for another half hour."

"Thank you." Walter smiled.

"Mercer." Phil called to his old friend to help him.

People removed their plastic food boxes from the card tables. No food was left. Mercer and Phil folded the card tables as the others folded their chairs.

Kasmir and Alida walked outside to his trailer. She thanked him again for allowing her to ride Mumtaz.

"Will you be hunting Thursday or Saturday?" He paused. "Of course, you will. You can ride Kavita Thursday and Mumtaz again on Saturday."

"Kasmir, I can't take advantage of you like that."

"You're not. My horses need to go out."

"Mumtaz is gray. Did you ever read Tesio?" She named the great Italian breeder of the first half of the twentieth century. "He thought grays a mutation."

"Yes. Tesio and the Aly Khan are worth study. But I don't agree with the mutation theory, do you?"

"No. But then I look at paints and pintos, color horses. I don't really know too much about their backgrounds but they aren't as refined as Thoroughbreds. Thoroughbreds don't come as paints. Although I bet there's one somewhere out there." She cupped her chin for a moment in her gloved hand.

"Bet not." Kasmir held up five fingers for a five-fingered bet.

"You're on."

They batted this back and forth, each becoming colder by the moment.

Freddie called from her truck. "Alida!"

"All right," Alida called back.

"I'll bring your horse Thursday."

"Kasmir, allow me to come to your stable. I can tack up my own horse. That way I'd get to know her a little bit."

"Well—"

"Really, I like doing my own grooming and tacking up."

"All right. Perhaps—Mmm, the fixture is forty minutes from my place—perhaps an hour and a half before the first cast?"

"I'll be there." Then with a mischievous glint to her eye she said over her shoulder, "I respect your opinion, but I think mine is better." She burst out laughing.

He laughed, too, slipped into the cab of his truck, and the tears came. His late wife would say that to him constantly.

"Thank you, my love," he whispered.

CHAPTER 24

S he kept good records," said Mercer. Asked by Ben Sidell, he reviewed the pedigrees of horses on whom Dr. Hinson worked.

Also asked by the sheriff, Sister sat next to Mercer at Penny's desk at the Westlake Equine Clinic. "Ben, certain strains in all the breeds carry problems. Penny was wise to know each horse's background if she could."

Mercer turned from the screen to Ben, in the chair next to him. "That's one of the problems with what I call backyard horses. Often Old Jose is bred to Sweet Sue because the owners think they're a good match. They have no idea what they're doing."

"Isn't there hybrid vigor among horses as well as people?" Ben smiled slightly.

"Yes," Sister answered. "We don't need to know names, but I'm assuming nothing in Penny's records points to crime. Or misuse of drugs?"

"No," said Ben. "But I don't know pedigrees like you two do. And what struck me is the amount of research she put in during the last month of her life," he added. "Could have been just a notion, as you Southerners say."

"Oh, come on, they say it in Ohio, too," Mercer shot back.

"Sister, what do you make of this fellow here?" Mercer pointed out a Quarter Horse cross.

"Poco Bueno blood, if you go back four generations. A very good Quarter Horse line. The dam, his mother, was that line and the sire, you know well, a chaser son of Damascus."

"Right." Mercer tapped away on the computer keys.

"And?" Ben asked.

"Whoever bred the gelding used two very good lines, sturdy. They looked for a mating they could afford. Ben, very few people could have afforded Damascus's stud fee when he was alive. So this person knew his or her stuff, and wanted an appendix, a Thoroughbred/Quarter Horse cross. You can find good blood if you look hard enough at a reasonable price, and anyone breeding an appendix horse would do just that."

Ben rubbed the flat of his palm on his cheek for a moment. "Do either of you have any idea why Penny would have studied all this, plus all her research on equine DNA?"

"Again, to see if a condition she was treating could possibly be passed by blood," Sister repeated. "Things like the inability to sweat, or hip problems—you'd be surprised what can show up. It's only in the last twenty years, really, that some of these conditions can be pinpointed genetically. Prior to that, a lot depended on a horseman's memory."

"And honesty," chirped Mercer, always quick to find a financial motive. "If a yearling looks fabulous, moves well but, you know, is a little screwy, how many sellers will tell? I worry a lot more about mental states than, say, a slightly crooked leg."

Sister crossed her arms over her chest. "Ben, you know her client list, we don't. Did Penny have any pedigree research not connected to her clients?"

"No."

"What about going back to the beginnings, like Eclipse or Matchem?" Mercer named two foundation sires of Thoroughbreds in the United States.

"Matchem 1748, right?" Sister was thinking.

"Right." Mercer then added, "Eclipse 1764."

"You can go back that far?" Ben interjected, amazed.

"Very often, you can," said Mercer. "Sometimes further. For instance, we know the names of some of Charles the First's horses in the royal stud long before the English started their stud book." He leaned back in the office work chair, stretched out his legs under the desk. "For instance, Navigator, the great founding stallion at Broad Creek, goes back to Matchem, whereas Broad Creek's two other founding stallions from the 1880s, Limelight and Loopy Lou, eventually trace back to Eclipse."

"What about his new stallion, St. Boniface?" Sister asked. "Phil is very shrewd about stallions."

"Goes straight back to Ribot 1952, which will finally get you back to Eclipse." He swiveled his chair to face Ben again. "Any breeding establishment tries to go with the percentages. If a stallion has been able to throw a high percentage of Grade One stakes winners, naturally, you push him forward."

"That's where I differ." Sister sat upright. "I pay more attention to the mare."

"Well, true enough but a mare produces one foal a year, if she catches," said Mercer. "Whereas a stallion can cover many mares. It's all numbers or, as I like to think of it, the economy of scale."

"So Broad Creek has great blood?" Ben, not versed in pedigrees, was interested.

"Kept the farm alive through thick and thin but the funny thing is, no one gave a fig for Navigator before he started to breed," Mercer told them. "He goes back to Matchem but his immediate sire, Seneca and his grandsire, Naughty Nero, so-so. No one paid much attention to the horse but Old Tom Chetwynd said, 'Hell, let's try him.' So he bred a couple of in-house mares. Those foals started winning at age three and every crop after that, there were a high percentage of winners. If you go back far enough, you'll find Australian 1858 in Navigator's pedigree, and finally you get back to Matchem. But you never know."

"Old Tom bred to his own mares?" Sister was very curious.

"Initially he did," said Mercer. "He loaded the dice and put Navigator to a few of his best. It was his only chance if the horse had any quality at all."

"Why didn't they race him?" Ben asked.

"As you know, Broad Creek has its own training track and I guess Navigator's times were slow. I don't know. Long before my time. Even Phil doesn't know. You never ever know. A lackluster runner can produce wonderful foals. Some stallions produce great colts, others great fillies or broodmares. Some horses run better on turf than dirt. It's roulette, genetic roulette."

"But study helps," Ben said.

"Sure." Mercer flicked a few more pedigrees on the screen. "Sister, you know more about Warmbloods than I do." He named a larger, heavier horse than a Thoroughbred, a horse much used for show jumping.

"Not a lot." She peered at the screen. "Holsteiner. Lovely." Then she smiled at Ben. "When I was a girl and even unto my forties, no Warmbloods. No horses of color in the field either. By that, I mean paints, palominos, et cetera. Because all you saw were Thoroughbreds. Anyway, the Warmblood craze started here in the 1970s. The old line is: When you start a hunt, you're glad you're on a Warmblood, when you finish you're glad you're on a Thoroughbred."

Mercer filled in the blanks. "Warmbloods are calmer but they don't necessarily have the extraordinary stamina of a Thoroughbred. However, if someone gets their horse-hunting fit, the animal can usually last at least two to three hours, depending on the pace."

"Crawford rides a Warmblood, a lovely animal," Sister informed Ben. "Okay, we've sat here and blabbed on. Why are we here, really?"

The sheriff turned his hands up, then let them drop. "Because I'm in the dark. I can't see even a pinprick of light in Penny's murder, so I'm trying anything."

"Like whether she knew someone was breeding a horse with a passable flaw?" Mercer inquired.

"That was one idea."

"Ben, that would certainly be an issue in terms of veterinary expense for an unsuspecting buyer but a lot of possibilities may never occur," said Mercer. "Your mother may have diabetes, it may be in her family. Doesn't mean you'll get it. We go back to percentages. And the stud fees are really an issue only in the Thoroughbred world. Other breeds are less expensive, the fees."

"And Penny couldn't prove wrongdoing," Sister added. "She could only note to a buyer, if asked to vet the horse, what those possibilities might be."

Ben grasped the issue. "Still, it could be a sales killer."

"Yes, but you take a field hunter. A vet comes along who vets the animal as though he is going to race. That's a real sales killer." She laughed.

Mercer, too, said with amusement, "You take someone new to horses, the vet comes along and points out every tiny flaw and the person panics, just panics. No sale. The key phrase for a fox-hunter is 'serviceably sound' and some vets can't do it. They are terrified of lawsuits. It's like just about any other profession these days. There's someone waiting in the wings to point the finger, bring a suit. I'm amazed any business ever gets done."

"Well, I don't think it's quite that bad but what Mercer says is true," Sister agreed. "But what he isn't saying is that a vet can be paid off."

This shut the other two right up.

"What?" Ben's eyebrows shot up.

Sister frowned. "A vet can pass a horse with a serious flaw if given enough money under the table. Some do. Corruption appears in all lines of work, Ben, even law enforcement."

A long pause followed this, then Ben, voice low, "Do you think Penny could have been party to that? Let's take Broad Creek Stables, since they are the biggest Thoroughbred breeder here. Do you think Phil would have given her money under the table?"

"No," both replied at once.

"But it happens," Sister calmly repeated the

idea. "When a couple of hundred thousand are at stake, a lot of folks with shaky ethics wobble."

"Not Penny," Mercer loudly defended her. "And not Phil. You have two of his youngsters. Look at how sound they are. They just aren't that fast and furthermore, Midshipman doesn't want to race. On the other hand, I am willing to bet he will love hunting. It's more natural than running around an oval."

"I don't mean to imply that Phil paid off Penny," said Sister. "It's a kind of conjecture. A payoff would only be worth the risk if large sums of money lay on the table. And buyers for Broad Creek Stables horses usually have their own vets anyway, because the best of those animals are sold at Keeneland or Fasig Tipton." She named two sales venues of high quality.

"I see," said Ben. "So Penny wouldn't be used?"

"No," Sister replied. "She might be consulted here before the animals are shipped. Kind of an insurance policy. But she wouldn't be a candidate for that kind of dishonesty. Nor would she have done it."

Both men nodded in agreement.

"I looked at the drawings she had of horses," said Ben. "You know, where the vet marks a problem. She was thorough." He could read the illustration because when he bought Nonni, he was given one by the vet, who happened to be Penny.

"Ben, I don't think we've helped you one bit," Sister said sorrowfully.

"Actually, you have. You've helped me understand where other kinds of crimes could be hidden. First, I was thinking about drugs. And then seeing all her research, I wondered if there was some kind of tie-in, something I wouldn't know because I'm not really a horseman. I'm just a rider. You two were born into horses. I wish I knew what you forgot." He smiled.

As Mercer turned off the computer, Sister pointed to the screen. "Hey, turn that back on a minute. Go to the DNA stuff."

Mercer did and she quickly read as he moved the text along for her.

"Forgive me. But now I'm curious. We know Midshipman goes ultimately back to Matchem."

"Right." Mercer looked at Sister.

"I want to run a DNA test and we'll see how it works," Sister said. "Maybe if I go through the process, there might be something in Penny's research that resonates. It's worth a try."

Ben shrugged.

"Who can you use?" Mercer could think of a lot of good vets.

"I'll tell you after the research. If word should leak out, it might look bad for Penny and Westlake. You know how people jump to conclusions and it might not be so good for the vet either, as he or she will be bombarded by a lot of people who stick their noses in other people's business."

"Not me." Mercer smiled sheepishly.

She fibbed. "Never gave you a second thought."

"So you don't think Penny's sudden interest in pedigree and DNA was just a notion?" Mercer posited triumphantly.

"No, I don't." Sister held up her hand to quiet him. "But I don't know why. A hunch."

CHAPTER 25

Midshipman stood in the cross ties in the center aisle of Sister's barn. Tootie was pulling his mane, a standard grooming procedure endured by horses though not especially liked by them. Two ropes with clips, each affixed to the side of the aisle, helped the horse stand still as the clip fit on his halter. They were literally cross ties.

Rickyroo was watching from his stall. *"You got a lot of mane, boy,"* the old horse said.

"Oh, just give him a buzz cut," Keepsake teased from the neighboring stall. *"He'll look like a marine."*

The youngster remained quiet. He knew the older horses were giving him the business, one of many tests they would throw at him. The other horses demanded more patience from him than the humans.

Nearby in his stall, Matchplay whinnied. *"No one's touching my mane."*

Lafayette snorted, *"Let me tell you something, son. You landed in a great place. These people know horses and they take care of us. You shut up and learn to take care of them."*

Matchplay's nostrils flared. Having been nipped once over the fence line by Matador, he thought better of sassing back to an older horse.

Sister came up to Tootie, opened a Ziploc bag. Tootie dropped a bit of pulled mane into it with the root bulbs attached.

"That should do it." The Master returned to the tack room where Betty and she cleaned tack. Under hanging tack hooks that looked like grappling hooks, two buckets of warm water, clean sponges, saddle soap, and even tooth-brushes had been laid out on towels.

Working on a bridle with a simple eggbutt snaffle, Betty said, "What's better than a heated tack room with a little kitchen?"

Sister smiled. "A bigger tack room with a bigger kitchen?"

"More to clean," Betty replied.

"I haven't done too good a job here." She looked down at the tartan rug. "All those years I polished the floor. Finally put this rug down and it is easier to vacuum than wash and polish but boy, it shows every single mud bit."

"Hard, hard winter. Ice. Mud. Snow. Sleet. And sometimes all in the same day. Have you noticed that on some of our fixtures, the footing is better?"

"Yes, I have. Time to break out the soil maps and review them all." Sister dipped a washrag into the warm water, then wrung it dry. "I wonder if I should put the mane hairs in the fridge?"

"No, why?"

"Things keep better if they're cool."

"Doesn't matter. Are you taking the mane to Greg or is he coming here?"

"He'll be by later. I miss seeing him. He travels so much now since he sold the practice."

Greg Schmidt, DVM, had sold his veterinary clinic with the idea to retire. In a sense he did retire, but his reputation meant people would call and beg him to speak at a conference, or to please just look at this one horse, et cetera and so forth. Despite not wanting to bother him, Sister had always relied on his superior judgment, discretion, and marvelous common sense. He was the only person she trusted to run a DNA test on Midshipman. It wasn't that most working vets were gabby, but something might slip out. She would take no chances. Greg was a deep well.

"Every now and then I dream about traveling like him," said Sister. "Cutting back on the responsibilities. I'd like to see South Africa and Namibia, Botswana. I've visited almost every former British colony but not those places nor India. Wherever the British were, there are good horses."

"Is this your revenge on the Empire speech?" Betty lifted one eyebrow like an arch actress.

Sister shook her head. "No. But I believe all of us once under the British flag have a great deal in common."

"Even India?" Betty was quick.

"Don't know. I haven't been there, but India is

the world's largest democracy. And they inherited that incredible British civil service."

"You read too much," Betty teased her.

"Not enough. And who's talking? Of course, you stuff yourself with those hideous romances." Sister then spoke in a breathy voice. "She noticed his rippling chest, his piercing green eyes, the black two-day-old stubble. Her heart beat faster."

"Sounds good to me. Maybe you should try writing one of those. Boost your income."

They laughed just as Dr. Greg Schmidt, early, walked into the tack room.

"A two-day-old stubble," Betty repeated, bent over laughing. "Love that!"

Greg, always a good sport, ran his hand over his cheek. "I'm getting lazy."

"Don't pay any more attention to her than if she was a goat barking," said Sister. "Greg, our Betty Franklin, a seemingly intelligent, level-headed woman, has become intoxicated by romances and all the male heroes sport stubble."

The retired vet beamed. "So I'm in good company."

"Always." Sister handed him the Ziploc. "What a good boy that horse is. Didn't fuss when Tootie pulled his mane. She's now giving Midshipman the Roughneck Farm day of beauty."

Greg peeped out the window in the door that opened into the center aisle. "You know, he reminds me of Curlin, who stands at Lane's End

Farm. One of the most beautiful Thoroughbreds I've ever seen."

"Lane's End." Betty said the establishment's name in such a way that confirmed its exalted status.

"Some of those farms in Kentucky are incredible," said Sister. "The knowledge is generations deep. Think of the Hancocks," she added, mentioning a prominent family.

Greg—Ziploc between his forefinger and thumb—leaned against the saddle rack. "Well, you know better than I that once upon a time Virginia and Maryland boasted horsemen of many generations."

"What is it they call people who leave to film outside of L.A.?" Betty paused. "Runaway production. That's it. Well, we've sure seen it here in the racing world."

"The Chenerys left. Ned Evans died. The late Clay Camp finally left Virginia for Kentucky. What a brain drain." Greg stated a bare truth. "People who come here now aren't racing people. It's three-day eventers, show people, foxhunters, of course, and great as all that is—clean money, no pollution, all that good stuff—still, it's not the same as racing. Racing brings millions into a state. Right now the equine industry brings one-point-three billion dollars into Virginia. Just imagine what that figure would be if the old days returned?"

"Greg, I think of it a lot." Sister wiped down the bridle with a clean dry cloth. "When people ask me how do I feel about getting old, I say, 'Wonderful, because I lived through some of the best years this country and the horse world ever had. I'm lucky.'"

"I caught some of that when I moved here from California." The tall, silver-haired man looked at the bridle Sister was cleaning. "Who are you hunting in an eggbutt snaffle?"

"Aztec," Sister replied. "He has such a sensitive mouth, I don't need much."

"I've always liked that bit. When you started hunting, Sister, I bet people rode in double bridles."

"Plenty did. The bit sewn into the bridle. I still use bridles, English, with the bit sewn in."

"Greg, you know what a stickler she is," said Betty. "I change my bits. Sister sniffs when she sees me do it and tells me I can afford the true hunting bridle."

"I do not." Sister defended herself.

"Ha. I once saw you tell a man he had his garters on backward."

"Well, Betty, he did. I considered the correction an act of kindness."

"Eagle eye." Greg smiled at Sister. "Well, ladies, I'd better head home. Called the lab. Not much going on. You'll have your DNA results quickly. Week at the most."

With his hand on the doorknob, Sister asked, "Greg, did you ever talk to Penny about pedigree research? Equine genome?"

He thought for a moment, looked down at the plaid rug, then up. "One of the biggest arguments I ever had with Penny was over just that. She showed me the papers on some appendix crosses, gave the history of the horse, which I knew, then compared them to some of the Thoroughbreds she saw."

"She saw a lot of horses," Betty added non-committally. "More once you retired."

Greg smiled. "She swore that a lot of Thoroughbreds were turning into hothouse flowers, the stamina and bone being bred right out of them. She wondered why the Jockey Club didn't wise up and allow judicious outcrosses." He frowned. "'Penny,' I said, 'Never. Never. Never. Never!' Well, we got into it. I said the problem wasn't the Thoroughbred, it was the people who breed them. If someone knew what they were doing, they could and would breed a strong horse. I believe the Thoroughbred is the greatest athlete ever. She couldn't believe I was that conservative; I think her word was conservative. Better than jerk, I suppose."

Greg smiled at the memory, then continued, "But Penny was young, remember. She hadn't seen many of the old-style Thoroughbreds, heavier cannon bone, you know what I'm saying.

306

I laid into her about paper breeders, people who look at bloodlines but not the horses. That and the real problem is writing racetrack conditions so inferior horses can make a buck. There's a race for every possible horse, especially inferior ones. She blew up at me. Whew!" He spiraled his forefinger up in the air.

"How long did it take before she spoke to you again?" Betty wondered aloud.

"Not long. She apologized for losing her temper. Penny had such a good heart. She cared so much for horses and it pained her to see so many leg injuries. For West Nile virus, stuff like that, we have vaccines, but fragile legs, there is no cure. That's breeding," Greg remarked with feeling.

"She did have a good heart." Sister's tone softened. "Greg, I have a feeling that her death is tied up in all this, even though there's no way that woman would ever be party to anything shadowy."

"No, never," Greg rapidly agreed. "Penny was straight up."

"And because of that, if she found wrongdoing, I think she would have blown the whistle," Sister said.

"Yes, she would." Greg looked at the mane hairs in the Ziploc. "Sister, I'll get right on this. I won't send it to the lab. I'll drive it down."

As he left, Sister knew he followed her line of thought, most especially what she didn't say.

Betty, too, had a vague sense. "Jane, what are you getting into?"

"I don't know."

"Be careful. We have no idea why Penny was killed or who did it, obviously. But if you blunder into something, well—"

Sister lifted up another bridle. "They have to catch me first."

"Don't be a smart-ass."

CHAPTER 26

Clytemnestra, mean as snakeshit, big as a house, glowered as the trailers parked at Foxglove Farm. The heifer's son, Orestes, now larger than his mother, evidenced a much sweeter personality. Nonetheless, if hounds traveled through their back pastures, the field certainly did not. No one wants to be chased by a giant bovine.

As this was Saturday, March 1, skies overcast, mercury hanging at 48°F, the field overflowed.

Cindy Chandler, owner of Foxglove, kept her foxes happy. She had a mating pair under the old schoolhouse, a mile and a half from the main barn. Another male fox lived at the eastern edge of her property and occasionally Comet would travel over from Roughneck Farm.

An accomplished gardener, one with a long knowledge of plants, Foxglove delighted all who hunted there unless they offended Clytemnestra. The clapboard barn, the old clapboard schoolhouse, the clapboard house, all sparkled in good condition, impressive given the hard winter. No paint peeled.

Painted fencecoat black, three-board fences marked off intelligently laid-out pastures and paddocks. However, what always excited comment from newcomers were the two ponds at different levels, a small water wheel between them.

Today, ice rimmed both ponds. The raised walkway between the ponds had some icy spots but the water wheel—quite simple as opposed to the enormous one at Mill Ruins—still flowed, the wheel lazily turning.

Hounds promptly moved off at 10:00 A.M. Shaker included all the young entry in today's draw. They'd been working all season, a couple here, a couple there, then two couple—until now, when all the youngsters could go.

With Clytemnestra at his back, glaring while she chewed expensive hay, Shaker prudently cast in the opposite direction from the brooding beast.

Near the front of First Flight, Phil looked over his shoulder. "That has to be the biggest heifer I have ever seen. Each year she's larger."

"Why does Cindy waste good hay on her?" complained Mercer. "Cows have four stomachs. She doesn't need the pricey stuff," he quipped.

"Oh, yes, she does," said Cindy, riding behind Mercer.

A flush over Mercer's face indicated that once again he had opened his mouth before looking around or thinking. Fortunately, Cindy possessed both charm and a great sense of humor. She wasn't the least offended by his criticism.

"Sorry, Cindy," Mercer apologized instantly. "I didn't realize you were back there."

"If he'd known, he might have babbled even more," Phil tormented Mercer.

"Well, gentlemen, if Clytemnestra eats four-star hay, she behaves herself. If not, she will smash right through a fence. Actually, I believe she could take out the barn if she'd a mind to."

Up front, Sister heard them chattering, as well as others. She loathed a chatty field but hounds had not yet been cast, spirits were high, why squelch them? If the blab continued once hounds were working, well, that's different.

"Lieu in." Shaker put the pack into a thin line of woods below the ponds, using the old Norman term now about one thousand years old.

This woods expanded to the north, providing good hiding places for foxes, bobcats, deer, raccoons, and the occasional weasel.

This morning, red-tailed hawks, red-shouldered hawks, and broad-tailed hawks sat motionless in treetops. All of them hoped hounds would scare up voles, moles, mice, and other little rodents. Perhaps those raptors were the original foodies.

Riding with Sybil today, Tootie trotted at woods' edge as they headed due east. If the pack had turned right, they would be heading south, finally running into Soldier Road. Foxglove Farm boundaries were more natural than man-made, with the exception of Soldier Road. Natural boundaries can be easier to hunt than man-made ones and Shaker was making the most of it.

Hounds worked the edge of the woods; a few, noses down, walked along the pasture by the woods while the bulk of the pack moved through the woods. For Sister, this was a complete cast. She wanted her hounds fanning out. Other Masters and huntsmen did not. Everyone had their own ways and their own reasons. Sister wanted her hounds to do what was called "Make good the ground." She wanted as much ground studied by those superb hound noses as possible.

The ponds—now above the field, to the right— lowered the temperature a bit as they all moved alongside them.

Older Asa, out today for his once-a-week hunt, widened his search heading to the bottom of the ponds' high banks.

Hounds, horses, and people really do become wiser with age and Asa, feeling the slight temperature drop, also could smell more moisture below those banks. He stopped, inhaled deeply, moved a few paces, inhaled again. His tail slowly waved to and fro, then that stern picked up speed.

"Hot. A hot line!" With that, he ran straight up until he was now level with the top pond.

No reason for any hound to check Asa, the pack immediately rushed to him. Shaker didn't even have to say, "Hark."

Within seconds the whole pack opened, the young entry beside themselves with excitement.

On the south side, Betty kept at two o'clock. She wanted to be on somewhat higher ground, which afforded her a wider view. The First Whipper-in, which Betty was, often sees the fox first. If a cast is like the face of a clock, Shaker is in the middle where the two hands meet. Hounds start at twelve o'clock. Betty was to their right at two o'clock. Sybil would ride at ten o'clock. Once a fox tore off, the staff did their best to maintain those positions but ground conditions could make it difficult.

If a hunt is fortunate enough to have a professional whipper-in, that individual is usually given the title of First Whipper-in. A few hunts in North America carried three to four paid whippers-in —wonderful for them and really wonderful for a young person starting out, say, being given the slot of Fourth Whipper-in. There's only one way to learn foxhunting, and that's by doing it.

Sister occasionally dreamed of a paid whipper-in or even two, say, young men or women in their middle twenties, but her two honorary whippers-in—loyal, reliable, shrewd in the ways of quarry—could have been professionals. Sister was proud of Betty and Sybil and knew that putting Tootie out with them would fast-forward the young woman's knowledge.

On a good trail in the woods, Sybil held hard, as did Tootie. A medium-sized red fox shot right in front of them, plunging deep down into a narrow crevice in the land. The two women counted to twenty, then bellowed, "Tallyho!"

The count to twenty is plenty sufficient for a fox.

Hearing the call, Shaker waited. His hounds were turning in that direction. In his mind, to pick them up and throw them into the woods would be to undermine them. Both Shaker and Sister wanted hounds to work on their own, be confident and not dependent on constant human interference.

Asa was no longer in the lead, as he wasn't fast enough. He worked in the middle of the pack. Irritating though it was to fall back to the middle, he knew he did his job. One of the youngsters, Zorro, shot over the line, then pulled up, confused. He wailed.

"Shut up, Zorro," Asa called to the tricolor in his deep voice. *"Come back to the middle."*

Zorro wanted to be first but he returned to the middle, for he had an inkling he'd messed up.

In their prime, Tattoo and Pickens now led the pack with Dreamboat, Diana, and Dasher close behind, the rest of the pack just behind them. They all headed into the woods, where their voices ricocheted off the trees. All slid down into the crevice, then clambered out as the humans circled round, losing time in the process.

Sister knew her fixtures. No need to kick on Matador. Keeping a steady pace, Shaker and hounds in sight, she put the field in a good position. They splashed across the narrow creek, running down the wide path on the other side. Then . . . silence.

Sister pulled up to see the pack gathered at the base of a tree. A fox, a beautiful gray in full winter coat, sat on a wide branch above. This was not the fox Sybil and Tootie had seen. Hounds had been on another fox's line that ended up at the tree.

Shaker blew "Gone to Ground" because there are no special notes for "Climbed a Tree."

Zorro, Zane, and Zandy couldn't believe a fox lounged over their heads. The other hounds, however, had seen this many times.

"You come down, this isn't fair," Zandy bitterly moaned in her high-pitched voice.

"Cheater," Zane added to the disgust of his sister. *"You're a cheater."*

Smiling, the gray called down, *"Well, why don't you get right under me, stand on your hind legs. Maybe you can grab my tail and pull me down."*

"Yeah. Right." Zorro did just that, with his two littermates now on their hind feet.

The fox taunted them a little more, swinging his butt over the tree limb and urinating all over them, laughing loudly.

"Ow, ow, ow. It stings!" Zorro blinked his eyes as the older hounds couldn't believe the youngsters would do what a fox told them to do.

Sitting on his haunches, Asa declared, *"Young and dumb."*

Hounds laughed, horses laughed, and the people laughed, although they had no idea what Asa had said.

Shaker, thumbs-up to the fox, turned his horse Showboat around. "Come along, hounds. Come along. No telling what he'll do next."

Having a girl moment, Tootsie wrinkled her nose at the humiliated Zandy. *"Don't get near me!"*

Poor thing. Zandy dropped her ears, falling back in the pack where Pookah walked beside her without saying a word.

Shaker left the woods and rode up on the hill. The ponds below sparkled as a shaft of light sliced through the clouds; then, like quicksilver, disappeared.

He cast hounds up toward the schoolhouse. Fox scent led to it, a short burst with singing ended at the foundation. A pair lived inside and had no incentive to open the front door.

Shaker sat by the schoolhouse. Sister waited, as did the field. Gray rode up with Phil and Mercer. The Bancrofts rode right behind Sister. Kasmir and Alida rode together behind Gray. As with any hunt, the longer one is out, the more the well-mounted, fit rider and horse move forward. Because of the recent weather, many people had not been able to keep their horses in as good a shape as they wished, but right now, all was well. No one was winded. Bobby Franklin kept an eye on his group, especially since new people usually started in Second Flight. He watched their horses for them. If a horse began to lag or tuck up a bit, Bobby would kindly send them back, with a guide always, at a walk.

Shaker motioned for his whippers-in to come up to him. The pack sat, waiting.

"Betty, go down to the wildflower meadow," he said. "If the pack crosses the road, you'll be with them. Sybil, parallel me on the other side of the fence and Tootie, you take the right. I'm casting west then south once we reach the meadow. Wind's come up a bit. We'll head into it."

He waited as they moved off, giving Betty an extra five minutes. Tootie, first time alone as a whipper-in, actually wasn't nervous. She loved it.

"All right, lieu in." Shaker asked the hounds to draw on the south side of the farm road.

They wiggled under the fence. Five minutes passed, ten, then fifteen. Shaker and Showboat walked on the farm road, ice crystals in the ruts.

A peep, then a bark sent the huntsman into a trot. Showboat took three strides to easily clear the coop, painted black like the fence. Sister and the field followed while Bobby trotted down to a large farm gate.

Hounds worked the line, not enough for a roaring chorus but the scent was warming.

The pack moved into the wildflower meadow, nothing but brown stalks now. Betty crashed through winter's debris, staying tight on their left shoulder while Sybil came out of the woods above her, behind Shaker. As the pack headed straight for the road, so did Sybil.

Betty crossed with them. Sybil—who always rode effortlessly, no fuss—brought up the rear, making certain no hound lagged on the macadam highway. Given that all the young entry hunted today, Sybil correctly flew up there with extra vigilance.

Also over the farm-road coop, Tootie stayed on the right, crossing the road minutes after Sybil. Tootie found herself in the mess below Hangman's Ridge. There was no easy way up or down on either side of the broad flat plateau. Given that she lived at Sister's, she knew where the deer trails were. Finally, on one she headed upward. Already halfway up the steep incline, Betty marveled at the pack. Hangman's Ridge harbors all manner of game and the youngsters, while being exposed to some of the scents, had not yet smelled others. They never took their noses or eyes off the correct line.

As Betty stood in the stirrups, reins in her left hand, right hand entwined in Magellan's mane, she was able to stay over her horse's center of balance.

Sybil picked her way to the left of this, finally

reaching the base of the ridge where she, too, picked up a narrow trail to circle the base. Given the distance, she had to move as fast as she could.

Betty finally reached the top of Hangman's Ridge, the wind blowing as always. Minks scattered about as the hounds flew across the flat plain.

Shaker now reached the top, stopped for a moment, saw Betty go down the Roughneck side. He followed. Sound echoed around the ridge but it seemed that hounds moved forward and down.

Sister galloped across the top, the huge centuries-old hangman's tree to her right.

Cursing the hounds, horses, and people all the while, minks ran across the top.

Not one bird sat in the hangman's tree. They didn't like it.

With great effort, Sybil had rounded the base, and now could see the old orchard on the other side of the Roughneck Farm road. To her delight, she also saw Comet. He skimmed the surface of the road as he ran hard, then turned left toward her. He knew who she was and, before he reached her, he zigged right, reached the stone ruins to pop into his den. Sybil remained motionless because she didn't want to cross the line.

Within minutes the pack ran right in front of her, Dreamboat, Giorgio, and young Pickens up front closely followed by the entire pack, Betty immediately behind and Shaker perhaps a football field behind her. Normally Betty would have ridden off the road, parallel to it, but there was no way to do that coming down from the ridge. The minute she hit the farm road, she jumped over the old orchard fence to parallel the pack, then jumped out again and into the stone ruins field, holding up at a bit of distance from the den.

By the time Shaker reached it, hounds dug at the stones, carried on in high excitement.

"Go ahead. Bloody your paws," Comet taunted.

Having been made a fool of once today, Zorro stopped digging at the stones.

Sister and the field came up as Shaker dismounted, blew "Gone to Ground," and praised each hound. He caught his breath as did everyone else.

The distance back to Foxglove Farm was perhaps three miles straight as an arrow and involved climbing, sliding down, rough terrain.

Sister waited for Shaker to mount up. He stood on the stones and stepped onto Showboat who stood still, as a huntsman's horse should. Horses get excited by the chase, too, so staff is always grateful when their mount does what he's supposed to do.

Sister then rode up. "We're near the kennels. Let's put them up and we can drive over to Cindy's to fetch the hound truck and Betty can drive the trailer back."

"Right."

She rode back to the field, telling them to return to Foxglove, she and staff would reach Cindy's place a little later.

Once at Roughneck, Tootie and Betty took care of the horses. Sybil also dismounted, stripped her tack off, sponged her horse, dried him, then borrowed a blanket. She'd come back later with her trailer.

Sister and Shaker walked hounds to the kennels.

"This last month has been so good." Sister beamed.

"Really has," he agreed.

As extra rations and lots of fresh water were poured into the buckets and hound troughs, Sister wiped her eyes. The fox piss scent was over-whelming. "What are we going to do with the smell?"

"Don't pick on me," Zorro cried. *"I didn't know."*

Hearing the puppy cry as he stared directly at her, Sister praised him. "You hunted very well today. And foxes are tricky."

Shaker and Sister praised each hound, calling every name and then when finished with the treats, calling each hound by name again to go to their special runs and petting everyone.

Shaker sniffed his hand. "Let's put these three in the medical run."

"Good idea. Zane, Zandy, Zorro, come along.

Special motel tonight." Sister and Shaker walked to one of the doors off the big draw room, opened it, and the three obediently followed.

Once they were given an extra cookie plus fresh straw for bedding in the warm enclosed recovery room, Shaker advised, "We can wash them tomorrow. I'll get the straw out first thing."

Both Shaker and Sister washed their hands in the deep stainless steel sink.

"All right. Tootie can help us." Sister glanced at the wall clock in the special medical room, which even had an operating table. "We'd best get over there. I'll borrow Gray's Land Cruiser. We can all squeeze in there."

"Sister, I'll drive my truck. You know how he is about his Land Cruiser."

She paused. "You're right. The girls and I will bounce over in my truck."

"I'll take Tootie," said Shaker, "then you only have to fit in three."

"Thank you. Good thing we're all slim, isn't it?"

In full swing, the breakfast greeted the staff as they walked into the Foxglove dining room, more eighteenth century than twenty-first.

Alida thanked Sister. "Another wonderful day and Kasmir lent me Mumtaz for Saturdays, Kavita for Tuesdays. And I can use my horse on Thursdays. Such fabulous horses."

Sister looked over the crowd to see Kasmir

talking to Gray. "He is a generous soul and a good, good man. We're all lucky to have him in our club." She prayed to herself that perhaps lightning would strike Alida.

The beauty glowed. "Yes. Yes, I can see that. I have never met a kinder man."

"Nor I." Sister took a chance. "You know, Alida, as I have aged I have learned just how sexy kindness and ethics are."

Alida looked into those bright hazel eyes with her own soft brown ones. "Yes. Yes, Master, how very true."

Before more could be said, Mercer charged up. "I have an idea."

"God help me," Sister joked.

Phil hurried over with Cindy, along with Betty and Ben. "Actually, Sister, it's a good one. We've all been discussing it."

"I know you e-mailed your curriculum sugges-tions to Crawford. Right?" Mercer referred to their Custis Hall board duties.

"I did," replied Sister. "Actually, I thought they were creative. At least I hope they are. I suggested we use hunting to teach the girls about the environment. And we don't always need to ride. We can do walking tours."

"Great idea," Phil said supportively.

"Well, here's what we've been thinking," said Mercer. "Next week is our next to last week and Woodford will be here from Kentucky for our

Thursday hunt and our Saturday hunt. So why not invite Crawford?" Mercer held his hands together as though suppressing a clap.

"Putting both packs together?" Sister wondered aloud.

Mercer immediately saw the problem. "Well—"

A born mediator, Cindy offered her idea. "Ask him for Thursday to make it a triple meet, even though he's an outlaw pack. We can say he's a farmer pack, which in essence he is if he'd just be halfway decent to the MFHA. They are far more reasonable than he is. Crawford brings his pack; his new huntsman and Sam can whip in if he wants. The fixture is Oakside. Not too far for him."

Sister wasn't entirely convinced. "Well, let me ask Walter. I'm not opposed, but we have to consider how the MFHA will respond to a triple meet with one club being an outlaw pack. My suggestion is just for us and Crawford to go out together the last hunt of the season. This also gives Shaker time to ride with Skiff. Sorry, but it really is politics."

Cindy smiled, realizing Sister wanted to find a middle path, wanted to avoid open conflict with the national organization. "That's why you're the Master. You have to consider everything, but I think doubling up for our last meet is a great idea."

Desperately needing a drink, Sister trod toward

the bar once the discussion wrapped up. She heard Phil say to Mercer, "Do you live to make life difficult?"

Mercer replied, "No, but I want to know really what's in my Dixie Do," he said, naming his horse.

"You know he goes back to Dixieland Band. He's a foxhunter, Mercer. It's irrelevant."

"I'm on a DNA kick," Mercer replied defiantly.

Sister thought that Mercer really couldn't let things go. She just hoped he wouldn't blurt out that Ben Sidell had asked them to review pedigrees. "He wouldn't," she thought.

Prudently, she sought out Ben once she had a cup of tea in her hand, and reported what she'd overheard. "Hopefully he'll stick to Dixie Do."

Ben shrugged. "I think he will, but I'll just give him a reminder." With that, the sheriff made straight for Mercer, grabbed his elbow, saying to Phil, "Excuse me one minute, Phil."

"Of course." Phil went looking for Sybil, as he wanted to know what the whipper-in thought of the day.

"Mercer." Ben fixed his gaze on the man. "Best not to discuss DNA or anything."

"I'm not." Mercer's eyes opened wide. "But I'm curious about my horse. That's all."

"Well, keep it at that, will you?"

Sister sidled up to Gray, who inhaled deeply. "Ah, yes, fresh fox."

"Honey, is it that bad? I walked the Z's to the back room. We'll wash them tomorrow."

"I've smelled expensive perfumes that weren't as potent," he teased her. "Hey, you can never predict what will happen."

She put her arm through his. "That's the truth."

CHAPTER 27

T hose little skulls with the glowing eyes have got to go," O.J. whispered as she rode up to the Saddlebred barn with Sister Jane.

"They are creepy," she agreed.

Woodford rode out with The Jefferson Hunt on Thursday at Oakside for the first of two joint meets. The field numbered thirty-five people— good for a cold rainy day.

Vicki Van Mater and Joe Kasputys drove down from Middleburg again to add to the mix. Along with their horses, their two German shepherds, Ben and Gandy Man, rode along. Vicki and Joe would laugh that the dog Ben was smart enough to do police work like the human Ben. While Vicki and Joe were intelligent, neither Ben nor Gandy felt their humans were in the German shepherd league. Much as they loved Vicki and Joe, they felt they needed guidance.

While the rain wasn't pounding, it slid inside collars and down the insides of boots if even the tiniest gap occurred. Cold feet were bad. Cold wet feet were even worse.

The Saddlebred barn emanated fright in the steady rain. The water washed the glowing skulls so the red eyes popped right out at you.

O.J. stiffened in the saddle as she caught sight of the hanging mannequin. "Dear God."

"Startling. I bet those pony clubbers screamed bloody murder when they saw that guy hanging," Joe teased.

Vicki gasped when she saw the hanged man.

Tedi Bancroft chuckled. "It really is awful."

Vicki replied, "I foxhunt so I can legally trespass and enjoy countryside I can only see from horseback. I may revise my opinion."

Joe laughed. "I'll mark the day you revise your opinion." He heard a hound open. "Then again, what's a barn of horrors if hounds open?"

The hound was Cora.

The two Masters shut up and squeezed their horses into a trot.

Hounds sang out but the pace stayed at a trot. Shaker stayed behind them, rain hitting him in the face.

Kasmir, Alida, Freddie, Phil, Mercer, Ronnie, Xavier—the stalwarts—filled First Flight, along with the guests. People in this part of the world organized their work schedules so they could hunt at least one day a week—if lucky, two.

Walter usually kept office hours on Thursdays and Bobby Franklin had an appointment today. He asked Ben Sidell to lead Second Flight, which he happily did.

The field crossed a meadow, took a log jump into another meadow, then threaded through woods, tree bark turning darker. Hounds continued after their fox at the same pace.

When they reached the back of this woods, everyone noticed swirling low mist rolling up from the abutting meadow. The swirl turned into a wall, a dense ground fog. The temperature dropped so rapidly everyone felt it. This wasn't a lower temperature in proximity to water or a dip in the terrain. The mercury headed straight down, the rain continued, but now a *pip, pip, pip* could be heard hitting helmets.

Joe tweaked Vicki. "Honey, just remember this was your idea."

As the freezing fog enveloped them, hounds opened wide.

In territory she was learning, Sister stayed on the widest path she could find. Ahead, she could just make out Shaker, thanks to the scarlet coat.

Hounds turned toward them, then veered into the woods again. Staying on the path, Shaker halted a moment to listen.

Twist's voice sounded the closest to Sister, then he, too, moved away. Sister couldn't see a thing except Rickyroo's ears and neck. If she stopped, everyone behind her would collide into one another. She thought moving along the outside of the woods, keeping between the trees and the back fence line might work. If nothing else, the fence line was a better guide than being in the middle of the woods in a pogonip.

Did Woodford drag this curse along with them?

No point wondering about that. She trotted along, reached the corner of the back fence and turned in what she felt was the direction back to the barn. No way to hunt in this. The problem now was getting everyone back.

Maria Johnson knew her property but she couldn't see anything either.

Hound voices echoed in the fog, near, then far, then near again. Sister heard the horn: two beeps to tell hounds and staff where Shaker was.

She thought she heard galloping hooves, perhaps a whipper-in, but that faded away.

"Maria," Sister called out loudly.

"Yes," a voice replied, seemingly from the middle of the riders.

"Come up here. Can you?"

"Yes."

As Sister waited, she felt O.J.'s horse now beside her. "Can you believe we're in this freezing pea soup again? I blame it on you."

"And how do I know you didn't bring it to Kentucky?" countered O.J. "Don't blame me if we're in this mess again." Her voice floated toward Sister.

"Can you see me?"

"Not well."

"So you can't see me flip you the bird?"

O.J. laughed. "Sister, I am shocked, deeply shocked."

O.J. felt a horse slide by her, then she saw Maria. O.J. fell back.

Sister minced no words. "How the hell do we get back?"

"We aren't far. I'll ride next to you and when we have to we'll go single file. I'll go up front. All right?" offered the blue-eyed Maria.

Sister kept her sense of humor. "Do I have a choice?"

"Come on." Maria asked her dark bay Thoroughbred, Annie, to walk out.

Ten minutes later they reached another fence corner. Maria turned right, still inside the fence. The freezing rain stung as it turned to sleet, lots of sleet.

People dropped their faces. Gloves became soaked. Those who did as was proper had white string gloves under their girths and pulled them out. They would become soaked, too, but the reins didn't slip.

There was abundant misery for all.

"We're almost there." Maria spoke to Sister.

The next ten minutes seemed like an eon. First one trailer appeared, then disappeared, then another. But everyone did find their trailers.

"Thank you," Sister said to the much younger woman.

"Do you need help? I can go look for hounds," Maria volunteered.

Just then they all heard the horn close by.

Giorgio appeared, Sister spied a few tricolor coats next to her. Then Shaker.

She sighed. "How glad I am to see you."

"Damn, this came out of nowhere." Shaker dismounted, walked his horse toward where he thought the trailer was. Wrong trailer. He looked at this one, getting up close, then remembered where the others had parked.

When he finally reached the right trailer, Betty was already there. She held open the door and hounds gratefully hurried inside, snuggling in the straw.

Shaker blew for Sybil and Tootie. "Betty, go on and see to your horse," he said. "I'll wait by the trailer."

Hojo, his mount today, usually rode in the trailer with the horses. Shaker had a divider for the horse so hounds wouldn't get underfoot. The hounds had a second story in the trailer with a rubber-covered walk so everyone could get in and not be crowded. Shaker didn't want to put Hojo inside until his other whippers-in showed up. He prayed they had the hounds Parker and Pickens with them.

As he waited, he threw a blanket over Hojo, over the saddle, too. "Hold on, buddy. Let's hope this doesn't take long. If it does, I promise I'll walk you to their barn, if I can find it."

A hound wiggled between his legs.

Sybil appeared. "That's Pickens. Would you

blow again? I think Parker was with me five minutes ago. Lost sight."

Shaker blew three long notes.

As Sybil dismounted, they both waited.

And waited.

Shaker was ready to walk Hojo into the stable, wherever it was, when he heard a little yell.

"Where are you? Where am I?" came Parker's mournful howl.

"Parker. Parker. Come along." Shaker's voice radiated warmth and within seconds, a sleety hound raced up to him, couldn't contain himself, stood on his hind feet to see the huntsman.

"I'm so happy. I was scared!"

"All right, Parker, in we go." Shaker opened the door and the youngster scooted in.

No one wanted to come outside.

"Sybil, go on to your trailer. We've got everyone. I'll see you in the house."

"I think we need a compass," she joked.

Curled up in the straw on the trailer, Ben and Gandy rose to greet their masters, Joe on Ali Kat and Vicki on Boo Bear.

Gandy shook himself. *"You all are crazy."*

"Not me," the TB/Shire mix replied. *"It's her."* The horse indicated the human.

Fortunately Vicki understood nothing of this exchange.

"Joe, hurry up and put me in the trailer," his TB/Hanoverian begged.

The two Middleburg Hunt members hurried as fast as they could. Once the horses were up and wiped down, they looked at the dogs.

"We'll put them in the truck when we leave," Joe said sensibly. "It's warmer here with the horses and the straw than in the truck with the heater turned off."

"Okay," Vicki agreed.

When the humans left to grope their way to the house, Ben lifted his head. *"Hmm."*

Gandy Man inhaled deeply. *"Filthy day but that smells too interesting."* With that, the shepherd left the comfort of the trailer for the driving sleet. Ben followed.

Taking care of their mounts took longer, but after twenty minutes most people had put up their horses and done whatever needed to be done. Then some, holding hands, made their way to the house.

"We could form a chain." Alida smiled.

"If we don't reach the house in the next two minutes, we'd better," Xavier added.

Once inside everyone started talking, hurrying for hot drinks, breathing a sigh of relief.

The Woodford group caught up on the Hinson news, as well as Middleburg Hunt news. Everyone wanted to know about everyone else's season.

Phil made his way through the crowd, looking around. He spoke to people one by one, then came up to Sister and Gray. "Have you all seen Mercer?" he asked.

"No."

"His horse was at the trailer but untied. I put him on the trailer. I figured maybe he slipped the knot. Mercer doesn't always tie the best knot." Phil looked at the door when someone opened it. "It will be a good story when he gets inside." Phil rejoined the circle.

Sister made sure to speak to each Woodford guest, most of whom she knew. Maria, Nate, and Sonia kept a shuttle between the kitchen and the dining room. A good cook, Nate outdid himself.

Sister inhaled. "Did he make shepherd's pie?"

"He knows it's your favorite," Gray replied.

"How did he know that?"

"I told him, and I bet he's saved you a big slice in the kitchen. Otherwise, you won't get any."

True enough, for people stood in line for a slice—plus Sister rarely got to eat much at these gatherings.

A half hour passed with food, drink, chat and feet warming.

Phil returned. "Still no Mercer."

"That is peculiar," Gray said.

"I'm going out to look for him," said Phil. "This isn't like him. Maybe he fell and his horse came back. Who would know?" He walked toward the hall to fetch his jacket.

"I'll come with you." Gray put his plate on a

small table and, as he walked away, he said to Sister, "Phil and I are going to look for Mercer."

"I'll come, too." She hurried to them.

Seeing them leave, worry on their faces, Xavier, Ronnie, and Kasmir also followed.

Once outside, the brutal weather hit them again.

"Won't do any good to look for hoofprints," Phil said. "They're all over the place."

"The only thing I can think to do is to back-track," said Kasmir. "Let's walk down the middle path, then turn toward the fence line. At least I think that's the fence line." He pointed west.

Staying together, they trudged through now stinging sleet. The fog hadn't thinned.

Two dogs howling alerted them to something in the barn.

They reached the edge of the Saddlebred barn but couldn't see the glowing skulls, the sleet was so thick.

"Blood." Ben held his nose up, following the scent inside the barn.

"Fresh." Then Gandy Man shouted, as he heard the humans outside.

The mannequin sprawled on the barn floor. Swinging slightly from the rafter was Mercer, blood dripping down his coat.

"Terrible trouble." The two German shepherds sang a dirge, hoping to hurry along the humans outside.

Following the cry as best they could Sister, Gray, Shaker, Phil, Kasmir, Ronnie, and Xavier stepped into the barn.

"Oh, my God," Phil gasped. "Mercer! Mercer!"

CHAPTER 28

In the old barn, Phil Chetwynd rolled old hay bales under Mercer's body. Being tall, he stepped upon them, holding Mercer's legs and, with great strength, lifted the body so the pressure was off the neck.

Ronnie Haslip, the most nimble, climbed up the rafters. Gray joined Phil. Gray knew Mercer was gone, but Phil, a man possessed, kept pleading, "We have to help him. Help me."

And so the other men did. Ronnie, like most foxhunters, carried a pocketknife. He cut the rope and Mercer dropped down into Gray and Phil's arms, the unexpected weight toppling them off the hay bales.

The two German shepherds, sitting down now, didn't budge.

Kasmir, Shaker, and Xavier, also by the hay bales, did their best to break the fall, trying to prevent Mercer's body from hitting the ground hard.

Xavier left the group to go back to the house and find Ben Sidell. Given the thick fog, he only found his way through the noise coming from the house.

Ben hurried out of the house with Xavier and Sister, groping their way to the Saddlebred barn.

Once inside, the sheriff walked over to Mercer, carefully laid on the ground, on his back, blood-shot eyes staring upward.

Ben removed his leather hunting glove, placing his finger on Mercer's neck. He said nothing, for it was obvious that Mercer was dead. He wanted to feel the temperature of the body. His guess was the body had cooled very slightly. Clearly the man's neck was broken. Putting his glove back on so as not to leave more finger-prints, he gingerly tilted Mercer's head to the side where his hair was matted with blood. He'd first been struck by a blunt instrument.

Phil leaned over on the other side of the body. "Let me perform CPR. He's not dead. He can't be dead."

Ben rose, "I'm afraid he is, Phil."

"No!" Phil knelt down to pump on Mercer's chest.

Gray and Shaker had to lift Phil up, protesting.

With kindness but firmness, Ben said, "He's gone. Anything any of us do to him will compromise this crime scene." Turning to Sister, he said, "Will you go inside, tell everyone there has been an accident and no one must leave the house? Oh, Sister, when you get inside stay there until I get there, which will be some time. Don't tell anyone what has happened, only that there has been an accident. I'm going to call the department right now and hope a team makes it out here in this miserable fog before too much time passes. Obviously, the faster we can go over all this, the better."

"He can't be dead." Tears filled Phil's eyes. "He can't really be dead."

"Phil, I'm going to ask you to sit down on one of the hay bales. Xavier, will you sit with him? Oh, Gray, perhaps you'd better go in with Sister. And whose dogs are these?"

Sister, before heading into the slashing weather, answered, "Vicki and Joe's. The Middleburg folks."

"Ah, well, they seem well behaved. They'll have to stay here until folks are free to leave the house."

Fortunately, Ben's team arrived within forty minutes, a good time considering the deplorable conditions. Two law enforcement officers, both women, were sent into the house. Ben knew the women would be very good at calming people and getting statements. The new head of his forensic team went immediately to work and another young man carried a bright flashlight, as the electric power had long ago been cut off in this barn used only for hay storage and odds and ends.

No matter what happens in our life if you're hunt staff, hounds and horses must be attended to. Sister, Shaker, O.J., and Tootie, due to the long delay at Oakside, finally reached Roughneck

Farm at 6:00 P.M. The hounds, subdued, ate warm kibble, then quietly returned to their lodges and sleeping quarters. Rickyroo, Hojo, and Iota, Tootie's horse, and O.J.'s mare, told everyone in the stable. Back at Oakside, Sister had asked Kasmir if he would take Phil's horse and Mercer's wonderful Dixie Do, to his farm. With Alida's help, Kasmir loaded them up.

At Tattenhall Station, the Indian gentleman watched as Alida brushed the horses and comforted them.

"My man can do that," Kasmir offered.

"They know something's wrong. Sometimes a bit of attention helps." Alida ran her fingers along Dixie Do's neck.

Kasmir bedded the stalls himself thinking here was a woman not afraid of work and one who was sensitive as well.

Gray called Sam and told him the news. He met his brother as soon as Ben Sidell released him from Oakside. They both drove to Daniella Laprade's. She took the grim news with steely calm, asked where her son's body was, and wanted to know when she could see him. Gray called Ben Sidell, who called back in twenty minutes, saying she could see her son now. Mercer wouldn't be sent to Richmond until tomorrow, assuming the weather improved.

So Gray and Sam drove their aunt to the county morgue. Using only a cane, Daniella stood firm as the large file cabinet, for that's what it looked like, was opened and the body slid out, feet first on the slab.

Both nephews stood on either side of her in case she collapsed.

"He was a good son." She then looked up at Gray. "Who did this?"

"Aunt D, we don't know."

"You'd better find him before I do. And it was a man. Women don't kill like this. Hear me?"

"Yes, ma'am," both brothers said.

Then she turned and walked out, barely using her cane.

Later, Sister, O.J., and Tootie, in the library at Roughneck Farm, discussed the remaining weekend.

O.J. leaned on soft cushions on the sofa. "I understand if you cancel Saturday's hunt, Sister. Perhaps you should."

"Mercer loved hunting. You all drove all the way from Kentucky. I think he'd want the hunt to go on. You know I'm a stickler for things being done properly. I wouldn't do this if I thought it would be slighting him." Sister stood up. "Let me call Walter. Best to discuss this with my Joint Master."

Walter had by now been informed of everything. As Sister sat at the desk, Tootie mulled over the awful happenings while talking to O.J.

"It's a strange coincidence," Tootie said. "The first pogonip and now this one and both—well, awful."

"Two murders." O.J. felt suddenly very tired.

"Three." Sister had hung up the landline. "You didn't know our local vet, Penny Hinson, but three. It can't be a coincidence. It can't be." She then returned to her chair, falling into it, also exhausted. "Walter agrees with me. Mercer would want the joint meet to continue and Saturday is the big day at the Bancrofts'. Always a beautiful fixture."

"Yes, it is," O.J. agreed.

They heard the back door open. The dogs ran to the kitchen, where Gray walked in from the mudroom.

"Gray." Sister rose to greet him. "Let me get you a drink."

He kissed her. "Thank you, honey."

Neither O.J. nor Tootie said anything until Sister handed him his drink and he was comfortably seated in an armchair. She held up an empty glass toward O.J.

"I believe I will." O.J. joined Sister at the bar. "I don't know why but I want an old-fashioned."

"Let's make two." Sister asked Tootie, "You're twenty-one. Anything?"

"No, thanks."

Once they were all seated and Gray had some

restorative scotch in him, Sister asked, "How did it go?"

"No tears. No raised voice. She's really a terrifying old woman." He took another deep sip. "But I feel for her. She looked at him and said he was a good son. Then she wanted to know who killed him and told Sam and me to find the killer before she did."

O.J. frowned. "Like a Greek tragedy."

"In a way, yes." Gray set his drink on a coaster. "You know, I keep thinking about that old barn, the House of Horrors barn. Whoever killed Mercer had a kind of sick sense of humor."

O.J. murmured, "I guess."

"And whoever killed him knew the place," Sister added.

Tootie curled her legs under her. "And the killer took advantage of the rotten weather. It doesn't seem like a planned murder."

"No, it doesn't," Sister agreed. "You're right about there being something spontaneous about this. The pogonip provided the chance and he or she was tremendously bold."

"He. Aunt D says women don't kill like that." Gray spoke, having picked up his drink again.

"She's right," O.J. agreed.

The phone rang, Sister got up to answer it. After listening to Greg for a bit, Sister asked, "Eclipse? Eclipse, not Matchem?"

344

"Yes." On the other end of the line, Greg Schmidt's voice was positive.

"Eclipse." She then recited. "Pot-8-Os, Waxy, Whalebone, Camel, Touchstone, Orlando, the second Eclipse, Alarm, Himyar, then Domino. That line. That Eclipse line?"

"Yes," he repeated.

"I suppose you've heard by now all that's transpired?" said Sister.

Greg replied, "Tedi Bancroft called me. I'm so very sorry."

"Yes, I am, too. Greg, does anyone else know this, know Midshipman's line back?"

"I couldn't rightly say."

"Thank you." Sister hung up the phone, turned to the others and stated definitively, "Benny Glitters."

CHAPTER 29

Daniella appraised Mercer's house as she directed Gray and Sam in the large bedroom. "A place for everything and everything in its place," she said.

"We won't have the body for at least a week, I would think, Aunt D." Gray stood in the large well-lighted closet.

"I want to select his clothes while it's on my mind." She leaned on her cane, the wheelchair in the living room should she tire.

Sam, allowed to go in to work a few hours late this morning, knelt down in the closet as his aunt shuffled through Mercer's shined shoes. "Not a speck of dirt, even on the soles," Sam observed.

"His idol was Cary Grant," Daniella said with uncharacteristic warmth. "Mercer always said if a man can dress half as well as Cary Grant he'll be smashing."

"True," Gray agreed. "Duke Ellington wasn't bad either."

"Those were the days, those were the days," she intoned with a kind of wonderment. "Gray, I don't want him buried in a black suit. The undertaker can wear a black suit, not my boy. He needs color. So"—she flicked her cane right under a navy suit, chalk pinstripes—"he always looked good in this and we can use an eggshell white shirt and, oh, the tie, the tie will be what makes it—that—and the pocket square."

"A rosebud on the lapel," Sam volunteered.

"I hadn't thought of that." She liked the idea. "Regimental stripes, so many regimental stripes, but I think for this, his last social occasion, we should use a solid-color silk tie. I say a glorious burnt orange or a cerise. Something that just says 'Mercer.'"

"Right." Gray, though not a man for a bright tie, did agree. "And the pocket square can be a darker color or a different color. Mercer always said matchups were boring."

Daniella nodded. "Yes, he did. Now Sam, the rosebud. If we use the cerise tie it could be pink, now that's bold, I think. If we use the burnt orange then I say a creamy white, not stark, and we won't know until we go to the funeral home. We'll have to hold the colors up to his face."

This thought did not appeal to Mercer's cousins, but dressing her son was of paramount importance to the ancient lady. They would do it. Both nodded.

A knock on the front door quieted them.

"I'll get it." Gray strode out of the room, glad for a moment out of the closet.

Opening the door, Phil—strained, drained, but composed—greeted him. "I thought you all would be here. The cars are here. I came to help."

The two men walked to the bedroom.

Phil bent down to hug Daniella. "I am so sorry, so very very sorry. Whatever you want, just ask." Tears rolled down his cheeks.

She kissed him and said, "I am not going to cry. Phil, don't you cry either."

He reached into his jacket, pulled out a linen handkerchief to wipe his eyes. "Yes, ma'am."

"We are going to celebrate him. Perhaps it's easier for me because I know I will be joining him before you all do."

"Auntie D, don't say that." Phil's eyes teared up again.

"It's the plain truth. The boys are helping me assemble his wardrobe. I think we've got it. Sam, why don't you carry his clothing over to my house? In fact, we can all repair there for a drink and to plan the service."

"Yes, but while we are here, I thought perhaps I could be of special service," said Phil. "I know he had quite a few contracts lined up. Usually the bloodline research for the breeding season is over by now so everyone has been billed. But if anything is outstanding, I will call the client."

Gray nodded his assent. "You know most of them anyway."

"Do you know where he kept his important papers? You know, insurance, stuff like that?" Sam asked Daniella.

"He used his computer but he backed up every

single thing. I told him all he was doing was making extra work. Just stick to the paperwork and throw out the computer." She paused. "Phil, let Gray call Sheriff Sidell. We want things done properly."

"Sure," Phil assented. "Didn't the sheriff go through his office?"

Daniella nodded. "Yes, but they said they would be back Monday. I guess they're shorthanded." She sighed deeply. "I don't know."

Mercer's small, bright office was as meticulously planned as his closet, where items were divided by season and color. Seeing the office made Phil dab his eyes again. He got hold of himself.

"All the insurance, car title, and tax returns are in that file cabinet. I know it looks like a pie safe but it's really his file cabinet. Phil, you know that," Daniella said.

Having quickly contacted Ben, Gray walked into the office. "Take the billing folder," Gray said to Phil while looking at his aunt. "Surely there's some outstanding monies."

"Mmm," came her compressed reply as the monies would go to her.

Phil opened the double doors, revealing long, thin editing drawers within. "He was certainly imaginative. Did he take in his papers to the accountant for this year's taxes—well, last year's, I mean?"

"Yes, but he made copies of all that, too," said Daniella. "His billings are in the top drawer, marked. Red means unpaid if there's a red tab on the folder. Green, paid." She touched the drawer under that. "He divided his research work up by states. So then he also alphabetized stallions in the drawers. He had cross-references and more cross-references. When a stallion moved, say, to Spendthrift Farm, he kept the former state file, made a new one, plus cited the move in the alphabetized file. His mind was so orderly."

She ran her forefinger lower. "These drawers here are miscellaneous. In his research he'd find a name from the past, like Foxhall Keene, and he'd put that information here. But everything is clearly marked. Owners files, mare files, progeny files, and percent of winners. All broken down and cross-referenced. Phil, take the billings file, but leave everything else. We can all go over that later."

"Quite right," Phil agreed.

"Auntie D, would you like me to take the computer?" asked Sam. "To double-check stuff?"

"No. The Sheriff's Department had a quick look and will return Monday. I told him Mercer backed up everything but Ben Sidell insisted. I suppose they're right." She sighed. "I guess a lot can be hidden in computers, not that he had anything to hide. He was an honest man."

"I'll go over everything the minute I get home

and bring it all back by Monday," said Phil. "I'm sure everything is in order but there are always a few laggards when it comes to payments." He frowned for a second.

As Sam helped Daniella on with her coat, Phil opened the front door. Gray quickly walked back into the office. He opened the pie safe, slid open the miscellaneous drawer, snatched the folder on top, sticking it under his jacket.

Once home, Gray smacked the folder on the kitchen table. "Janie! Janie!"

"In the library."

"Come here."

While she walked down the hall he was already recounting what had transpired. "Let's go over this now."

"Yes." Sister needed no prodding.

Gray pulled up a chair next to Sister. They opened the folder.

Golly hopped right onto it. *"I love paper,"* she purred.

"Golly, get off," Sister commanded and, of course, the cat paid her no mind. "The things I do to keep peace in this house."

Golly leapt off as Sister had gotten up to give her tiny dried-liver treats. The aroma brought the dogs; out came large GREENIES. The three pets chewed happily.

Sister sat back down, examining each page

or newspaper clipping that Gray now handed her.

"A lot of stuff here on the Aga Khan. His breeding theories." She looked over the next paper. "The racing stables of King Edward the Seventh."

"Here you go." Gray slid over a genetic blueprint for Dixie Do, Mercer's hunt horse. "One of the Broad Creek Stables horses Phil called back from the western tracks."

"Right, Dixie had one-fourth Quarter Horse blood. We don't have any Quarter Horse tracks here, as you know. A very nice horse and"—she inhaled sharply—"back to Eclipse. Mercer knew! He knew if the DNA was what it was supposed to be, and you can trace male ancestors back a few centuries, he'd find Matchem. Dixie would go back to Matchem. He figured out that Navigator and Benny Glitters had been switched. Both were handsome bay horses much resembling each other."

"But when did he know?" Gray looked to see if there was a date at the top of the page, tiny print along the top. "He knew Wednesday."

"Let me call Ben."

"Before you do, should we call Meg and Alan?"

"Not until we are 100 percent sure. There's no point in creating uproar at Walnut Hall or worse, danger. A killer can board an airplane as easily as someone else and we don't want to jeopardize anyone at Walnut Hall. We know he was here to kill Penny and Mercer. Let's wait."

She rose, phoned Ben, told him what they had, and her fears for the wonderful people at Walnut Hall. Finally, she sat back down. "We're between the Devil and the deep blue sea."

Gray put his large, strong hand over hers. "Janie, don't go out tomorrow."

"Sweetheart, I have to. It's a big Saturday joint meet. O.J. and Tootie are up there at Horse Country buying out the store with the rest of the Woodford gang. We can't disappoint them. And I suspect we are safer in the hunt field than inside."

"Mercer wasn't."

She thought long and hard. "True, but the pogonip provided opportunity. Tomorrow it's supposed to be clear."

"All we have is circumstantial evidence. With a little luck, maybe we can flush him out in the open. Ben can't make an arrest just yet, but we can help him. It seems impossible and yet . . ." Gray gazed off in the distance for a moment. "And yet it makes sense."

"Let me make a suggestion. Have Sam take Daniella to the home place. Just the outside chance that she might get close to figuring this out and endanger herself—because I know she'll pick the phone right up for a loud accusation."

"Kill Daniella? That's crazy," Gray said.

"Exactly. But he is now a little crazy."

CHAPTER 30

Smoke curled upward, then flattened out from the two chimneys at the Lorillard Farm. Given Saturday off by Crawford so he could help his aunt, Sam fed the wood-burning stove. The fireplace in the living room also roared. The mantelpiece had the flourish of a Grecian scroll. The fire screen, almost as old as the house, had a hunt scene in metalwork across the center. Made at Pattypan Forge along with the fireplace utensils, it bore witness to the artistic urges of those long-dead workers.

Aunt Daniella, wrapped in a rich cashmere shawl, watched him feed more large heavy oak logs to the living room fire, then replace the screen. "You could have ridden today. Mercer would have liked that."

"Mercer would have liked it but Crawford wouldn't. He hunts on Saturdays, too."

She pursed her lips, a thin line of dark lipstick spread on them. "Foolish"—she took a breath—"but entertaining. Mercer never could get him interested in racing. You'd think someone with that big an ego would have jumped right in."

"A big ego but also a big brain. Very few people make money racing. Crawford believes in profit."

"Foxhunting is hardly profitable," she fired back.

"No, but he feels he gets a lot of bang for his buck. His words."

"Common. Such a common expression." She sniffed. She shifted in the comfortable chair placed before the fire. "While I enjoy your company, Sam, I don't see why I must be here. I'm perfectly fine at home."

"Of course you are, Auntie D, but the sheriff thought you might be tempted to go back into Mercer's house before they do."

"He gave us permission to select his funeral attire and Ben allowed Phil to take the current billing file since we have copies and"—she paused—"is there anything else?"

"No." He lied, nor was he about to tell her about Gray taking the miscellaneous file, which he had already replaced. Gray had gone early to Mercer's house, before the hunt. "Auntie D, did Mercer ever talk to you about horses' bloodlines?"

"All the time." She smiled.

"Did it ever interest you?"

She tugged at the corner of the cashmere shawl. "Not so much, although last week he was completely transfixed—transfixed, I tell you—with DNA stuff. Related to bloodlines, but he started off about a horse bone that is seven hundred thousand years old. He was so caught up—truly caught up and excited—I let him rattle on. That was the only way with Mercer. Even as a child. Remember when he decided to become the marbles champion of central Virginia? I told him there was no marbles champion." She waved her hand. "So he trooped down to the county courthouse and wrote out a plan for a marbles tournament, handing it to the county commissioners." She laughed.

"I remember he beat me all the time." Sam stood up, thinking this would be a good day for hunting as opposed to marbles. "But he didn't call your attention to anything peculiar last week?"

"Not in so many words, but he was troubled. Penny Hinson's murder deeply upset him." She sighed. "He was too sensitive. And overly curious about other people's lives." She spoke a bit louder. "Oh, I told Chantal to stay in Atlanta. No need to return. We'll take care of my boy. I think she was offended but she can be claustrophobic. Well, she makes me feel claustrophobic, although I know she means well." She gave Sam a sharp look. "Is there no making peace with her?"

"You can answer that better than I. I'm polite."

"Mmm." She pursed her lips together, one of her signature expressions.

As the two talked, Sam didn't let on that Ben didn't want Aunt Daniella left alone until the department had a bit more clarity, which he hoped might occur today.

Meanwhile, Uncle Yancy had returned to the Lorillards' mudroom. Knowing two people sat in

356

the house, he was circumspect. That quickly evaporated as Aunt Netty popped up through the hole he'd dug in the floorboards, casting away the rag pile.

"How cozy." She beamed.

"Netty, what are you doing here?" Burled up in old saddle pads, he lifted his head.

"I wanted to see your place. You have two dens over here, plus this room. My, aren't you living high? Anyway, I miss you."

He knew that was a major fib. *"What do you want, my beloved?"*

"A little warmth. My den at Pattypan is cold." She was half telling the truth.

"How can it be cold? You've got the den lined with straw and grass, every rag you could find and the old roof and sides still stand. That cuts the wind."

"It's the chill, Yancy. I feel such a chill."

He stated flatly, *"Life gets colder."*

They shut up and listened intently as Sam had walked into the kitchen. He opened the refrigerator door, then closed it.

"Does he ever throw out anything good?"

Yancy whispered, *"Juicy bones, coffee grounds which are too bitter, but he's been eating a lot of soybeans and he throws out the shells. I've gotten fond of them."*

"Enough for two?"

"Netty, you are not living with me. You'll try to

throw me out again and I'm not leaving." He paused. *"And I'm not leaving Sam. He's a sweet fellow but sad, so very sad. Every now and then I'll show myself and he stands still as a statue. I make him happy."*

She frowned. *"It doesn't do to care too much about humans."*

"I know, but I like some of them, and look at Inky. She lives in the old orchard and knows the silver-haired Master well. She gets treats all the time."

Aunt Netty considered this. *"That's a Master and a Master takes care of foxes. By and large it's best to be wary of humans, if for no other reason than that they are sublimely stupid. Name another animal that breeds past the food supply or uses up all the water. Remember the new people who ran their well dry, then dammed up the creek? See? No brains."*

"I don't remember that." He stopped, cocked his head. *"The horn. They're at the covered bridge."*

With her fabulous ears she, too, heard the hunting horn. The sound carried this morning. Using the farm roads, After All lay a mile and a half from the Lorillard place.

"They might pick up my line if they head east," Aunt Netty said. *"Doesn't matter, we're safe."*

The "we're" alerted him. *"You can't stay."*

"I need the warmth."

"Then take some rags and be gone. He's got piles of them, the dirty ones and the neatly folded ones."

"Throwing me out when hounds are running? You can't be serious!" She fumed.

"After the hunt then." He listened as Shaker blew for hounds to move off. *"Let's hide on the top shelf. In case Sam opens the mudroom door. He likes to hunt, but today he's got old Auntie D with him."*

"She's two years older than God." Aunt Netty giggled as she leapt from shelf to shelf.

Yancy wanted to say, *"So are you!"* Then realized he was, too. He kept that to himself.

Seventy-one people rode out this Saturday as Sister had sent an e-mail asking members to come to honor Mercer with this joint meet with Woodford hounds. She also requested that The Jefferson Hunt members wear black armbands. Most everyone had to make one, but that was easy enough. Mercer would have been touched.

There were low clouds and decent footing—at least it wasn't icy. A starting temperature of 42°F promised a good day, perhaps even a great one. Sister asked O.J. to ride up with her as always. Other First Flight Woodford people could also ride forward. The Bancrofts, Phil, Ronnie, Gray, Xavier, Kasmir, Alida, Freddie, and Felicity all rode up behind them. Lila Repton was trying First

Flight again and After All Farm was a good place for a novice First Flight rider; the jumps were so well set, most creek crossings were solid. Second Flight found Bobby Franklin leading, and Ben Sidell rode with him. If necessary, Ben would move up.

The sheriff had men placed at strategic points in After All, Roughneck Farm, and the Lorillard place, as all abutted one another. He did not put any officers on the other side of Soldier Road, figuring the hunt would stay on the south side.

The clatter of seventy-one sets of hooves reverberated through the red-painted covered bridge. Hounds, sterns held high, couldn't wait to be cast, but all their training ensured they didn't scoot off.

On the right, Betty crossed the creek, as did Sybil on the left, neither one riding through the bridge. The steep crossings didn't faze the whippers-in.

Shaker was on Kilowatt, a Thoroughbred of great power. He had planned to ride to the front fields of After All, then turn inward, avoiding the woods and riding toward Roughneck Farm. Then he would ultimately turn eastward again after drawing the Roughneck fields, jump back into After All and draw through the woods. Given the promising conditions, he thought this would allow people to see the hound work—at least in the beginning.

And they did, but not as Shaker planned.

Once cast, Diana loped into the middle of the field, streaks of snow still in the deeper folds. She stopped, stern upright. She blew out of her nostrils, then sucked air in. Pickens desperately wanted to be a forward hound, so he immediately ran over to the reliable, driven Diana.

Putting his nose down, he whimpered for a moment, *"Umm."*

Diana sharply told him, *"Open or shut up."*

She continued on, nose down, and he shut up but by now the whole pack spread out around her. Everyone knew she had something, but would it heat up or grow cold?

Aztec jigged a little. He wanted to go and so did Sister.

To Diana's right, Thimble opened, followed by Diana who ran on the line up to where a bouquet of fox scent just burst into her nose. Everyone spoke at once, tore off at first in a line, then bunched up, running a bit like a rugby scrum.

The field witnessed this beautiful sight; it sends chills down a foxhunter's spine and often does the same to someone seeing for the first time hounds work as a team.

The fast pace right off the mark thrilled Sister. Much as she loved hunting, there were times when she was eager to find a line, or disappointed on a poor day. Impatience, a fault with her, had to be curbed. A lovely jump—twenty-four feet long, three fence panels long—sat square in the fence line. Edward Bancroft had built this stone jump thirty-five years ago and it held up. He actually bought the stone because he wanted to practice stone fences. Sister and O.J., grinning and laughing—they couldn't help it—took that fence as a pairs team, as did many of the riders behind them. If two or three people can clear an obstacle together, so much the better. That got everyone high; hearts beat faster. Poor Bobby had to hustle to a gate but many of the Second Flight people managed to catch up, observing the wonderful jumping in pairs and determining then and there they would be doing that next year.

Flying through the second large field, hounds hooked sharply left; they took the hog's-back jump first, followed by Shaker, then Sister, then O.J.—as this jump was maybe twelve feet long. Although three feet by six and using thick railroad ties, it was not a solid jump; one could see through the ties. Not that it was terribly airy, but a horse not encountering a hog's-back before might well put on the brakes. Not one did today because the pace was too good and The Jefferson Hunt horses had flown over this jump many a time. The Woodford horses were Thoroughbreds and that had to count for something.

Those seventy-one people thundered over the field, jumped a coop into the wildflower field between Sister's and the Bancrofts', roared up to the ruins, and stopped. Hounds crawled over the ruins.

Inside his den, Comet remained silent. He'd retreated to the deepest part of his lair. Happy for a rousing start, Shaker dismounted, blew "Gone to Ground," and praised everyone. He took Kilowatt's reins from Kasmir, who had ridden up at Sister's direction to hold Shaker's horse.

Stepping on the wall ruins, Shaker threw his leg over.

"Thanks, Kasmir."

"My pleasure." Kasmir slightly inclined his head, then rode back to Alida Dalzell. He was resplendent in a weazlebelly and top hat, riding his flaming chestnut mare, Lucille Ball. That mare had such a fluid stride the sight of her moving could bring tears to the eyes of any true horseman.

Sister smiled at O.J. As Masters, both knew to be asked to perform any service in the field was a singular honor. The harder, dirtier, or more dangerous the chore, the greater the honor. And while this was an easy chore, it did mean all eyes fell on Kasmir. He was marked by Shaker as a trusted man.

Sometimes, riding back to the trailers after a hard hunt, Sister would muse that this was one of the last sports where the warrior ethic prevailed. The point of foxhunting was not to make the sport easy but to make it superb sport enhanced by elegance. She could hear her mother's words, "Jane, face danger with elegance!"

Not that the blazing run had been particularly dangerous. The footing was pretty good, no steep incline or decline troubled them. Nor had there been any difficult crossings, but people had to put on the afterburners and jump some decent jumps, interesting jumps.

Shaker pointed the stag end of his crop toward Betty, then swept it forward. She moved forward on the right and Sybil shadowed her on the left. They knew he was heading back over the field at the base of Hangman's Ridge, toward the tiger trap into the woods of After All. A hog's-back jump was also placed in this fence line about three football fields farther down, should anyone have difficulty with the tiger trap, which looks like a big coop with logs vertically next to one another. Again, an easy enough jump, but it helps if a horse has seen one before.

Somehow no matter how many gates one puts into a fence line they never seem to be in the right place when hounds are running. Bobby, as Second Flight Master, dealt with this frustration constantly.

Hounds left Comet as they walked along the bottom of Hangman's Ridge.

"Ooo," Pookah exclaimed, *"bear tracks."*

Feeling especially good today, Dreamboat said, *"Pookah, don't fret over a bear. We'll get plenty of fox today. It's a perfect day. Low clouds, the right temperature, moisture in the earth and best of all, no wind. Perfect, perfect, perfect."*

As they rode along the foot of the eerie ridge, some trees grew out horizontally from the earth. There were also odd, dark rock formations.

Sister thought it was a perfect day, a day Mercer would have loved. She prayed he could see all this and appreciate the tribute. He was truly loved.

Not one given to expressing deep emotions, she felt them. Irrational as it was, Sister often sensed her son or husband near and she thought other people who had lost someone dearly loved could feel their spirits as well. Somehow she believed Mercer was with them today and if they saw their quarry, she would know it for certain.

Shaker popped over the tiger trap, Kilowatt floating over, followed shortly by Aztec, a smaller horse than Kilowatt, but such a handy fellow. One by one, the field jumped into the woods while Bobby, once through the gate, shepherded the Second Flight toward them by a different trail.

Hounds cleared. Fifteen minutes elapsed, then Dreamboat shifted into third gear, shouted, *"Follow me!"* and once again, all on! The hounds' music swirled around the trees, intensified as they crossed Broad Creek, then moved up along the fast rushing waters only to cross again. Within ten minutes, the pack was at Pattypan, always so difficult.

Athena, the great horned owl, had been lazily dozing inside the forge. Mice were everywhere. It was a bit like taking a nap in the supermarket. She cursed when the hounds lurched through the long high windows. *"Damn you all!"*

No hound bothered to reply because they hurried to Aunt Netty's den—tidy, as always.

"She's not here!" Cora surmised.

"Maybe she'll come back," Pansy said hopefully.

"Oh, we'll give the old girl a run for her money," Ardent promised, for Aunt Netty had teased him many times.

Hounds jumped out the other side of the forge.

Anticipating the direction once Dreamboat headed again into the woods, Sybil loped onto the narrow deer trail to head toward the Lorillard farm. She had to gallop, as this was a longer route, but there was no way through the thick undergrowth, the reason Pattypan was such a good place for a den. There was one way in and pretty much one way out. At least that old farm road ran in both directions.

Sister pushed Aztec onto the road but hounds circled the woods before they shot toward the Lorillard farm. She had a lot of territory to make up. Right behind her, O.J. twisted so many times in the saddle to avoid low-hanging branches, she knew she wouldn't be needing Pilates today. Behind her, Ginny Howard had the same thought, with Walter moving up behind as other people fell back.

Back on the good road between After All and the Lorillard place, hounds could be heard screaming toward the old home place. By the time the entire field reached the white clapboard home, hounds scratched at the back door.

Sam stood outside in front with Aunt Daniella, who used her cane. Hearing the hounds, she wanted to see the show. Sam didn't want to leave her, even though hounds blazed for his mudroom door.

Inside, Uncle Yancy cursed a blue streak. Aunt Netty had led the entire hunt right to his best place! She pretended she hadn't done a thing but she did flatten herself on the top shelf, along with Uncle Yancy.

As the field waited, Shaker dismounted, walked to his hounds.

"Good hounds, good hounds. Come along now."

"*Two foxes!*" Pickens screamed, totally beside himself. "*Two.*"

"*Open the door,*" Taz begged. "*Please open the door. Let me at 'em!*"

Tempted as Shaker was because he knew his hounds had to be right, he led them away. If he had opened the door to the Lorillard's mudroom, they would have ripped it up, and it's never a good idea to desecrate a landowner's property.

Waiting, Sister looked back at Ben. Tapping the

brim of her hunt cap with her crop, she rode to Phil as Ben came forward.

"Great run," Phil enthused as Gray came alongside him.

"Phil"—Sister leaned forward on Aztec's gleaming neck—"we know that Navigator was actually Benny Glitters. Why don't you tell us about how the horses were switched? That's why Harlan was killed, wasn't it? He knew."

Wedged in, Phil couldn't take off, but he threw his leg over his horse, dropping to one side, and ran like hell toward Aunt Daniella.

Sam stepped in front of her as Sister, also wedged in, tried to stay clear of Phil's horse. Ben, too, but Phil had a head start and they were at this moment encumbered by being mounted. Ben reached inside his coat and took out a .38 from his chest holster, well hidden by his heavy winter frock coat.

A tall man, Phil threw Sam to the ground but the slight man gamely rose to try to fight the bigger, heavier man. Phil reached for Aunt Daniella.

Without flickering an eye, she brought up her ebony cane between his legs with great force.

He bent over and that fast, Sam, using both hands, smashed him with an uppercut that sent teeth flying. Phil hit the ground. Ben dismounted, holding his gun to Phil's temple.

With Kasmir holding Kilowatt, Shaker ran over just as Sam hit Phil again. Shaker put Phil's arm up behind his back, lifted him up and held him tight.

Sam got control of himself.

"You have the right to remain silent . . ." Ben began reading Phil his rights, as Phil would be charged with murder.

It had happened so fast. Not one of those now seventy people said a word. Even the hounds stood still, waiting for a command from the huntsman.

Sam took Aunt Daniella by the elbow, for the exertion had cost her. He supported her while Gray, also dismounted, gently took his aunt's other arm. He handed her her ebony cane, which she had dropped after whacking Phil.

She looked stunned, then looked at all the people wearing black armbands. Her mouth opened. Nothing came out. She put her head on Gray's shoulder and the tears flooded out.

"He would be so proud," she gasped, oblivious of Phil or anything else.

"Yes, he would. And he would be proud of you." Gray kissed her cheek as he and Sam gently walked her to the front door.

Uncle Yancy couldn't help it. All this commotion. He snuck out, creeping around the back of the mudroom to look. Sister saw him and tears came to her eyes. Mercer had indeed sent a sign.

CHAPTER 31

Two weeks later, a lovely service was held for Mercer, who was buried in the Lorillard plot next to his grandfather. Daniella had requested that his horse Dixie Do be at the service, along with the entire pack of The Jefferson Hunt.

Gray held Dixie's reins. Mercer's tack glowed, the run-up stirrups gleamed. The hounds sat silent as stone, with Shaker on foot, in livery, at their head.

The entire hunt club attended, as did many members of Keswick, Farmington, Oak Ridge, Stonewall, Bedford, Deep Run, Casanova, Rockbridge, and Glenmore. Mercer had hunted with so many people over the years.

The glorious day saw a few crocuses peeping up out of the ground. If one stared intently, red could be seen returning to buds, although the trees still looked barren. Spring was stirring.

After the service, everyone retired to the Bancroft residence because the Lorillard place wasn't big enough to hold all these people. The Bancrofts had paid for everything, as well as opening their home.

Uncle Yancy—still stuck with Aunt Netty, and back in the mudroom—was glad the party was held elsewhere.

A large framed photograph of Mercer as a child on his first pony stood next to an identically-sized photograph of Mercer in full formal kit wearing a weazlebelly and top hat on Dixie Do, braided for Opening Hunt.

O.J. had flown back from Kentucky for the service. She talked with guests eager to catch up with her, with Kentucky hunting. Sister, Gray, Betty, and Tootie gathered for a moment by the punch bowl.

"It was an ingenious crime." Betty did give the Chetwynds credit. "And it made their fortune for 121 years."

O.J. joined them. "Alan and Meg did have tests run on Benny's, I mean Navigator's, lineage. Sure enough, he goes back to Matchem. I guess Harlan and who knows, another worker or Old Tom himself, switched the stallions at night. They greatly looked alike. Sometimes the cleverest crimes are the simplest."

Gray shook his head. "Can you imagine the work? Now the Jockey Club has to go through all the pedigrees for the last 121 years to correct them."

"They can do it." Sister smiled. "I have great faith in them. Remember, the founding member of the Jockey Club was Domino's owner, James Keene."

"Lucky Phil confessed," Tootie remarked. "Just spilled it all out."

"Well, honey." Betty put down her punch glass. "He had nothing to lose anymore and I don't think he was in his right mind at the end. The strain of that remarkable dishonesty, the knowledge, the weight of the crime passed to the oldest son from generation to generation, and then the horror of two murders. He told Ben he didn't really want to kill anyone. He couldn't see a way out."

Ben joined them. "I heard my name."

The small group reviewed what they'd just said.

The sheriff sighed, then said, "You know, Phil cried and cried, and said it was like killing his brother. He loved Mercer. And he said they were actually related. His grandfather had a long affair with Mercer's grandmother, Daniella's mother. He said he really felt he'd killed his brother. Obviously, the Chetwynds can afford the best lawyers but he says he wants to be put away." Ben shrugged. "For what, for reputation? For the money? Kill for that? Even if he had to shut down Broad Creek Stables because of the scandal, Phil would never have been poor."

"He couldn't live with the shame," Sister posited quietly. "Old name, old ways, old money."

"It's crazy." Tootie couldn't quite understand it. "So he creates more shame. Crazy."

"That it is." Sister put her arm around Tootie's waist. "People have been doing irrational things for thousands of years. We aren't going to stop now."

O.J. asked Ben, "Okay, the stallions were switched, but why did Old Tom Chetwynd have Harlan Laprade killed when he brought the slate memorial to Walnut Hall?"

"Money," said Sister. "Harlan must have been asking for more and more. Blackmail. Harlan loaded Benny Glitters on a big boxcar full of horses going to Broad Creek. No one would really notice that Navigator, who'd ridden on the train from Virginia, was switched. Harlan was in charge of the shipping. Only Old Tom and Harlan knew."

"And was Harlan a frequenter of houses of ill repute?" Betty couldn't help but ask.

Ben nodded. "Not that his wife didn't know he'd done such things in the past, but no one wanted her to know where his clothes were found. The disappearance was bad enough. Making it look like Harlan died in a whorehouse gave Old Tom a cover. Also, Old Tom was sleeping with Daniella's mother. He didn't mind getting rid of her husband, who by all accounts was a good horseman but a bad husband. King David did it too, remember?"

"Does Daniella know now?" O.J. asked.

Gray's voice was low. "She probably does but like her own mother, there are some things a lady doesn't want to investigate. All this has been quite enough."

Ben spoke again. "Phil killed Mercer then

strung him up. He's a strong man. If the pogonip lifted, he hoped no one would look closely as they'd become accustomed to the hanging dummy. He wanted to go to the breakfast, look for Mercer, then worry about his friend not showing up. Then he could go out and look for him. Bold and clever."

And just then, Sam, next to his aunt, her ebony cane in hand, walked in front of the enormous silver punch bowl.

Ed Bancroft tapped a glass. The room fell silent.

"I thank you all for your tribute to my son," said Daniella. "He was a good son, a good horseman, and a good businessman. I was and will always be proud of him. There are over two hundred years of Laprades and Lorillards buried at the old home place and soon I will rest next to my son." A murmur went up but she held up her hand. "To everything there is a season. I think Mercer went before his time but we do as the Lord commands. So it was his time and I look forward to mine. All good things must come to an end. When I go, don't mourn me. If there is any quality of mine you admire, make it your own. The quality I most admired in my son, apart from his love, was his eagerness for life.

"Thank you again and I especially thank Tedi and Edward Bancroft for giving Mercer his last social engagement." She smiled. "I thank my nephews, Gray and Sam, and I thank Jane Arnold for Mercer's hunt.

"I wish you all a good life and I know Mercer would want me to say, 'Good hunting.'"

Everyone applauded and Daniella was mobbed. Sensing her fatigue, Sam walked her to a chair. Gray left the small group to attend to his aunt, get her another drink, do all the things Mercer used to do.

That night, Sister visited the stables at Roughneck, saying good night to each of her horses, including the two newcomers from Broad Creek. Then she walked across to the kennels, careful not to awaken anyone if possible. She spied Inky looking at her from the edge of the orchard.

She winked at the beautiful vixen who remained motionless. Then Sister walked back up to her house, the pale smoke curling from the chimney.

She thought the Three Fates had cut the threads of two good lives recently as they were spinning out the lives of others. Spinning, spinning, spinning, and she prayed she would live a much longer life to be part of the tapestry.

To the Reader,

You might wonder how The Jefferson Hunt could have such a good season in such nasty weather. I have no idea.

Our season (Oak Ridge Foxhunt Club) from January to March 2014, proved bitter, snowy with odd, wild temperature bounces as in fifty degrees. Yes, fifty degrees. Without gilding the lily, it was the strangest, worst winter I've ever experienced, yet the hunting was terrific. On the days of the huge temperature bounces it was not terrific, granted. The rest of the time, we picked up fox after fox and ran as best we could in snow and sometimes over ice patches. When the snows melted, we ran in mud, returning splattered to the trailers. But when we smiled our teeth were white.

Parking proved more of a problem than hunting.

For those of you who do not foxhunt, most of us who do, do not go out in a deep powdery snow. For one thing, should a fox be out they can't get away from you. Usually they are tight and warm in their dens. If there is a good crust on the snow, I will take hounds out because the fox, being light, can get away. However, one must be careful because if the crust is too thick it will cut hound pads. One has to use judgment, obviously. Also, if the snow is deep it tires horses and hounds quickly.

A light snow, a few inches on the ground is perfect and to hunt while flakes are twirling down is the best. The horses and hounds become so excited, hounds will throw up snow at one another and people ignore the snow sliding down their collars. It's too much fun to complain.

If nothing else, I hope the Sister Jane novels impart the respect we have for our quarry and the care we give to our partners: horses and hounds.

Given that 80 percent plus of the U.S. population lives in cities and suburbs, the connection with nature is fading to the detriment of all living creatures. You and I are medium-sized predators. All mammalian creatures divide into predator and prey. To know where one falls on that scale goes a long way to integration in that scale. In other words, sisters and brothers, we are not the crown of creation. But we sure can be fun.

Up and over,
Rita Mae Brown

During hunt season, mid-September to mid-March, you can follow some of our hunts at http://www.facebook.com/sisterjanearnold

ACKNOWLEDGMENTS

The oldest equine graveyard in the United States is at Walnut Hall. Benny Glitters, however, is a fictional horse.

The owners of Walnut Hall, Meg Jewett and Alan Leavitt, are not fictional, and Lexington, Kentucky, is grateful for this. Their generosity and kindness is legendary. I especially call attention to their support of the library.

And I thank Alan again for the exciting tour he gave me of his stables and its residents.

As for Jane Winegardner, MFH of Woodford Hounds, what can I say about a beloved friend of years and an inspiring Master? Whenever I think of this hard riding lady, I remember the laughter first.

I also thank Robert M. Lyons, MFH, and Justin Sautter, MFH, of Woodford for their hospitality to Oak Ridge members and myself when we visit.

My much abused whipper-in, Dee Phillips, walked me through most of the DNA material, all that stuff about a mother's DNA, etc. Thank God, she is a tolerant soul as well as a terrific whipper-in to myself as well as Deep Run, the grand hunt outside of Richmond. The history of that group alone would make a fabulous novel. Deep Run has experienced everything: war, fast women, beautiful horses, men too handsome for their own good and the good of the ladies, and all of this shining with that Virginia veneer of perfect manners. Ah, yes.

I suspect this could be said of most hunts in the United States and Canada. Dull people don't foxhunt.

Thank you to Kathleen King, Oak Ridge member, and lawyer who digs into my research keeping me this side of trouble. We also hunt bassetts together.

And one last request. Please do not visit Walnut Hall. It is a private residence and the equine graveyard is also private. Peace should be preserved.

To anyone I might have forgotten, just cuss me out.

Always and Ever,

Rita Mae Brown

ABOUT THE AUTHOR

Rita Mae Brown is the bestselling author of the Sister Jane foxhunting novels—*Let Sleeping Dogs Lie*, *Fox Tracks*, *Hounded to Death*, *The Tell-Tale Horse*, *The Hounds and the Fury*, *The Hunt Ball*, *Full Cry*, *Hotspur*, and *Outfoxed*—the *New York Times* bestselling Sneaky Pie Brown mysteries, and *Rubyfruit Jungle*, *In Her Day*, and *Six of One*, among many other novels. An Emmy-nominated screenwriter and a poet, she lives in Afton, Virginia, where she is Master of fox-hounds and huntsman of Oak Ridge Hunt Club and one of the directors of Virginia Hunt Week. She founded the first all-women's polo club, Blue Ridge Polo, in 1988. She was also Visiting Faculty at the University of Nebraska in Lincoln.
www.ritamaebrown.com

Center Point Large Print
600 Brooks Road / PO Box 1
Thorndike, ME 04986-0001 USA

(207) 568-3717

US & Canada:
1 800 929-9108
www.centerpointlargeprint.com

X